COURTING MURDER
2012

"HERE COMES THE JUDGE—HE'S stubborn, cranky, a bit sarcastic, and completely charming. Bill Hopkins nails the voice! This is a big-time mystery in a small town—and you'll fall in love with the place. *Courting Murder* is guilty—of being terrific." –HANK PHILLIPPI RYAN, Agatha Anthony, and Macavity-winner. Her thriller, *SAY NO MORE*, was a *Library Journal* BEST OF 2016!

RIVER MOURN
2013

"BILL HOPKINS BLENDS HIGH STAKES with hi-jinks in this harrowing adventure set above the mighty Mississippi, as quirky, appealing Judge Rosswell Carew tracks a criminal with a deadly, and personal, agenda. A fast-paced, energetic read." –LESLIE BUDEWITZ. *AS THE CHRISTMAS COOKIE CRUMBLES*, A FOOD LOVERS' VILLAGE MYSTERY, will be published in 2018.

BLOODY EARTH
2014

"JUDGE ROSSWELL CAREW SCOURS THE countryside with his Mensan sidekick looking for bad guys once again. This time it's not just the cops telling him to keep his nose out of it; his job is on the line. This doesn't stop the judge, and by now we wouldn't expect anything less. One of the reasons that this has become my favorite series is that each word, each phrase had entertainment value. Some books simply get skimmed because there's so much fluff and stuff. Bill Hopkins delivers comedic gold on every page with just enough suspense to keep me pleasantly in the edge of my seat (or rather snuggled in the depths of my couch with my kindle)." – AMAZON REVIEWER

Unfinished Grave
2015

"THIS IS HOW YOU KNOW that you've thoroughly enjoyed a good book: you're really sorry when it comes to an end. I got hooked on Book 1 and devoured Books 2, 3, and 4. Although each one can be appreciated on its own, you're going to want to read them all. Bill Hopkins has created a cast of quirky characters who I became quite fond of and will certainly miss (unless the author can be persuaded to write Book 5). Lots of suspenseful action, witty repartee peppered with a dash of humor and some downright scary moments kept me up turning the page until crazy o'clock in the wee hours. Judge Rosswell Carew, (please, don't ever call him Ross) if the author is kind, I hope to find you and your crew in another adventure chasing the bad guys." – **AMAZON REVIEWER**

Dishonest Corpse
2016

"EVERY BOOK IN THIS SERIES is superb and can be enjoyed on its own but be warned: the author gets you hooked and keeps you wanting more. With a quirky cast of characters (the good ones you will love and the bad ones you will love to hate and sometimes you can't be sure which is which) along with exceptional storytelling, Bill Hopkins will keep you turning the page into the wee hours. If he has a heart, the author will continue delighting his readers with further escapades of the good Judge Carew turned detective. More, please!" – **AMAZON REVIEWER**

Harvest Death
2018

"A THRILLING MURDER MYSTERY WITH fantastic narrative and dialog" – **COZY READERS**.

The
Angel Spoke
MURDER

Bill Hopkins
Sharon Woods Hopkins

A Judge Rosswell Carew Mystery
Book Seven

DEADLY WRITES PUBLISHING, LLC

THE ANGEL SPOKE MURDER by Bill Hopkins and Sharon Woods Hopkins

A Judge Rosswell Carew Mystery – Book Seven

Copyright © 2021 by Bill Hopkins and Sharon Woods Hopkins

Deadly Writes and the Deadly Writes image and colophon are trademarks of Deadly Writes Publishing, LLC

Edited by Donna Essner
Book cover and interior designed by Ellie Searl, Publishista®
www.publishista.com

ISBN: 9780997591125
LCCN: 2021909136

www.deadlyduo.net
deadlywritespublishing@yahoo.com

DEADLY WRITES PUBLISHING, LLC
Marble Hill, MO

To our friend, Ed Searl.
You left us way too soon.

ACKNOWLEDGMENTS

To our friends both Facebook and real life, who kindly loaned us their names for special characters in the story. They are all wonderful people who are not at all like we wrote them.

Reverend Ed Searl
JoEllen Jansen
Brian Reeves
Martha Bailey Wurl
Dennis West

"The darkness of night strives to quench the brightness of day."
—Anonymous

"Crazy men do not dream."
—Anonymous

CHAPTER 1

==

Father Michael Smothers' descent into hell sprang to life on Courthouse Hill.

As was his custom after lunch, the priest climbed the steps on the side of the Common Pleas Courthouse until he reached his favorite bench in the shade of a two-hundred-year-old oak tree. He stood for a moment contemplating the puzzle of what surrounded him.

The August sun and the humidity rolling in from the Mississippi River zoomed the temperature up to the far side of miserable. He wondered how the air could be stifling and soggy, yet the heavens refused to produce rain for over a month now. The grass, what there was left of it on the hillside, mirrored the muddy water of the Mississippi, rather than the rich, blue-green when rain was plentiful. Even the dust, he thought, lay in wait for wind to gather it up and blow it away, or, at some point, rain to wash it down to the streets below. Even the dandelions, along with all the other summer weeds, slept.

The priest shook the thoughts from his brain with the ferocity of a dog flinging muddy water off his body and lowered himself on to the bench for prayer. *Nothing I can do about the weather, but maybe I can salvage my soul.* He crossed himself, all the while peering up at the courthouse. He never tired of gazing at the majestic building built before his grandfather was a man. He then turned his attention to the steps descending to Themis Street, named for the Greek goddess, The Lady of Good Counsel. Appropriate, the priest contemplated since she was the personification of divine order. Just beyond, he watched as vacationers and residents crossed the railroad tracks past the floodwall, toward the river, trying to walk off their lunch. The wall, stretching a little over a mile to the north and south, protected the merchants along the shore of the river from flooding.

After a half hour of prayer, he stood and stretched his legs once again ready to head back to Holy Cross Church. Lots of paperwork faced him when he returned to his office. He thought back to when he entered the priesthood. He was a mere boy, a teenager, and innocent in the ways of the secular world. At nineteen, he hoped his life as a priest would be filled with delivering the faith to worshippers and dispensing forgiveness for sinners. He longed to be what Saint Matthew called a shepherd. He wanted to feed the hungry, give water to the thirsty, welcome the homeless, clothe the naked, attend the sick, and visit prisoners. The priest blew out an exasperated breath. Today, ten years after his ordination, he found himself swamped with paperwork, consumed with complaining parishioners, and overwhelmed by the demands of the Continuing Theological Education, all which cut into his prayer time. *Such is life*, he mused.

As Father Mike descended the steps, he grasped the metal handrail to steady himself. Oddly, the rail felt cold. He stopped, raised his hand, and looked at it. Then he wrapped his hand around the rail again, immediately jerking it away. *Impossible.* His hand felt like it was on the receiving end of freezer burn, as though the metal rail had been dipped in liquid nitrogen. He continued down the steps without the aid of the rail, but after a few steps, he noticed a buzzing, like that of a distant hummingbird, slight at first, then louder with each step he took. He closed his eyes as the droning penetrated his brain and jittered down his neck and into every nerve of his spine. It was as if a snake—a snake made of ice—vibrated down along his backbone and back up into his brain again.

Before he could take another step, a light—white, iridescent and bright, like icicles on a tree—encircled him and washed the color from everything—the trees, the buildings below, the steps, the rail, his hands and arms, and even his black suit. Everything glowed as if a bolt of lightning turned his surroundings the color of salt-water taffy. In an instant, the light changed and bombarded him with a prism of colors in all sizes, and in textures like he'd never seen. Never in his life had he ever witnessed anything so glorious. A diamond set in a gold band flew past his right ear, flashing like a strobe. Another cartwheeled in front of his nose. Chinese silkworms of every color, distinct and bold like that of a Picasso painting wriggled past his eyes. Finally, the wondrous parade winked out. Surprised at the sudden disappearance of light, the priest blinked several times to adjust his vision. To no avail. In stark contrast to the blinding light, he now saw nothing. It was as if the density of midnight on a starless and moon-free night claimed his sight.

Dizziness overcame him and the priest slumped down onto a step. He pinched the bridge of his nose, thinking it might restore his sight. It did not.

"Oh my dear Lord, I'm blind!"

He rubbed his eyes again, and again. Still nothing. He knew better than to move. If he did, he'd probably tumble head over heels down to the street and plow headlong into a lunchtime jogger sprinting up the steps to the courthouse. Or lawyers hurrying back to court after a quick lunch at a nearby restaurant. If he stumbled over one of them, it would be disastrous. He sat there, trying to ponder his fate.

Surely, he could call to someone for help. What would he tell them? "I touched the handrail and it was cold as ice, and then a bright light blinded me." They'd think he'd gone 'round the bend. Besides, unless someone was next to him, he doubted they would hear him. *So many noises,* he thought. *Noises I didn't hear until now.*

A short distance away behind the courthouse, one of those lawnmowers the size of a field tractor ran full-tilt boogie. The streets below were chaotic with pedestrians and traffic. Even if he yelled at the top of his lungs, no one would likely hear him. Cars whipped along to their next destination, their passengers unlikely to notice a man sitting on the steps. He doubted any of them would have their windows down in this heat. The pounding of jackhammers he hadn't noticed before battered the concrete in need of repair a block away, and the daily train just then blasted its ear-piercing whistle. So imprisoned by darkness and noise, he remained seated. *Surely someone will come along soon and ask me if I'm OK.*

Then he remembered his phone. He leaned back and tugged it from a pants pocket. When he clicked it on, all he heard was a low hum. Even rebooting it did no good. The hum continued regular and loud. And menacing. Whether the glitch was a phenomenon the phone company would try to explain away later or something else, he didn't know. He shoved the phone back into his pocket. After all, he couldn't see to call anyone anyway. Now, he wished he still had his first cellphone. The one that reminded him of Captain Kirk's communicator: flip it open, punch the raised buttons, speak. Easy. Anyone—even a blind man—could do it in the dark. He chuckled then. The only "buttons" on his current phone were pictures of buttons, useless to a blind man.

After that realization, a nauseating sensation struck him. Here he sat, outside, in the light, visible to everyone but himself. This complete darkness propelled him toward sickening fear—a fear he'd be totally blind forever. Panic overcame him.

"Can anyone hear me?" he yelled. *Did I say that out loud?* He repeated his question. "Can anyone hear me?" He knew he'd spoken out loud the second time because he felt the vibration of the words in his throat. Then another reality struck. His hearing. Except for the humming of his cellphone, he'd heard nothing since . . . the jackhammers. *Am I losing my mind?* Had he had a stroke? Or maybe he imagined everything.

No, not everything.

He was blind as a bat. And now . . . deaf.

No! The priest stuck his fingers in his ears and shook his head back and forth.

Nothing.

He turned his ear toward the street and listened intently for the slightest noise. Nothing. A deep unexplained quiet he'd never experienced added to his confusion and fear. He tottered on the chasm of horror, where, if he fell in, he knew he might never return. *Calm down, Mike. Calm down.* After a few deep breaths, he regained his perspective. *This is a dream. That's all. Before long, you'll wake up and all will be OK.* To convince himself, he pinched his arm to the point of bruising. The pain was real. Yet everything was black as pitch and more quiet than death.

Maybe that was it! *I'm dead.* He thought he should do something, if for no other reason than to verify his death, or life. If he stood there on the hill yelling and waving his arms, he'd certainly attract attention. Then again, he could garner attention that wouldn't be of the helpful sort. Some might think he'd consumed a bit too much of the wine before Mass. Or maybe, he'd finally gone looney tunes from too much paper work. A disturbing-the-peace violation filed against him would not set well with his parishioners, and certainly not the bishop. So again, he just sat there.

The rumbling in his stomach ratcheted up to the point where bile rose in his throat. He swallowed several times to keep from vomiting. Along with everything else happening, he had no desire to upchuck his lunch.

"OK, enough," he said aloud. Father Mike took a deep breath, got up, and steadied himself before continuing down the steps. At this point, he thought breaking his neck was better than just sitting there. Again, he grabbed the rail. Again, he jerked his hand away at the intense cold, doubled his fist, and jammed it close to his mouth and blew onto his freezing hand. It was numb. If he hadn't known better, he would have thought it was the dead of winter. *On the bright side, I still have my sense of touch.* The pain disappeared.

Without grabbing the rail, Father Mike stepped gingerly down one step. No sooner than both feet were planted, his sight returned.

Elated, he said, "Thank yo—.

The priest froze.

He blinked repeatedly and leaned forward to get a better look at the spectacle in front of him; then he pulled back aghast at what he saw. *What is that?* A man—no—not a man, and no, not a woman. Whatever it was hovered above him on a cloud. *It's not human!* No human looks like that. *An alien?* He shook off that notion. *Surely not an angel! Why would God send an angel to me, a lowly priest?*

The entity wrapped in eye piercing gold floated toward him.

Father Mike squeezed his eyes into slits. Just as he opened them wide, the being touched him.

Wake up!

At the command, Father Mike jerked back and looked around. Everything was back to normal. The jackhammer started up again. *And I can hear! I must have fallen asleep while saying my prayers.* Relief washed over him. He realized he was sitting on the stairs, not the bench. And . . . the being still floated in front of him. Did he hear him out loud? No, he heard him inside his head!

Who—what—are you? His words were from his mind instead of his mouth. Then he repeated them aloud.

When it is time I will tell you. The angel pointed to something on the ground. *Eat.*

The priest looked down but didn't see anything edible.

"There's nothing there." A fierce wave of nausea overtook him. He lowered his head and raised his hands toward the entity. "Go away—whoever—whatever you are!"

When he looked up, the angel came even closer. Again, it said, *Eat.*

Incredulous, the priest shook his head and pointed to the ground. "There's nothing there."

That's when a whisper of a breeze enveloped him. Immediately, he was comforted.

The rush of sensory images and the buzz of otherwise mundane noises, akin to waking up to the brightest and loudest movie exploded in his head and knocked him backward. He fell backward.

After regaining his senses, he sat up and searched around for his glasses and prayer book. Before he could find them, the angel deposited them next to him. He stopped short of thanking the entity. When he put on his glasses, he noticed a small, low burning fire.

Am I seeing things again? Unattended fires outside were frowned upon in the city, especially downtown. Even burning leaves and lawn trash was forbidden. He squinted to get a better look. The fire didn't appear to be spreading. Just like the burning bush Moses saw, he told himself. A flame without destruction. Atop the fire, one, flat, cake-like bread baked in a small pan. Next to the fire sat a crude earthen jar of water. There again was the angel. The priest hung his head in frustration and warded off an expletive. Immediately, the bread and water were in front of him. The angel—for that is what he'd begun to call it—motioned for him to eat. He ate without question.

After eating, a heavy sense of lethargy overcame Father Mike and he fell asleep. No sooner it seemed than he'd closed his eyes, that the angel touched him and uttered one word.

Scrapbook.

"Scrapbook?" the priest repeated. *Nothing angelic? Or spiritual? Or Godly?* Like he would have expected. Rather, the word was, well . . . mundane. Unimaginative. Boring.

The angel spoke again.

Murder.

When the angel touched Father Mike's forehead, the priest fainted.

CHAPTER 2

The Raggedy Man
A couple of weeks ago

TONIGHT I SHIFTED INTO *THAT* mode. Again. After enjoying a stolen cigar and snifter of high-dollar brandy, the mode intensified, enveloped him, owned him.

As it always did. And anytime this happens, I have to *do* something about it.

Cape Girardeau. What a town. Great town . . . no, not really. Yes, it is better than Lockerbie, of course, but that's not saying anything you could spit through your teeth. The town is ripe for the harvest. And that's why I'm here.

Raggedy Man, Raggedy Man,
Who must you be?
A killer who likes the name, Lockerbie.

After I arrived, I scoured the town in order to get my bearings. Once that was done, I decided last night—just for practice—to break into several houses and apartments downtown. Unlike the mall, the businesses shuttered their windows before the sun even evaporated into the horizon, so I figured it was easy pickins. I highly doubted many places had alarms, and if they did, I knew how to disarm them. The first place I broke into was a second-story apartment that faced the floodwall. (I'm not really a second-story guy, but hey, we all have to increase our skills.) I tiptoed up the outside steps to the back door, wrapped my fist in my shirt and smashed the window, and crawled in. I looked around, but didn't take anything; just left by way of the front door, which had been left unlocked. See what I mean about this being child's play?

My last break-in for the night was successful, too. I crawled in through a bedroom window. Just like the other place, no one was home. Except me, of course. The room smelled like lavender, which was nice. That, however, isn't really important.

I knew a woman lived there because I'd been watching her over the past week. Frequently, there was a younger woman with her.

Finally, after about thirty minutes of me hiding in the closet twiddling my thumbs, she came home. The younger woman was with her. I found out later that they were mother and daughter.

Believe me, when they came in, I didn't know what was going to happen. Sometimes I just let come what may. Sometimes I just tie the person up and go through their stuff, take something valuable, and leave. Last night, *THAT* mode hit me. And when opportunity knocks, I listen. Wouldn't you?

The women walked into the bedroom and laid a bunch of packages on the bed. They were talking and laughing about the great deals they'd gotten that day. I watched them through the slats of the door. After a few minutes, they walked out of the bedroom to another room on the other side of the house. As soon as they left the room, I followed them. All quiet-like.

I waited until they were in the living room and then I ran into the room yelling like a banshee. They screamed. Terror struck their faces.

"Be . . . be . . . be quiet," I stuttered. With my hand in my shirt, I pointed it at them. "Kneel do—do—down."

"No," the older woman said. "What do you want? I've got money."

I put my finger to my lips. That's the only thing I could say without wobbling my words.

Then I sang, "I'm not a stutterer. It's spasmodic dysphonia." Singing is easier than talking, and that's how I relax and stop my stuttering.

The older woman, I could tell, thought I was crazy, which irked me. So, I sang, "I'm not crazy. It's a nerve sickness. If you are normal, air from your lungs is pushed through your vocal chords and words come out all in one piece. Sometimes when I try to talk, my vocal chords spasm and no words come out." Of course, I added mannerisms to help them understand.

They looked at one another as though thinking me harmless. Which really set me off. And since I was in *THAT* mode, when someone thinks I don't mean business, I turn mean.

I pulled the gun from my pocket and pointed it at them. This time, they raised their hands and did what I told them. Of course, the older woman again tried to bribe me with money. I just shook my head.

After I got them all tied up, I shot the younger woman in the back of the head.

Her mama screamed, of course, and bless her, she vomited before she wet herself.

"Shut up! Turn o-o-over!" I screamed. Because she didn't obey, I kicked her in the side and then shoved her over so she was facing me. I shot her in the chest.

Next, I searched the house, looking for anything valuable. I found a billfold in a desk in the den. It had a hundred dollars in it. I took that. That's when I heard something. I went back in the bedroom. The mother was still alive and sobbing. She'd turned on her side next to her daughter. I fired another shot. Right into the back of the head.

Then I left.

On the way out, I said to myself in my head—so I wouldn't stutter, "They should be thankful I didn't rape them."

All in all, it was a good night for practicing and honing my craft. It was a lot of work for not much money, though. You may be asking me why I sweated through the night for practically nothing.

Like I said, when I'm in *THAT* mode, opportunity finds a way to knock.

Especially since Martha asked me to take care of those meddling Fribeau sisters.

Raggedy Man Raggedy Man, what do you offer?
Nothing but a mother-daughter slaughter!

CHAPTER 3

Day 1, continued
River City Unitarian Congregation

AFTER THE ENCOUNTER WITH THE angel, Father Mike mulled over where he should seek help with this extraordinary problem. Surely, someone in the bishop's office could refer him to a specialist in angels. However, before he consulted with his ladder of superiors, he wanted to speak to an outsider. No way did he want a reputation as a priest who saw things—angels or otherwise. Angelic visitations happened. Of that, no doubt existed. The problem, however, was that people, including priests, viewed a visitation by a divine messenger as peculiar. He knew he'd been privy to something spectacular, and he much preferred a visit from an angel rather than a ghost. Still, other priests, parishioners, and Cape citizens would look at him funny. He just knew it. Not to mention the media would have a heyday.

Thus, his first step was easy. Visit with an old acquaintance who had no connection with his church and someone Father Mike knew would be discreet. He set off to find Reverend Ed Searl at the River City Unitarian Congregation.

At first, he'd thought of meeting the minister on the riverfront where they often met and chatted about immensely important things and, more often than not, incredibly trivial subjects. Father Mike needed to see the reverend now. No time for niceties, he marched to Ed's church.

The priest slipped into the entrance of the small chapel, slinking in the shadows at the back of the church to avoid attracting attention. There was a funeral service in progress, so he decided to sit in the last pew and wait.

The early afternoon sun cast its rays through the stained glass windows, spreading rainbow colors across the blood-red carpeting of the main service area. He never tired of the serenity that the glass murals cast over his own congregation during Mass.

Curious about the identity of the deceased, he quietly picked up the pamphlet that contained the obituary: Anna Fribeau. Who now lay in an urn, her body reduced to ashes. He remembered the woman had been murdered.

He looked toward the front of the church.

A lace runner ran the length of a plain dark table. On the table, a black-and-white photograph of the woman rested by the urn. She appeared to be in her early thirties. Candles graced the setting. He imagined that one in particular, a large white candle set in a blue ceramic bowl must've represented Miss Fribeau. A cone of incense burned in a brass holder next to her picture. The aroma of cinnamon permeated his nose and reminded him of his favorite doughnut.

Father Mike became mesmerized by Ed's liturgy entitled, "A Meditation of Candles." The priest consulted the booklet so he could follow the service.

Ed, wearing a purple and white stole with golden six-pointed stars dotting it, lit the large candle and stood silently before the crowd for a few moments. The gray-haired minister sported a salt-and-pepper beard, but no mustache. Father Mike always wondered why. He'd imagined only Amish men wore facial hair in that fashion. *Did the Unitarians have an Amish branch?* He'd have to ask Ed one of these days.

"In awe and wonder, our thoughts leap to understand about our lives as humans, along with the mystery of where we come from when we are born, and where we go when we die." Ed continued in that vein for several minutes, impressing Father Mike with his sincerity.

When he finished, he invited the mourners to offer their memories of the woman. Some told funny stories; others, like her sister, walked up to the table and lit a red candle for her. She wept in silence for a few minutes, then said, "I will miss my beloved sister, and I pray that her killer is found and brought to justice."

Anna's brother fondly spoke of how he and his sister fished at night on the Mississippi River when they were kids. He lit a white candle for her.

The last mourner came up to the table, turned, and spoke eloquently of Miss Fribeau. Father Mike thought he recognized the man, an occurrence that wasn't impossible in the small city, although he failed to put a name to the face.

Thereafter, the minister and mourners stood in silence for a few minutes. Finally, Ed dismissed the congregation with soothing words meant to heal.

The priest waited for the people to leave before approaching Reverend Ed. The man he'd recognized but couldn't place, had remained as well.

"Shall I help you straighten up?" the man asked the minister.

"Yes, please. Thank you."

Without another word, the man went to work gathering the items on the table.

The man asked Ed, "Does the family want these items? And is this airline ticket any good?"

Ed examined each item and then said, "The family said the phone no longer worked and they'd already cut off the service. The brother said he couldn't bear to use his sister's fishing rod, so he wants us to donate it to someone who could use it. Take it if you want. I don't fish. The airline ticket, too, was nonrefundable. And they didn't know who left the flash drive. Everything can go."

"All right. I'll go and look for a box to put all of it in. I'll be back in a moment."

After the man left, the priest walked up to Reverend Ed, who had his back to him. He coughed to get his attention. "Reverend, do you have a few moments for me?"

Reverend Ed jumped, clearly surprised that anyone was still there. He whirled around and put his hand on his heart.

"Mike! You scared the bajeebies out of me."

"Sorry, Ed. My apologies."

Ed removed and folded the brightly colored stole he'd worn over his black suit. "It's been a while. The last time I saw you, if I remember correctly, was when we both served on the Interfaith First Responder Chaplain Team." He straightened his tie. "What can I do for you today, my friend?"

In answer, Father Mike pointed to the things lying on the table. "What an odd assortment. May I look at these? I'm always curious about what others consider important in their lives."

"Be my guest. Sometimes the family asks us to put everyday things up here during the service to remind us of the deceased. The ancients in practically every culture on Earth put common things in graves."

"Catholics have relics of saints in our churches."

"The things here are nothing now. Junk is probably a better term."

Mike clasped his hands behind his back and leaned over the montage, like a prospective buyer at an auction. He wondered why Ed continued to emphasize the worthlessness of what was or had been important to others.

"Look at this," Ed said. He held up a book. *The Slave Next Door: Human Trafficking and Slavery in America Today*. And this: a flash drive. An unused airplane ticket. It's certainly a motley lot."

"Are you going to toss all these things?" Mike asked.

The man in the blue suit came back and loaded all the items in a cardboard box.

"Yes, except the fishing rod," Ed said. "On second thought, wait." The man stopped and looked at Ed. "Let me keep that book. It could be a useful item for my library." The man handed the book to Ed.

With the box in hand, he said, "I'll be leaving now." He nodded to Father Mike and then turned to leave.

"Would you mind to lock the doors when you leave?" The man nodded.

Ed glanced around the chapel. "So, you said you wished to talk to me."

"Yes, that is if you have time."

"Certainly."

As wisps of gray smoke from the wicks of paraffin candles found his nose, Father Mike recalled birthday parties and fireworks of long ago, not to mention, of course, the candles that had once been in his church. The Unitarians still used the old-fashioned paraffin candles that smoked when extinguished, whereas the Catholics preferred clean-burning beeswax candles, which had little aroma.

"Talk. That's what I want to do." Ed coughed and waved his hand in front of his face, dispersing the smoke. "I'm all in favor of beeswax, yet a few diehards on the candle committee are opposed to non-vegan—"air finger quotes"—candles." Father Mike watched the minister tilt his head first left and then right, which told him what Ed thought of the candle committee. "And soy candles do contain some paraffin, which makes them stink, too."

"There are always naysayers who stand in the way of progress," said Father Mike. "Usuallly, the more meaningless the fight, the more vicious the tactics."

"Quite right," Ed said. "It's what happens when there's little at stake." A grin surfaced on his face. "So be it." The minister motioned his friend to the first pew. "OK, let's chat."

After they sat, Father Mike sat back. He squirmed to get comfortable. "I have one thing to say, Ed. Doubtless anyone naps during your services."

Ed's laughter peeled throughout the church. "Have to do something to keep their attention. Now," Ed issued a refined lip smack, and then set his hands with straightened arms on his knees, "it's been a while since the chaplain response team. We had only a few interesting conversations there. I'm still doing it, you know. Responding, I mean. I also make a lot of visits to the hospital and go to the houses of anyone who invites me. I have many interesting conversations."

"Me, too, on all counts. Our responding rotations obviously don't coincide. We should talk to someone to assign us together."

Ed nodded. "Indeed. It would be nice to see you more often. You're an interesting fellow."

Father Mike chuckled. "You mean for a Roman Catholic?"

They both laughed.

"You and I, and our churches, interpret writings and tradition and history in different ways. That won't keep us from being frank and open with each other, right?" Ed reached into his pocket and withdrew a hanky the size of Delaware.

"Exactly. There are a few priests up around Boston who proclaim that a lot of our faith is mostly symbolic. Although I suspect that's more prevalent in your neck of the woods. Anyway, a discussion on either side would be interesting." Father Mike picked at an annoying cuticle.

"As long as it didn't melt into a heated argument."

"Unfortunately, as in politics, sometimes it happens."

"Maybe those priests would live life more fully at my seminary. Meadville-Lombard Theological. There we joked about an atheist who stood before the throne of God, perched at the middle of the universe on Judgment Day, and said, 'Lord, you didn't give us enough evidence.'" Ed laughed.

"Your atheist was too busy not looking."

Ed shook a finger at him. "You may well be right. Now I know you didn't come over here to chat about the wonderful days at seminary. What brought you here to my little chapel today?"

Father Mike didn't hesitate. "Do you believe in ghosts or angels? Because I think I had a brush with the supernatural." He explained in detail his vision of the angel. When he finished, he asked Ed, "Any ideas what all that could be?"

""Oh, my." Ed pinched his lips and closed his eyes. After a minute, he leaned his head back and opened his eyes. "Let me think." He removed a pencil from his pocket, from where he also retrieved a small notebook. He jotted a few words in the book. "I've got a question." He glanced up at the priest. "Why do you come to me? You and your church have other priests around, probably one every five or ten miles in every direction. This part of Missouri is loaded with Catholics. Or, you could go to Saint Louis or Memphis, walk into any confessional, and have a long talk. No priest would remember you even if you identified yourself in the confessional as a priest. In big cities, no one is surprised by any confession. That's my guess. Why chat up some Unitarian you know?"

"True enough. I don't want any of my fellow priests in the area knowing about this, confessional or otherwise. When I talk with you, I ask for complete confidentiality. If you have a form of minister-penitent privilege, that is, I can tell you anything." Ed nodded agreement. "And," the priest continued, "what I will now tell you must never be revealed, even under pain of imprisonment."

Ed's eyebrows shot up. "There's more?"

"Yes." Father Mike looked down at his hands and vowed again to quit picking at his cuticles. What do his parishioners think when he distributed Communion?

"Mike, I get it. There will never be any revelations on my part, even under pain of death."

Father Mike straightened against the backrest of the pew and rubbed the back of his neck to relieve his tension, as well as easing the knots in his shoulders.

"Our bishop said he never wanted two things to happen in this diocese. First, a visit from the Pope. Second, an apparition of the Blessed Virgin. The Bishop thinks the Pope and the Blessed Virgin are both too busy to mess with this diocese. I decided I'm not saying anything to the Bishop, even if it is *not* Mary, but an angel or even God, talking to me." He waved his hand in the air. "For whatever reason."

Ed sat in silence for a minute. Then he turned toward his friend, his eyes wide, his breath shallow, a sheen of perspiration on his face. "Perhaps . . . something else?

"If by something else, do you mean Lucifer, the once beautiful angel, and his minions?"

Ed nodded. "Lucifer, the 'Star of the Morning?' Yes. Or maybe it was electrical impulses in your brain?" He looked at Mike questioningly.

"You mean nothing happened and I imagined the whole thing?"

Ed shrugged, stood and walked up to the table holding the murdered girl's ashes. He turned back toward the priest. "Or, as I might say if this was the '60s, 'Are you having a flashback due to a bad trip?'"

"I don't do drugs. Never smoked pot or took speed, LSD, opioids, anything. I don't even do alcohol. I'm the only priest I know who doesn't ever touch alcohol. Except, of course, for Mass. No tobacco, either, except for an occasional cigar. And I only have one or two cups of coffee with or after breakfast."

Ed rearranged the candles, and turned back toward Father Mike. "You and I don't have the same idea about what God is, or what the devil is. Even if we did believe the same, there's usually more than one explanation for anything on earth, and at times, there is no explanation at all."

Jittery as a grasshopper, the Reverend Ed continued fiddling with the candles, then assumed a most pious attitude. He strolled back to the pew, peered down at the priest. Nearly whispering, he said, "The devil, the brain, exterior substances. You, sir, are telling me that none of my guesses is correct."

"Exactly."

"OK. I have an issue about the early New England Puritans who maintained that rigid theology was helpful. It shouldn't suffocate the lives of the people it was meant to help."

Father Mike inclined his head. "That's why I came to you. No offense, but you folks in the Unitarian camp come off more skeptical about these things than some of us—most of us—in the Catholic camp." He returned Ed's somber stare. "I figured you would help me look at this from a different angle."

"No offense taken," Ed said. "The best advice I have for you is that you must get more rest, eat properly, exercise more, and evict the monkeys running loose in your mind. And, of course, stay out of this oppressive heat."

A long silence ensued. Finally, Father Mike stood and stepped out of the pew. "I disagree." He rubbed the stubble on his face with the back of his hand. The morning's shave hadn't been close. "Maybe we don't know each other intimately, Ed, but you surely know me better than that. I'm a practical person. Do you really think I'm delusional because of the heat?" His voice scratched like a fine violin with defective strings. "I came to you for real advice, not some stock answer you'd hand out to your parishioners."

Ed slid his hand into his jacket like that famous picture of Napoleon. To Father Mike, it formed a scoffing portrait of a judgmental man. Ed began pacing, his eyes half-shut, his bushy eyebrows (reminding Father Mike of caterpillars) sticking out away from his face. After a bit, Ed clasped his hands behind his back, and twisted toward the priest, shook his head, and then bowed. "Father, forgive me for I have sinned by giving you stock answers."

"Nonsense. It's me actually, who's acting the part of a difficult parishioner. You're not the one who's sinning. It's me sinning by being impatient."

"A doctor—"

He interrupted Ed. "No. I'm not going to a doctor."

Ed launched into what sounded to the priest like a hellfire and damnation sermon. "Father Mike, be reasonable. You need to rule out stroke or some kind of brain event that neither you nor I could diagnose." Ed pointed at Father Mike in an obvious ploy of making sure the subject of the rant was paying attention. "You lost your sight and your hearing at the same time, and then they both returned at the same time. That is not a normal event. You could be risking permanent and irreversible damage to yourself. That's something you never want to happen, is it?" The rhetorical question couldn't be answered any way except with a yes. The literary device was known and used by lots of preachers, including himself.

"Priests," Father Mike said, "stand out in a crowd, as you well know. I couldn't go to a doctor even in Saint Louis or Memphis without the chance of discovery. Even when you're in a town as a stranger, people want to talk to you when they see your collar."

"That's what you signed up for." A smile played on Ed's face when he pointed to Father Mike's black shirt, black pants, black socks, black shoes, and a white Roman collar. "Instead of your uniform, wear an old sweater and new blue jeans. Sunglasses. A ball cap. No one will notice you. No one will speak to you."

"Is that the only idea you have?"

Ed thought a moment. "No, of course not. There's a way around going to a medical doctor who's actually practicing. I have, as a member of my flock, a man named Ferdinand. He claims to be a medical doctor, as well as a lot of other things. I've not verified any of those claims. He never asks money of anyone he helps. I suspect he's wealthy. He doesn't show it at all. If I ask him for a favor for you, he will grant it."

Father Mike eyes widened. "You want me to see a quack?"

Ed shrugged. "Or, you can go to Saint Louis or Memphis. Or perhaps just stay in Cape Girardeau."

"I'm not going to let him inject me with anything *or* let him perform surgery."

"I doubt that will be a problem. So . . . tell me what you want me to do."

Father Mike chewed the inside of his cheek, weighing his options for a bit before he answered, "Yes. No, I mean, no, I'm not going to a doctor here or in any other city. Period."

"You'll see Ferdinand?"

"I'll see Ferdinand."

Ed added, "If Ferdinand examines you and finds something physically or mentally wrong, you'll seek further help?"

"Of course. I'm not suicidal."

"I'll contact him for you."

"Thank you." Father Mike shook Ed's hand. "I think."

"Thinking is good."

"I also reserve the right to refuse using him at any time."

"That won't hurt his feelings. Unitarians are tough that way."

"Yeah, well, okay." Father Mike stared at his shoes for a few moments. "Thank you." He extended a hand again. "Thank you very much."

The minister refused the second handshake and instead pointed to the pew. "Sit." Father Mike sat and Ed walked to his office door, opened it, then reached for a large edition of the Holy Bible. When he returned to the priest in the pew, he opened the book. "You may be familiar with these ancient writings." Ed winked and smiled at Father Mike. "Let me try something else by looking into the Hebrew Scriptures."

"Please do."

"Before we go any further, you told me once you went to seminary in New England. Correct?"

"Correct. Sacred Word of God Seminary, outside of Bangor, Maine. A Maine winter will freeze all occasions of sin and leave you numb and holy. The cold served as a means to immobilize any interest in women. One of the nuns who taught us loved to say, 'Don't chase the women! You're no good at it. That's why you're here!'"

"Bitter."

"Yes, but the summers are quite pleasant."

"I meant the nun."

Father Mike snickered. "I've heard that the Pope has ordered that at least one mean nun must work at every seminary. Keeps the rowdy boys humble."

"Now," Ed asked, "haven't the Catholics up there in New England . . . well . . . caught up with Unitarians? Shall I say, dispensed with miracles and such? In fact, haven't they even gone so far as expressing doubts that God exists?"

Father Mike breathed in deeply. He'd heard this before. Before he answered, he lowered his head and said a brief prayer. After the Amen, he looked up and said, "I shouldn't speak for anyone else's beliefs."

"As it should be," Ed said, taking up the book and leafing through it. "Ah! Here we are. In the Hebrew Scriptures, Elijah took an arduous trip and when he grew depressed, he laid down under a broom tree and prayed for death before he fell asleep. Let me read. 'Suddenly an angel touched him. "Get up and eat." Elijah looked and saw a cake baked on hot stones, and a jar of water. He ate and drank, and lay down again. The angel came a second time, and said, "Get up and eat, otherwise the journey will be too much for you.'"

Ed closed the book. "That sounds like what happened to you. Maybe you're supposed to go on a journey."

The priest raised both arms in mock puzzlement. "And where am I supposed to find a broom tree?"

"You don't find renewal in a broom tree. They aren't really trees. They're dense bushes that grow up to twelve feet high. Honeybees love their flowers and their roots make excellent charcoal." Ed rubbed his beard. "Forgive me. It's the professor in me."

"Okay, Professor Ed. You have me hooked. Keep preaching."

"You find renewed strength in yourself when you expose your roots and the petals of your flowers, both of which are useful to God's creatures. When you do that, your light shines among your brothers and sisters and they are warmed by your work."

Silence filled the chapel except for the ticking of a clock.

"OK, Reverend Ed," the priest said. "There's one good way to end this meeting." The priest reached into his pocket and withdrew a medal on a chain. After he blessed it, he handed it to Ed. "It's the Holy Virgin. The Blessed Mother."

"Mary." Ed nodded and then slipped the chain over his neck. "She is a fine woman. In fact, the most humble woman we find in Christian scriptures. She's doing a good job. Wherever she is. I will never take this off."

"This may not be the right time. Or maybe it is. I'll just ask," Father Mike said. " Do you have a wife? Children? A significant other?"

Ed smiled. "Unlike priests, I didn't take a vow of chastity, abstinence, and celibacy, but I may as well have. Like you, I never found time for another person in my life. In my actions, I took a vow never to allow sex into my life." Ed frowned and patted his lips. "That's too harsh. No sex doesn't mean no love. My congregation and anyone else who needs my help always come first. My family isn't small. It is, in fact, huge. All of my people are people I love and I help them the best I can." Ed closed his eyes. "Some of my flock help me without my asking. Besides Ferdinand, Brian—the fellow in the blue suit—attends to sacristan duties. He sets up for worship, stocks candles, makes sure everyone has a hymnal, things like that."

"Brian? He looks so familiar."

"Brian Reeves. The prosecuting attorney for Cape Girardeau County."

"Of course! I've seen him on television and seen his picture in the newspapers."

Father Mike stood and stepped into the aisle. "Ed, I'm glad we talked."

"You may consult me day or night without asking. And I will do the same to you."

"I'll wait for your call about Ferdinand. Might do me good. Any final words of wisdom?"

Ed walked to the front door of the chapel with the priest, opened it, and walked outside with him. "You must pay attention to the visitor who does not name himself. Or herself. Or . . . itself."

Before Father Mike could ask, the minister patted him on the shoulder, walked back in, closed the door, and locked it.

———◆———

After he was sure the priest was gone, Ed opened his small notebook to an entry made exactly two weeks ago to the day. Beneath that notation, he wrote the date, and then wrote the fresh entry: *It happened again. This time with the priest, Father Mike.*

Must see Ferdinand.

Then, he re-read the old entry: *Spirit. Scrapbook. Murder.*

CHAPTER 4

THE RAGGEDY MAN

> *The Raggedy Man*
> *Doing what he can.*
> *The Raggedy Man*
> *Thinking up a plan.*
> *The Raggedy Man*
> *Killing he began.*
> *The Raggedy Man*
> *The Raggedy Man*
> *O, The Raggedy Man*
> *The bloody, Raggedy Man*
> *The bloody, bloody Raggedy Man*
> *The bloody, bloody, bloody Raggedy Man*

CHAPTER 5

Day 1, continued
Holy Cross Church

F ATHER MIKE KNELT IN THE front pew before the main altar of his church and crossed himself. Seeing the flames of the vigil candles as they burned low and gently flickered in an unfelt breeze, soothed him. The scent of incense from an earlier celebration lingered, which reminded him, too, of Christmas.

After a short prayer, he glanced up at the crucifix. It looked like the eyes of Jesus peered down directly at him and darkened.

A sense of dread overcame him. He looked back over his shoulder. No one or nothing was there. When he turned back, he said, "Jesus, is someone after me?"

Not expecting any answer, he leaned his head into his hands and continued his prayers. As he prayed, he thought of his Southern Baptist grandmother, Granny Smothers. When he was twelve years old, Granny caught him swearing. She grabbed his ear and pinched it. "The next time I hear the name of Jesus coming out your mouth, you best be on your knees praying!" She released his ear then, hugged him, and sent him on his way. And at least once a day, she'd tell him, "Michael, you think of Jesus every day of the year. You think of Jesus every hour of every day of the year. You think of Jesus every minute of every hour of every day of the year. And, Michael, your Granny Smothers is telling you to think of Jesus every second of every minute of every hour of every day of the year." Then she'd plant a wet kiss on his forehead. "Keep on lovin' Jesus." He smiled to himself at his favorite memory.

A few years later as a young man, questions surfaced. Why, he asked himself is there something instead of nothing? Why is there an infinite universe that offers only stars and planets that have no life? Why is earth the only one of those planets that has life? How did it, and humans, come to be? Because of his grandmother's constant reminders to keep Jesus in his life, the questions about life eventually led him to the Catholic Church, bound for the seminary.

Now, on his knees, he meditated searching for answers to his recent experience. It didn't help. Palpitations in his chest drilled blood from his heart to his brain directly into his soul and back again.

The relentless critter Paranoia overtook him. The priest, now on the verge of panic for what he'd experienced began to shake. Was it an angel? If it were something other than an angel, he reasoned, it would have hurt him, right? No, he hadn't been hurt. Still he patted himself down from head to toe. Everything appeared normal. No pain. No blood. Relief washed over him. "Thank you, Jesus."

His senses told him he'd imagined the entire thing. Maybe he had dozed off while sitting on the bench. That's why no one else saw what he saw. Yes. That was it. He had dreamed the entire episode.

With that, there was absolutely no reason to see Ferdinand, or a doctor. Maybe now, too, he'd get a good night's sleep and things would be pink and rosy at dawn.

Father Mike exhaled and relaxed. He began his nightly prayer.

"Dear God . . .

Click.

come . . .

Click.

to my assistance."

He raised his head and listened.

Nothing.

He shook his head, closed his eyes, and continued, "Heavenly Father. . ."

Click.

"Protect me—"

No sooner were the words spoken than a raptor-like creature overtook the priest. His voice failed him, his body paralyzed. Death, he thought. *I am going to die.* He was going to be sliced in two by the beast. Just as it reached him, the bird swung sideways and dragged its bloody talons across the marble tiles of the floor, which sounded like a tiny machine gun.

Rat-a-tat-tat.

The massive bird with wings like that of dragon again took flight.

Womp. Whoosh. Womp.

With each thump of its wings, every candle died out. Drool sprayed from its mouth as it flew overhead, coating the priest with a veil of warm, yellow slime. The stench, which might have risen from a thousand corpses, gagged him.

The beast shrieked as it came round again. Father Mike shut his eyes and clamped his hands over his ears.

Womp, womp. Pause. *Whoosh..*

"Stop! Stop!" the priest begged.

The creature descended toward him. Claws, open wide and the size of grappling hooks, like those used on barges, swung at him. Thankfully, he only felt a whisper of wind as it flew past his face.

The demonic phantasm dropped directly in front of him.

He clamped his eyes shut. "I must be . . . I am . . . This is not real!" he screamed. "Only an illusion!" He opened his eyes.

In a deliberate motion, he leaned back to stare at the being. The creature towered over him, enveloping the entire church.

The thing bent down and eyed the priest.

"No," said the priest. "You're not real."

The entity leaned in close to him. So close, its acrid breath gagged the priest.

A low chuckle erupted from its mouth. Barely above a whisper, the entity said, *Listen. Listen to everything I say.*

Father Mike leaned away from the foul fowl, scooted out of the pew, and backed away.

"What do you want?" In hopes that someone—anyone—had come into the church to pray, he scanned the area. He wanted a witness. But no one was there.

The Nearness, which still peered at him, did not move.

"Please," the priest gasped, "what do you want?"

It whispered, *Scrapbook.*

Incredulous, the priest repeated, "Scrapbook?"

It nodded. *Be not afraid.*

"What are you?"

I am not a demon. Then without warning, the thing roared, *Murder!*

As in his previous visitation with the angel, Father Mike understood what the being said in his head.

I am a messenger sent from the throne of God.

"Like . . . like the other angel?"

Ed

Father Mike jerked straight up. "Wait! Ed? I just saw him! Is he all right? Are you saying Ed's been murdered?"

Ed

The priest fumbled for his phone, dropping it onto the floor. He bent down and retrieved it and quickly searched for Ed's number.

"Calm down," he whispered. If anyone were to see him, they'd think he was having a seizure. That was exactly what he was doing. That had to be the explanation. Again, he checked the church for anyone who might be in there. No one. His actions would be difficult to explain.

Whatever it was, spoke again. *The Hivite Horror stalks you. Beware the Hivite Horror.*

"What's a Hivite Horror?" Father Mike backed away from the creature.

When he turned around to run, he stumbled headlong into Alexander Comana. "Alexander!" Father Mike gasped before he checked himself. He grabbed the man. *No slime. No dust. Nothing.* "Thank God it's you, Alexander!"

In an instant, all the candles in the church re-ignited. Alexander's eyes grew wide with surprise. He made the sign of the cross.

"Father, you okay? When I heard you, I rushed in here." The old man, talking around a unlit cigar, squinted at the priest. "Say, you don't look so good. You sick?" Alexander brushed his long dirty gray hair away from his face. "Let me call someone." The janitor yanked his phone from his overalls.

"No, no! I'm . . . fine." The church had returned to normal. "Must've been a dream," he muttered to himself.

"Are you sure? You look a bit green." Alexander took his cigar from his mouth and waved it at the priest. "If I didn't know better, I'd say you looked like you've seen a ghost."

Father Mike breathed slowly and deeply for a few breaths. "Alexander, did *you* see anything . . . odd . . . when you came in just now?"

The janitor stuck the stogie back in his mouth but didn't answer.

"Please, have you seen anyone in here? Or outside maybe?"

Alexander brushed charcoal dust from his hair onto the floor. "Sorry. No one except you."

The priest nodded

"I've been out back repairing the barbecue pit." He worked his cigar to the other side of his mouth. "Oh! Wait! There was someone."

"Just now?"

"Yes, yesterday morning after Mass. I saw that Scotch fellow, the one who lives down by the river, take and stuff a twenty-dollar bill into the poor box. I see him around here and there, but I believe that's the first time I've ever seen him give a penny to the parish. Actually, I don't think he's Catholic, but we take money when it's given to us, no?" The janitor winked at the priest.

"Yes." The priest nodded. 'But you saw no one today, or in the last few minutes?"

"Not a soul."

"Do you know his name, this Scotch fellow?"

"Hold fast there, Father." Alexander felt his pockets. "When I thanked him on behalf of the parish, he gave me his card." The old man stared at it a moment, then said, "Rosswell Carew. Detective or lawyer or something." Alexander stuffed the card back in his pocket. "Never know when I might need this." His grin glowed even in the semi-darkness of the church.

"That's a bit odd, getting a freewill offering from a lawyer." The priest blew out a puff of air. "Although right now, I'm not surprised about anything odd that happens around here."

Alexander twisted his head and body around in a full circle. "Did you see something, Father? Something that shouldn't be here?" He leaned in close to the priest and stared at his eyes. Before the priest could answer, the old man lifted both hands, palms up and said, "Okay. Got much work to do. You need to barbecue, you got a clean grill now."

The janitor stopped and picked up something just as Father Mike remembered what the being had said. "Ed!"

"Beg pardon?"

"Nothing."

"Oh, look here, Father, you must have dropped this." The janitor picked up a holy card lying on the floor. "Well, really look here. Saint Dymphna. The Little Fawn, patron saint of the mentally ill. She was murdered by her father, you know, a pagan warlord." The man shrugged. "I guess you already knew that." He handed the card to the priest. "You may need this. Never know, it may come in handy."

"Thank you." Father Mike stuffed the card into his prayer book. He dialed Ed's number.

No answer.

The priest ran for his car.

◆

When Father Mike arrived at the River City Unitarian Congregation church, he jumped from his car and hurtled toward the front door. Tacked to the door was a paper with this typed notice:

> **Reverend Ed Searl will be away for a few days on a personal retreat. If you need assistance before he returns, please call this number. Ferdinand,**
>
> **The Church Secretary.**

Father Mike punched in the number at the bottom of the notice, which was the same one Ed had already given him.

After a few rings, a man answered.

"Hullo." A long and loud yawn followed. "What is it?" The man spoke with a strong British accent.

"Ferdinand?"

"'Tis me."

Father Mike said he needed to reach Reverend Searl immediately, and that it was an emergency. The priest didn't bother revealing the details about Ed forcing a promise from him to consult Ferdinand in a professional capacity.

"We've met once or twice before if I am not mistaken," the secretary answered. "And I am rarely mistaken. I'm sorry, Father, but I do not know where Ed is."

Father Mike said, "Any good secretary knows where his boss is at all times." His accusatory tone didn't seem to phase the man. "This is literally a case of life or death, Ferdinand."

The church secretary said, "I found his note on my desk and I typed it and stuck it on the front door. As instructed."

"Please have him contact me as soon as possible!"

"I'm sorry but I can't help. Goodbye."

"Wait!" Father Mike said a quick prayer for patience. "You and I both know you know where Ed is. He explained who he was and that he feared for Ed's life. This is an emergency, Ferdinand."

Ferdinand said nothing for a few seconds. Finally, he said, "Look. I've told you all I know." Through the phone's cheap speakers, the secretary's voice sounded like marbles bouncing on a tin roof. "Sometimes he gets calls for buying Girl Scout cookies or such. I refuse to bother him with trivial pursuits."

"This isn't about Girl Scout cookies. This is his life on the line. Didn't you hear me?" Father Mike gritted his teeth, praying for patience. "I am the priest you saw talking to Ed after the funeral service he just performed."

After a slight pause, Ferdinand said, "I saw lots of people."

"Let me ask you something. Did anyone at the funeral mention murder?"

Silence fell on the other end of the line. Ferdinand cleared his throat. "Well, no, but there is something odd."

"What, what, what?"

"Ed . . . I believe his brain's gone off into the woods. He kept saying that something is after him."

"Something after him?" Father Mike rubbed his forehead.

"And one more thing. I'm pretty sure Ed is armed."

"Armed? With what?"

"A gun."

Father Mike felt like he'd been punched in the gut.

"Why would he have a gun? He's always said he was a pacifist. What kind of gun?"

Ferdinand's heavy breathing interfered with his words. "Some kind of pistol he got a bit ago from his pal, Judge Rosswell Carew. Fine man, Judge Carew."

Alarmed at what he was telling him, Father Mike said, "Ferdinand, I need to find Ed right now. If you want to keep him safe, then you'll tell me where I can find him." *God, please give me patience, and I need it right now.*

Ferdinand groaned. "All right, all right. Are you familiar with the primitive camping area at the Trail of Tears State Park?"

"Yes."

"Try there."

"Why do you think Ed would be there?"

"Ed calls that place his meditation area. For the last six months, he's gone up there to be alone. Ruminate on things. Meditate. You know, by some, he's labeled as a heavy meditator. They call him Rev Ed. When you meditate, you're supposed to slow down, you know, but when Ed does it, he speeds up. Get it? Rev Ed."

The priest didn't see the humor, so he didn't respond.

"Anyway," Ferdinand said, "From what I've heard, the path to the camping area is an overgrown weed patch. You'd never catch me out there traipsing through briars and vines. Ticks. Chiggers. Snakes. Spiders. Varmints. Mind where you step out there. Nope, not for me."

Finally, Ferdinand quit talking.

"Anything more?"

"No."

"Thank you, thank you, very much."

"Father Mike?"

"Yes?"

"I'm afraid Ed's on the verge of a mental breakdown. Carew may be sorry he armed him."

Yeah? Well, you ought to follow me around and you'd see who is verging on a mental breakdown. "A mental breakdown? Why do you say that? Has he been violent with anyone?"

"No, no, no," the secretary said. "It started several days ago. He mentioned something was bothering him. When I asked him to be more specific, he told me that I wouldn't believe him."

Instantly, he realized Ed and he had both encountered the same spirit being.

He knew all along when I told him about my experience that he had also met the same force. The same angel. He tugged at his collar. "Why didn't he say something?"

"Beg pardon?"

"Are you sure you don't know what's bothering him?"

"You priests have to keep things secret, don't you?"

"In confession, yes we do."

"Then I'll tell you if you promise to keep it secret."

"You have my word."

"Reverend Searl told me an angel was visiting him. Hard to believe, hey?"

I kncw it!

Since he made no immediate comment, Ferdinand increased his volume. "You heard me, right? He said it was an actual angel. Not a vision. A *real* angel. That's when I knew he was losing it. Never would've dreamed he'd fall for something like that."

"I understand what he saw."

"Or *thought* he saw, you mean. Wish he'd never told me. Such a shame, a good man like him losing his mind."

"All right, so tell me what Ed thought he saw."

"He told me the angel wanted him to take a journey . . . of forty days and forty nights."

"Like Jesus."

Ferdinand grumbled. "I don't know about that. Like many, Ed doesn't usually take those scriptures literally. But this time when he was talking to me, he did."

"What was his destination to be?"

"I don't have a clue. He didn't tell me that. He did say that he has a scrapbook about what started the appearances."

"A scrapbook?" The priest imagined the guy he was talking to was a dolt who had struggled through third grade or whatever they called it in England. His heart racing, he told Ferdinand as gently, yet as forcefully as he could, "Ferdinand, please get over here right now. I need to search Reverend Butcher's office."

The priest hated the bristly impatience he often exhibited toward others. Although now, with practice and prayer he grew stronger every day in hiding the flaming thorn bush of anxious fidgeting that plagued him when others didn't think or act as quickly as he wanted them to.

"I'm on my way."

"I'm at the front door of the chapel. Please hur—"

The phone went silent.

CHAPTER 6

Day 1, continued
River City Unitarian Church

I N THE LAST RAYS OF the sun, a vehicle, silent as a vacant building, eased to the curb in front of Ed's church. Father Mike recognized the car as a Porsche that had been converted by Electric Auto Works in Cape Girardeau. The man that got out of the car was dressed in a ratty military jacket and his blue jeans were punctured with holes. His oversized clothes (by two sizes at least) sported stains of questionable origin. Neither his scraggly white beard shooting out in every direction, nor his hair snaking out from under a camo jungle hat, had met a pair of scissors, or a razor in months.

Accompanying the man, and now disembarking on the passenger side, was the short barrel called Mrs. Bolzoni. Everyone in Cape knew the woman. She regarded the world through glasses that matched the bottoms of antique Coke bottles.

Why is she here?

"Father Mike!" the hobo-looking man yelled for the entire neighborhood to hear. "I hope you've been praying we find Ed in good health and sound mind."

"Ferdinand?" The man's in-person British accent was thicker than a ball of wax. And in person, he looked and talked like Sherlock Holmes as portrayed by Basil Rathbone in the early part of the twentieth century, except that Ferdinand flaunted a wild, wiry white beard.

"One and the same!"

"Mister Ferdinand." Father Mike strode toward the driver.

Ferdinand chuckled and the men shook hands.

Mrs. Bolzoni nudged Ferdinand in the ribs. "Did the little Italian woman what you have riding in this fancy car suddenly forever disappear?"

Ferdinand took her hand and patted it. "I believe you and Father Mike have met before."

Everyone knows of Mrs. Bolzoni.

"Mrs. Bolzoni and I are old acquaintances."

She ignored his outstretched hand and proceeded with her familiar tirade.

"Of courses I have done! Old my baloney! Does this mean that he should ignore me now? The Father here has the niece who does the works for the friend of his who is also the friend of me, Ollie, who runs The Purple Star restaurant where the niece of the Father here, and that should mean I don't want the shaking of the hands and the courtesy stuff?" Mrs. Bolzoni turned to Ferdinand, waggling her finger under his nose. "How should I learn the customs of this country of barbarians not like the sunny Italy where all is peaceful and loving? Answer that to me. No? You can't." To Father Mike she said, "You should bless this crazy car what makes no noise right now that the old Ferdinand drives with much care and I thank you and you welcome."

Father Mike knew better than to ignore Mrs. Bolzoni's request— actually her orders—and quickly blessed the car. Afterwards, he bowed and said, "Nice to see you again, Mrs. Bolzoni."

"You should live so long in the blink of an eye."

Familiar with the old woman's manner of speaking, he didn't bother reacting to her garbled proverbs.

Without another word, Ferdinand grabbed Mrs. Bolzoni's arm and sidestepped the priest to unlock the door. Father Mike turned and followed at a brisk pace. The old, odd couple in front of him hustled at a gait of people less than half their age.

Ed's office, a room with no windows, had four walls lined with shelves stuffed and spilling over with books, magazines, photos, and piles of yellow legal pads full of scribblings. Ferdinand walked over to the wooden desk shoved into a corner. He turned on the lamp, scattering a few stacked papers onto the floor, unveiling a laptop on the corner of the desk. Father Mike appreciated the arrangement of the room. To others, it might very well look a mess. The priest was sure that there was a method to the madness of the shelves. As he walked alongside, he saw books aligned according to subject. On the desk, ballpoint pens filled one coffee mug. Pencils filled another. Paper was stacked neatly beside the open laptop.

Ferdinand and Father Mike fell at once to searching for the scrapbook. Mrs. Bolzoni stood by, her arms folded, her eyes half shut. Her lips pursed as usual. After several minutes, the men gave up, the search proving as fruitless as the Garden of Eden after Adam and Eve had sinned.

"I don't think there's a scrapbook of any kind in here."

Ferdinand said, "I agree."

"Ha! You say nothing is not here never." Mrs. Bolzoni shuffled over to the desk and lifted high a pile of theology books next to the laptop, revealing the scrapbook. "This, boys, is your needed book of scraps. You must learn to observe the things better."

Father Mike, befuzzled, said, "Why did you look there?"

She blew him a raspberry and waved her hand in front of her face. "You probably read already all those books of the theology so you didn't see the stack, much the less what the stack hidden laid underneath." She then pointed to Ferdinand. "And him. He reads nothing only if it the things you see and touch and feel and smell. Big scientist brain is all he sees. He doesn't think with his heart." She pounded her hand over her chest. "Only his head. So he didn't see the stack neither much the less what the stack laid underneath."

Father Mike bowed. "I'm pleading guilty to your charge. I didn't even notice the stack once I'd decided they were all books similar to the ones I'd struggled with at seminary."

Mrs. Bolzoni shook her fingers at the men. "You both should read the Sherlock Holmes. Only one lady did ever deceive him and it was that the Irene Adler, who was some kind of German. She tricked him in to recognizing his name when she dressed as a boy on a dark night and strolled past Sherlock Holmes who was in the disguise and she says 'Good-night, Mister Sherlock Holmes.' He says he knows that voice when he sees too late down the dim street. He learned his lesson good. I learned the lesson from Sherlock." She held out the scrapbook. "We had such books of the scraps when I was a child and we hid notes in the paper covering the back and the front."

"Yes. Ah. Well." Ferdinand coughed and accepted the find from her outstretched hand. "This, I'll assume, is the only scrapbook in the room."

"Good assumption," said Father Mike. "I'll assume the same thing."

"I am as happy to help." Mrs. Bolzoni curtsied.

Father Mike looked over Ferdinand's shoulder. He had seen a similar kind of scrapbook at his grandmother's house when he was a kid. It was wide with pages made from some old, dark paper. "Where did Ed get this?"

"I'm not sure," Ferdinand said. "It's like one day it wasn't here, and the next day it was."

With Mrs. Bolzoni peering over his other shoulder, Ferdinand gently opened the book. He found ten pages with newspaper articles taped on each side of every page. It took only a glance to realize that the articles were about five unsolved murders in the area from only a few years ago. All of the victims were women. Young women. Beautiful women. All killed on or around Interstate 55 in Cape Girardeau County, Missouri.

Father Mike tapped one of the pages. "These killings are all familiar." Something else was familiar. Then it hit him. The thing in the church tried telling him about the murders. "I remember now. The newspapers labeled the killings—and the murderer—the Hivite Horror."

Father Mike pointed to one of the clippings. "The first murder happened in 2006. A young pregnant woman parked at a rest stop to call her boyfriend on the payphone. She told him a suspicious male in a red truck was following her. Then the boyfriend heard a scream over the phone, then nothing. He jumped into his car, raced to the rest stop where he spied a restored red '55 GMC pickup speeding away. The word HIVITE was stenciled on the tailgate. He described the suspect as a male with wild, black hair. The woman was never found. The boyfriend was eventually cleared by the cops."

Mrs. Bolzoni returned to the scrapbook. "Sometimes we live in beautiful world and sometimes we live in awful world." After a moment, she dabbed her eyes with a handkerchief and remained silent, rocking, cradling the grief of the deaths of women she never knew.

Father Mike continued, pointing to a second clipping. "The second murder was in 2007. That time it was a young, married woman who disappeared close to I-55. The police learned from neighbors, that she and her husband had argued loudly and publicly for a long time in the driveway of their home. Her husband couldn't account for his whereabouts during the period when she disappeared. A week after her disappearance, a human skull devoid of any hair or skin arrived on his doorstep. DNA profiling linked the grisly souvenir to the wife. Carved into the skull was the word HIVITE. There were no suspects. The husband was never charged with anything. He did disappear right after that, though.

The last murder—actually, three murders at once—happened about a year later. After their high school graduation ceremony, three female friends partied all night. They showed up drunk in the early morning at a boy's house located off I-55. He left to get some breakfast for the girls. When he returned, they were gone. The word HIVITE was sprayed on the sidewalk with red paint."

After the priest finished his briefing of the murders, the trio fell silent. "May God have mercy on all the souls involved in this horror," Father Mike whispered.

Mrs. Bolzoni removed her eyeglasses and wiped her face. "Horrible for all the souls."

"It is very bad." Ferdinand leaned down to give Mrs. Bolzoni a hug. "Anyway. Why was Reverend Searl interested in these murders? He must've thought there was a common thread or two running through this quilt of murder." He bent low over the book. "Hivite, eh?"

Father Mike said, "The Hivites were a group of the descendants of Canaan, son of Ham."

Ferdinand leafed through the scrapbook. "And, of course, we shan't forget that Schechem, son of Hamor the Hivite who raped Dina. The Hivites today continue to rape and enslave women."

"It's a puzzle without many clues," Father Mike said. "I sure don't have any answers."

Mrs. Bolzoni clapped her hands. "Then we must do like in the Hollywood. We should go off to see the wizard."

"The wizard?" Father Mike's eyes widened. "Who is this wizard?"

Mrs. Bolzoni said, "The wizard Judge Rosswell Carew."

Father Mike chuckled. "I know him. So he's a wizard, too?"

"Bravo." Ferdinand scribbled an address on a business card, closed the scrapbook, and motioned the priest to follow. "Then we shall go talk to him in the morning. Just after dawn."

"Sunrise comes early," said Father Mike. "I'll certainly be up. But will he?"

"Oh, yes, he'll be up."

Mrs. Bolzoni thumped her chest. "And I must keep the idiot wizard and his tasty wife and delicious baby from all harm."

CHAPTER 7

Day 2
The following day, before dawn
The Carew Residence

LOUNGING IN ONE OF HIS favorite folding chairs on the deck of his house overlooking the Mississippi River, Rosswell heard the front doorbell ring several times. He leaned forward and peered down at the door. The day still wasn't light enough to make out the figures standing there.

Rosswell enjoyed hearing the sound of his own voice, thus said to himself, "Who could that be this early in the morning?" Tina, he knew, would open the door. He leaned back in his chair. His lounging could last a few minutes longer. The doorbell rang again. He whistled through his fingers, sending a loud shriek that echoed all over the neighborhood.

His phone sprang into action, playing *I Fought the Law and the Law Won*. When he answered, Tina said, "What was that?"

"I learned how to whistle through my fingers. You put the tip of your fingers under your tongue right where the fingers join. Then you push the tip of your tongue—"

"Don't whistle for me. *Ever*. I'm not your dog. You be courteous and text like normal gentlemen do." She clicked off.

He sipped the boiling espresso sitting next to him. "Texting, my love." Rosswell's fingers plucked his keypad. After several mistakes in spelling, he managed to ask Tina politely if she'd answer the door. Then, as happened every morning, he opened his laptop to consult the local news.

In the opening shot, a Ford minivan emblazoned with *Cape's First News* sat near the river. A reporterette posed in front of the truck, her microphone stuck under her chin. The sound crawled from the speakers of the computer like it had been beaten, eaten, then upchucked. Even with his superb hearing, (no matter what Tina said), he couldn't make out every syllable of her chattering. Ignoring the hot wind tousling her curls, she slid the microphone closer to her mouth and gazed directly into the camera, which remedied some of the garbled words. Somewhat.

The doorbell rang again. After putting on his tri-focal glasses and studying his phone for a few seconds, Rosswell found the *AtTheDoor* app and clicked on it. Two men appeared on the tiny screen. Both of them waved. He paged his wife who was in the living room. "Please let those gentlemen in. I know Ferdinand, and I expect I know that other fellow, the one without a necktie. Thank you."

When Tina reached the door, Rosswell heard the two men and his wife discussing something in low tones. Everything they said was unintelligible. *My super hearing does have limits.* He clicked off the app and enjoyed a few seconds of meditating on the dirty brown river water flowing downstream.

"Judge Carew?"

Rosswell twisted around to discover Tina, Ferdinand, and Father Michael Smothers standing there. Except for his full head of prematurely frosted white hair, as though he'd wandered through a snowstorm, the priest could've passed for the twin brother of a young Saint Pope John Paul II. His skin was lighter—no, grayer—than the late Pope's. Dressed in his black priestly outfit complete with a Roman collar, he carried an aura of power about him, which Rosswell longed for in his own life. Such an aura could come in handy in his line of business, he thought.

"Father Mike," Rosswell said as he got up and walked to the priest and shook hands. "Please, sit down. I haven't seen you since you visited me in the hospital."

"I heard, though, that you know where the church is." Father Mike smiled.

Does he know I made that donation? Now I'll have to give more.

"Ferdinand," Rosswell said, extending his hand to the old man. "Always great to see you."

Rosswell sat in a folding chair piled with newspapers. Perching atop the stack, he didn't bother to remove them.

Tina said, "Yesterday, Ferdinand gave Father Mike our office emergency number. Then last night, after you fell asleep, Rosswell, Father Mike called and left a message." She turned to the priest. "Sorry. We don't have operators standing by twenty-four hours a day." Tina walked over and put her hands on the back of Rosswell's chair. "Anyway, he said he needed to talk to you about something spiritual. I called him back and told him to come over early this morning. And here he is."

"Something spiritual?" Rosswell said. "That's a switch. What is it you need to know?"

The priest pivoted his head and checked the deck. Then he rose and walked along the bannister as though surveying the streets and alleys.

Tina raised her eyebrows and shrugged. Ferdinand watched the unfolding drama in total silence, his usual stone face showing not a flicker except for a quick lip twitch.

"If you're looking for someone slinking around on the highways and byways," Rosswell said, "I can assure you we're quite alone."

"Judge Carew," said the priest, "I can't help but notice that you and your wife both have side arms."

"Yes, we do," Tina answered for both of them. "We are always armed. A sidearm that's not available immediately is nothing more than a paperweight."

Rosswell added, "We both have a lot of people who don't particularly like us. If there's a problem—not caused by us of course—we intend to leave that problem behind us, while keeping us healthy and whole."

For a long while, Father Mike stayed silent. "I understand," he said finally. He paused again and watched the gradually lightening sky. Finally, he looked at Rosswell, took a deep breath, and leaned in close to him. "An angel spoke to me."

Eyes blinking wide as a frown furrowed his brow, Rosswell drew himself up, stood, yet remained silent. Eventually he said, "I'd rather expect that happens a lot in your line of work."

Tina held up her hands in exasperation. "Ferdinand. Father Mike. Excuse us a minute." She gripped Rosswell's elbow, and then steered her husband toward the doorway leading into the house. Gritting her teeth, she whispered in his ear, "Shut up. Straighten up. And listen up."

Knowing when to listen to his wife, Rosswell shut up, straightened up, and listened up.

"Sorry for the interruption," Tina said upon their return. "Please, tell us what the angel did. Or said. Or whatever."

The priest folded his hands in a prayer-like gesture and closed his eyes. He spoke softly when he said, "The angel spoke murder."

Tina and Ferdinand both gasped. Rosswell choked on his coffee. Father Mike hung his head, a bit embarrassed.

"Let's go talk around the big one." Rosswell nodded toward the large table on the deck.

"I'll grab some drinks," said Tina. She returned shortly and placed the refreshments on the table. She handed each man a fresh espresso and enjoyed a real Coca-Cola—one with sugar, not corn syrup, for herself.

"All right," said Rosswell, "We might have a visitation on our hands. Let's figure this out." He dashed his espresso with salt and another teaspoon of sugar. "There must be mischief afoot." Gulping down the hot drink, a smile of contentment spread over his face and he promptly sneezed. He removed his tri-focals and scratched his scrawny mustache as he always did when he pondered the weighty matters of the infinite universe. "I'm assuming that a serious crime has happened, or you all would not be here in the predawn gloom, disturbing our early morning meditations on the deck."

"What he means," Tina said, "is that we just now got Jonathan David asleep for his nap."

"Our son is a night owl," Rosswell pointed out. "Tell me—who died?"

"Not simply *died*," Father Mike said.

"That's right," Ferdinand said. "And, not simply died, but killed. Sad to say, several. And they were murdered."

"Oh. Dear. A mass murder." Rosswell held his head in his hands. Mass murders were never good. "I hadn't heard. This morning I got up early when I couldn't sleep and came out here for fresh air. It was so nice and I hated to spoil it with television or radio or the Internet until just before you all got here and that's when I turned on the news. But, this mass murder wasn't being reported. When did this happen? And where?"

Ferdinand said, "Two thousand six, seven, and eight." He laid the scrapbook on the table and opened it. "Behold. Not a mass murder. A series of murders."

"Serial killings?" Rosswell leafed through the scrapbook. "I remember these. The worst part is that no one in law enforcement has ever found any of these items mentioned in the articles. After the initial investigations, everything tangible disappeared. Scary, but quite sad. And after interest in the investigations waned, no further evidence popped up. In fact, a lot of the people and things mentioned in those newspaper articles can't be found today." He leafed backward through the book. "This is a documentation of something terrible. Who compiled this information and why?"

"I wish I knew." Ferdinand shook his head. "We have no idea where this came from or why it was made in the first place."

"Who is we?"

"Me," said Ferdinand. "And my minister, Reverend Ed."

Tina said, "Doesn't anyone have a guess?"

"Perhaps I do," Father Mike said. "This reminds me of a story in scripture. It's about the Hivites and Dina in Genesis. She was raped by one of the Hivites—whose name in their native tongue meant serpents."

"We know about the story." Rosswell stared at Tina who nodded and then looked back at both men. Neither Rosswell nor Tina commented on the priest's theory. Tina and I discussed this a while back. I need more time to research the questions you've raised. Especially since snakes are involved." Rosswell shivered and rubbed his hands together. "I remember a lot of people investigating these killings."

Rosswell aimed his stare at Ferdinand, who said, "Oh, my yes, Judge Carew. I suspect there must've been hours, days, weeks, and years spent on peering into what the media has lumped together and now calls the Hivite Horror."

"Where did you get this?" Tina asked.

Ferdinand said, "We swiped it from Reverend Ed's office."

"Ed?" Rosswell clutched the scrapbook and jumped to his feet. "Ed Searl? The Unitarian preacher?" Ferdinand and Father Mike, both surprised at Rosswell's reaction, nodded. "Has something happened to my friend?"

Father Mike held up his hands in a stop gesture. "No . . . maybe. . . . Actually, we don't know. Let me try to explain."

"Yes. Calm down, Rosswell," said Tina. She patted him on the arm and pointed to the chair.

After the priest had recounted everything that happened to him on the side of the courthouse hill, and in the church, including the details of all the murders in the scrapbook, he propositioned Rosswell. "Rosswell, I have no money to pay you. Nevertheless, I need your help. I must find Ed."

"You called the cops I hope?"

"Yes, of course I called them. They're not interested in a competent and healthy man who's gone to a park to meditate. That's not against the law and it doesn't mean he's fallen in harm's way. He hasn't been gone long enough to be declared a missing person. Plus, he left a note that he was leaving."

Tina nudged Rosswell. "He asked you if you would help him find Ed. Answer the question."

"Yes. Absolutely. No money? No problem." Rosswell smiled and stuck a forefinger in the air. "However, I'll need help in order to give you my help." He angled his head toward Ferdinand. "Do you want to help me so I can help the Father?"

Ferdinand stroked his beard. "Ed is the head of the sacred space where I plant myself at least once a week. He hath bespoke many lessons unto me. Things that I never knew needed answering, Ed answered. Things I never knew needed asking, Ed asked. I am left refreshed after the words of healing Ed hath spoken to me." Ferdinand stared upward. "Thus and so."

Rosswell coughed a small cough and then picked up a spoon. He scratched the back of his ear with the handle. "I'm not sure what all that means. You're a member of his congregation?"

Ferdinand huffed out a big breath like a chipmunk with cheeks full of nuts, followed by a frosty stare. "I just said that."

With the most contrite voice in the universe, Rosswell said, "Oh. Begging your gracious and undeserved pardon. So, that's a yes?"

Tina patted Rosswell's hand. "That's what he said, dear."

Rosswell certainly didn't want to irritate Ferdinand, who had earlier proven himself nearly as valuable as Ollie, Rosswell's research assistant, especially the time he spotted a deadly snake and kicked Rosswell out of the path of the reptile's strike. Such a thing as alienating Ferdinand, would set Rosswell and Tina's detective agency back a century to the days of Sherlock Holmes. Now, he turned to the priest. "And you? You asked me for help. Will you, in turn, help me?"

"Of course. That is part of my job . . . to help people," Father Mike said. "When I asked you for your help, I committed myself to help you as well. That's how that works."

"Gentlemen and my dear lady," Rosswell said, bowing to his wife. "I've always wanted to say this. 'We ride at dawn! Otherwise we'll be burning daylight!'"

"*Clash of the Titans* and *The Cowboys.*" Father Mike laughed. "You're quoting two different movies, you know."

Tina hung her head and shook it, then added, "Okay, dawn's soon to show its face, therefore the early morning daylight is fixin' to start burning."

"Wait! You can't just drop everything and rush out to scrabble through the woods looking for someone," Rosswell said. He pointed to the men. "I will call you two when it's time to rendezvous. Right now, I do need one more thing before we can meet again and begin this operation."

CHAPTER 8

Day 2, continued
The Purple Star

ROSSWELL TRUDGED IN THE WANING dark to The Purple Star, only a block and a half from his house. Five minutes by foot over fairly smooth sidewalks and he arrived. His night vision bordered on extraordinary. Yes, streetlights glowed along the way, but they were the dulled orange kind that buzzed loudly, attracted hordes of bugs that flew down in his face, and only glimmered the minimum amount of light required by law. Fortunately, he didn't stumble once on the way to the front door of the café that had taken over the remnants of another downtown building—an old department store. Although the building had suffered many floods in its history, now, like all the other buildings along the riverfront, it was protected by the floodwall along the river. Now, the interior of the cafe, with its walls painted a multitude of pastel colors, gave no indication of any previous assaults on its dignity. Instead, the place proclaimed itself a fun place to eat.

All of this, thanks to Father Michael Smothers' niece, Mabel Smothers and her father, Ollie Groton, who'd once served as Rosswell's research assistant (everyone else called him a snitch) in their former hometown of Marble Hill. When Rosswell was on the bench, he had tossed Ollie in the clink a few times. During one of those residencies, Ollie received a purple star tattooed atop his bald head. Thus was named the restaurant.

"I have you to thank you for this ink, Rosswell," he'd said. "Free for a bit of info I traded to the artist, who had been thrown in jail for being drunk and obnoxious. When he sobered up, I bargained for the tattoo."

Even now, Rosswell and Ollie were the best of buds. Rosswell was of the mind that a felony or two shouldn't come between friends, especially when the same fish they both chased were tough as nails to fry. And everyone—except Ollie—loved Benita Smothers, Mabel's mother, and Ollie's ex-girlfriend. She was also the nurse who'd introduced Father Mike—her brother—to Rosswell when he was a patient in the hospital. Small world.

Rosswell positioned himself at the locked front door waiting for Ollie, who was late. Punctuality reigned as Ollie's powerful suit, which irritated Rosswell when Ollie fell off that particular wagon. No other potential customers were in the vicinity. *Thank goodness for that small favor.* He'd rather listen to the crickets chitter and morning birds sing than to make nice with others this early. Rosswell looked around and noted the beginnings of a false dawn in the eastern skies, casting a weak glow of gold across the streets of downtown. It would be an hour or so before the real dawn. A few wispy clouds bounced along the lightening sky. A breeze blew from the south, warming things up even more. As he stood there, a street sweeper rumbled around a corner and ran up and down the street brushing trash from the curbs, which flew out into the middle of the street.

Lot of good that does. Rosswell scrunched up his nose as a lackluster wind hoisted a rancid bouquet off the dark and steamy river. The stench of dead animals and human sewage floating down to New Orleans hung in the air like the aroma on the third day of the visitation of uninvited in-laws. Rosswell felt happy that he was no closer to the river. Even at this distance, the mile-wide expanse of dirty water threatened to make his allergies erupt. Not a good time for that to happen.

Rosswell's concentration was broken when the voice mail alert on his phone chirped. He clicked play and listened.

A weasel-like, whiny voice—clearly male—sang, "Oh, my sweet Rosswell you've stepped into it now. There will be stumbles and bumbles on the way to your grave. Hope it hurts a lot before you die."

Rosswell jerked the phone from his ear and stared at it.

What the hell? Weirdos. Oh, well, goes along with the private detective game since my telephone number is spread wide over Missouri,

Illinois, Kentucky, Tennessee, and Arkansas. Bound to be a nutcase or two in the mix.

At that moment, Ollie arrived.

Rosswell strained to keep himself from screaming, "Where have you been?" Instead, he snarled.

Ollie worked at the lock and calmly replied, "Stop barking until you've had your coffee."

"I've had several cups already."

"And I'm not late."

"You're late." Rosswell held up his phone, showing Ollie the correct time. "If you're on time, you're late. But you're never late. And if you're late, you're careless." Once again, he asked Ollie, "Where have you been? And what's wrong?" The light from Rosswell's phone shined on Ollie's face, which, like the rest of his body, was bare of any hair. Including his eyebrows. But not eyelashes. Sanitary purposes and all.

"One minute late." Ollie again busied himself with the door. "Come on in and I'll give you a free breakfast." Without whipping around to see if Rosswell had accepted his offer, Ollie hustled into the restaurant, flipping on lights, turning on appliances, and doing whatever else one does to make sure a restaurant is ready for customers. Last of all, he snapped on a switch that connected with the local oldies station on the hidden receiver. Ollie turned around and confronted Rosswell. "What will it be? Steak and eggs? Grits and honey? Wheat toast and apple butter? All of the above? Anything and everything is on the house for you."

The fear of the unknown struck Rosswell's gut with the cold of an icicle. Assuming his life had turned worthless, he still hadn't moved from the front door. Nothing to live for. This, clearly, was the end for Rosswell.

"What have you done with the real Ollie?" Rosswell pinched the bridge of his nose. This couldn't be the real Ollie. The real Ollie had *never* given away any food to him. At least not in The Purple Star. And Rosswell didn't rise to the level of a credit customer either. Cash on the barrelhead. Ollie didn't trust Rosswell.

"Fine by me," said Ollie, spinning around and returning to work. "See you later."

"I didn't come to eat." Rosswell shook off his confusion like an old dog that shakes while limping into a hot room after walking through a freezing rain. "Don't you want to hear about your brother-in-law?"

"Nope." Ollie stopped and yelled over his shoulder, "Father Michael Smothers is not my brother-in-law. Never has been. Goodbye." He commenced storming toward the back of the restaurant.

"You sound as if you hate him. How could you hate Father Mike, the coolest preacher in Cape Girardeau? As they say in the courts, let me rephrase the question. Don't you want to hear about your daughter's uncle?"

"I already know what Mabel's uncle said. At least the highlights."

"Ferdinand briefed you. That's what happened, isn't it?"

"I'm not allowed to reveal my sources. It's in the research assistant's code of honor."

"Baloney."

"No." Ollie sneaked a peek over Rosswell's head, searching for customers. "Salami is the research assistant's meat of choice."

Rosswell marched up close to Ollie, clasped both of his hands onto Ollie's shoulders, and looked up at him. Then got close. Up close and personal, which is a violation of Rosswell's personal space by Rosswell himself. Something that, by Ollie, would never be forgotten. But this was different. This counted as important beyond all measures.

"Ollie, this is different . . . and important. Real important."

The research assistant plucked Rosswell's hands from his body and then stepped away. "Are you trying to kiss me?" A grin smeared across Ollie's face. "I'm still not going to work for you." The smirk looked as if it was stolen from a drunk possum sipping the remains from old beer bottles. Rosswell considered the smirk unpleasant to behold. Ollie was not only skinny, but he towered above Rosswell by about a foot, which, at the minimum, turned the kiss question into a stalker's query.

Rosswell pretended to spit on the floor. "I was not going to kiss you. Not now. Not ever. Not even on the cheek. Not even if you're dying and mighty near to drawing your last breath will I kiss you anywhere on your body. But, this situation here is important enough for me to put my hands on your shoulders. Serious up."

The smile slid from Ollie's face. "Serious here." Obviously, he could tell when Rosswell had finished firing jokes at him.

"Preacher Ed is missing. And he's armed. And he's probably in the deep boonies inside Trail of Tears State Park, namely Sheppard Point Trail." Rosswell dropped his hands. "I have no direct evidence of any of that."

Ollie said, "Then you have circumstantial evidence. 'Some circumstantial evidence is very strong, as when you find a trout in the milk.' Henry David Thoreau said that. He knew a lot about how life worked."

"Then, yes," said Rosswell. "It's as bad as a trout in the milk, especially considering the scrapbook Father Mike found in his office."

"Are you talking about Reverend Ed Searl?"

"I am."

"And Father Michael Smothers?"

"Ollie, I already told you that."

"You think Ed's a murderer? A serial killer? Or a mass murderer? Or a killer of only one person? And he kept a scrapbook of his murders? Do you really think that?"

"Never."

"I've known Ed a long time. I could never believe—"

Rosswell's hands flew up, palms toward Ollie. Rosswell yelled, "BUT. . . ."

Ollie's eyes popped open wide when he jumped back. "I can't imagine what you could tell me about Ed that would lower his standing in my eyes." Ollie's mouth snapped shut with no sign of humor. He crossed his arms. "Okay. Give it to me."

Rosswell rubbed his hands together. "Here's my theory of detection. When you come on to a crime scene, you have, in essence, discovered a blank piece of paper. You're surrounded by lots of things to draw on that paper. It's up to you to produce a map that leads from the evidence to the perpetrator and to the crime and then to the facts that connect the perpetrator *with* the crime. If you bring a bunch of preconceptions and mark all over that map before you start the investigation, then you may never solve the crime because you've blurred the path which leads to the solution. You'll never make it home because you've lost yourself in a tangle of brush that you yourself created." Rosswell bowed his head and said "Amen."

"That's good." Ollie sat and wiped his bald head with a Kleenex covered with Vaseline, and then cradled his chin in his hand for a few moments. "That's good. That's very good." He shook a finger at Rosswell. "You know, that is *really very good.* Did Sherlock Holmes say that?"

Rosswell straightened and threw back his shoulders. "No, you did. About two years ago. I then wrote it in my journal and I re-read it before I came over here. Thank you."

Ollie scratched behind his ear for a bit. "That explains everything." He also stared at his shoes. "I owe you for thinking I said something that was truthful and helpful."

"I owe you for letting me borrow your thinking."

Candy Lavaliere danced through the front door just then.

"Hey, pal," Rosswell said, offering his hand in greeting.

Both men watched as she floated toward them. She, whom Rosswell had known for a decade, was a blonde woman with a gentle face, soft and clear to the point of translucence. Tanned and buff, she smelled like Ivory soap. Big charm bracelets on her arms rattled and clanked as she danced toward them. Rings on every finger. Rumor had it that this expert shooter also lifted weights and had read every book in the public library. . . twice. Ollie's intellectual equal was Candy, the former cosmetologist who loved to dance.

When she spotted Rosswell and Ollie's faces, she jerked to a stop, like a queen checkmating. She threw up her hands. "Don't 'Hey, pal me!'" She ogled both men. In her best flirty voice, she said, "Land sakes, you can butter my butt and call me a biscuit!" Then sensing the two had been cooking something up, she said, "I see that The He-man Women Haters Club is in session. Let me guess. You big old boys are fixing to hit the hard road in a quest to save the world by playing cops and robbers."

The blood pathways opened in Rosswell's face wide enough to paint it red. Withholding his anger, he snapped his teeth shut until his jaws hurt. Then he opened his mouth. Slowly. "I need Ollie for one day. No longer than. The mission won't run over one day." Rosswell massaged his jaws. "Someone's missing. We're almost certain he's at Trail of Tears."

Candy propped a hand on her right hip. "Mister Mensa," she said, pointing to Ollie, "And Your Lordship Judge," she said, pointing to Rosswell, "If you know where someone is . . . then he's not *missing*."

Rosswell closed his eyes and shook his head. "The sarcasm is so thick around here, I can't breathe. I'm leaving."

"Wait," said Candy. "Who is missing but not missing?"

"Ed Searl."

Candy frowned, as her attention focused immediately on Rosswell. "The preacher from the Unitarian church?"

"The same."

Candy concentrated on the floor. Then she plopped into a chair and covered her face with two hands. A single teardrop spilled down her cheek. Her voice edged toward breaking. "He sends all his members down here to eat every Saturday since we're not open on Sundays after their church lets out. He's a good man." She lifted her head high, stood, and slapped Ollie on the back. "I hope you find him. Alive and well. Now, get, and get gone. I've got this restaurant under control. And tell that nice Reverend Searl when you find him that he eats here free from now on."

"Wait." Rosswell frowned, pointing both forefingers at Candy. "You've never offered that reward to me."

Ollie said, "I offered you a free meal this morning."

"I meant a lifetime of free meals."

"Can it, Rosswell, and stop with the devil horn fingers," Candy said. "You boys need Sonya Blanco leading this expedition. I suggest you go find her before you get lost in the parking lot at Trail of Tears."

"Why Sonya?" Rosswell asked. "There are lots of good cops around here."

"Maybe, but I know sex slavers are your main target. Sonya's great-grandma was a slave and she made sure her whole family knew the horrors of buying and selling people."

Ollie raised his hands. "No argument from me."

"Nor me," said Rosswell. Candy, however, would never hear from him that it would take a ton and a half of red tape spread out over two days and twenty acres to get Sonya assigned to investigate what was, in reality, locating a sane and grown man out walking on a popular path in a state park. Not exactly a barnburner of a missing person case. He thought a moment. "It's impossible to get her. That's all I can say."

"Right," Candy said to Rosswell. "It's too complicated to get Sonya? As Ollie says, 'Unadulterated bullshit.' So. Okay. Sure. Get out of here. And you're family. That means you pay." She turned to Ollie. "Now you go on along, too. You get one day off. That's all it will take." She pushed them both out the door and shut it behind them.

"One question," Ollie said to Rosswell as they stood on the sidewalk. "You said Ed is armed. Or, at least you think he's armed."

"Correct." Rosswell scratched the back of his ear. "If he is armed, and if he's got a pistol, it's probably a Glock 43, complete with a Crimson Trace laser. Total point and click interface. Needed that because he hasn't learned to aim too good yet."

Ollie, his voice lowering, said, "And you know this how?"

"I helped him pick it out. So what?"

Ollie's eyes opened wide. "You mean to tell me that you fixed up a pacifist Unitarian minister with a 9 mil?"

"Yep. And I stuffed it full of RIP ammo, but I didn't tell him. Those loads are way nastier than hollow points. If he shoots and hits something, it's dead."

"Mighty good thinking there, Rosswell. But why did you give him a cannon when all he needed was a pea shooter?"

"Ed isn't going to hurt anyone. Remember, he's a pacifist," Rosswell scoffed. "And another thing, it's not a cannon. No one calls it a cannon."

"I do." Ollie returned to his low, threatening voice. "If a cat had kittens in the oven, you wouldn't call them buns."

"Ed didn't need a kitten. Or a bun. I gave him a cannon because he *needed* a cannon. Or whatever else you want to call it. Listen, Ollie, think about this. Yes, I know that Ed is an avowed pacifist. Now what happens? All of a sudden one day he starts seeing angels and he gets scared. He needs heavy-duty armament. Someone is trying to drive him nutso."

"Oh, right. He starts having delusions about heavenly visitors and you—brilliant you—slip him a gun that could wipe out half of downtown Cape before it runs out of bullets. Is he going to shoot an angel? That's great. What if he kills somebody when he thinks he's chasing a hobgoblin?"

The traffic increased as they stood there arguing. Noise bothered Rosswell. The one thing that irritated him about living in a city, even one as small as Cape Girardeau. Noise. Also the stink of the noisy cars in the growing heat of the day didn't soothe his nerves, either. He needed to be gone to the woods to search for Ed.

"Here's my assessment," Rosswell said. "The Reverend Ed Searl is one of the most stable and sanest people I've ever met. He won't use a gun in an unlawful manner. I guarantee it."

Ollie chewed on the inside of his cheek for a moment. "Guarantee or not, I question whether we are in danger going after a man toting a cannon who receives visits from angels."

Rosswell shook his head. "Stay here if you're worried about your safety." He angled onto the street and stalked away, but quickly stopped and turned on his heel. His voicemail alert vibrated. He pulled it from his pocket and put it to his ear—he kept the playback low for privacy—and listened. It sounded a lot like the other weirdo message. Then he played it again. Frowning, he turned back and stomped toward Ollie. "There's just one thing."

"What is it, Columbo?"

Rosswell walked close to Ollie, "Some guy *singing* messages that aren't nice. In fact, it was scary. Threatening. Dangerous."

Rosswell punched play while shoving the phone to Ollie's ear. Ollie said, "Shut up and let me listen to it."

When the replay finished, Rosswell said, "What is that all about?" Why is he singing?"

Ollie said, "I bet it's a kind of aphasia. Whoever recorded that may be able to talk normally, but if he's stressed out, he'll start singing, which is easier than talking. He's a stutterer." Ollie pointed to Rosswell's phone. "You just now got that? Do you know who it is?"

"Yes and nope. This is the second one. Not one Sherlock Holmes clue. The caller ID says UNKNOWN. I know lots of weirdos—nothing personal—although I don't know who this one is." Rosswell listened again and shook his head. "Maybe it's nothing. My days are filled with weird things. I'll worry about it later. Now, let's go."

Ollie hustled onto the street after Rosswell, and both hustled back towards Rosswell's home, and into the driveway. Rosswell unlocked his parked Monarch Orange Volkswagen, the car his mother bought brand new right after he was born and named Vicky, after her college roommate.

"Rosswell, hold on!"

"Let's go get the priest!" Rosswell yelled at Ollie. "Get in this car before I slap you sideways into silly."

That time, Ollie followed orders.

CHAPTER 9

Day 2, continued
Trail of Tears State Park

THE SUN HAD NOW RISEN full on. Heat spiraled from the ground into the sky like a tornado as Father Mike, Rosswell and Ollie, stumped toward the top of the hill next to the parking lot. Now, a half hour later, the sun warmed the group in a blanket of wavy, liquid air. The trail, well-marked with logs, piles of rocks, and an occasional hand-lettered sign, snaked up high and low on the steep limestone cliffs, crossing several streams. Rosswell and Ollie, who in the past had traipsed across several rugged areas of Missouri, savored this kind of country. As long as they didn't get lost. Or snake bit. Or otherwise injured.

Nevertheless, in case anyone within hearing range would think Rosswell loved the outdoors, he'd reserved several complaints that spewed forth when he grew tired.

"Slow down," Rosswell said. "My ears are popping."

"The slow speed of your climb allows time for the air pressure in your ears to equalize," said Ollie.

"Thank you, Mister Science Man." Rosswell sneezed. "I'm allergic to everything growing here."

"You don't know everything that is growing here," Ollie said. "And, you're fortunate. The medicine of the twenty-first century will cure you. Big Pharma loves you."

Father Mike, quite a bit younger than either Rosswell or Ollie, had never hiked the path, yet he led the pack, his strong legs pumping out a brutal pace. Rosswell took the priest's pace as a sign that he had neither the inclination nor the wind to waste on the sniping whines coming from Rosswell and the nasty retorts from Ollie.

Trying not to appear obvious, Rosswell surveyed the forest, which reminded him of vegetation more typical of the southern Appalachian Mountains than the eastern Ozarks. He loved being able to identify the abundance of plants. Other than oaks, he recognized the American beech, tulip poplar, and the cucumber magnolia that grew in abundance. Thick, invasive bush honeysuckle spread through the undergrowth. The forest floor was carpeted with wildflowers of all colors. Rosswell especially loved the yellow ones: coreopsis, Missouri primrose, and others he couldn't name. All the vines, too, competed for precious ground space, like fat snakes wriggling to claim a comfortable nest. In the more open areas, ragweed, hemlock, and goldenrod sprouted healthy and strong, waiting for the coming fall when they could spread their seeds. At the end of this trek, he was going to pay dearly. Of all the numerous types of ferns, ranging from tiny to giant, Rosswell's favorite was the Resurrection Fern, which grew in gargantuan clumps that, according to the lore passed down by old hillbillies, could never be killed. That bit of folk knowledge led to old timers wearing sprigs of the fern on their hats in the belief that it also saved a person from harm. Rosswell broke the tip off one as he passed by. *I'll use whatever it takes to keep me out of harm's way.* He stuck it in his pocket since he didn't have a hat.

"It's against the law to pick wild flowers," Ollie said. Rosswell ignored him.

———◆———

About halfway into their mission, Ollie fell against a tree and put his hand on his chest. "I'm going fast," he muttered. "It's time for Father Mike to give me the last rites."

"Pardon me," said Rosswell, "but weren't you earlier bitching at me about me being a bit of a whiner? You're anemic. Counting your money isn't much of an exercise. I can see you're not physically fit. Has the soft life of a restaurant magnate led you to grow spongy?"

"Spongy? No way. My muscles are iron." Ollie replenished himself with a long drink of water before he could go on. "How do we even know if Ed is up here?"

"Ferdinand said he was."

"Ferdinand? That—"

"Careful there. If Mrs. Bolzoni gets wind of you saying anything about Ferdinand, she'll be ready with a frying pan. Now, scan for shoe prints."

Ollie pushed himself away from the tree trunk and peered closely at it.

"No, Ollie. On the ground." Rosswell pointed to the pathway.

"Funny man," said Ollie, "there won't be any shoe prints. For one thing, too much ground cover. For another, it hasn't rained here for a month."

"We don't know for sure if he's up here," said Rosswell.

"Then what are we doing here?"

Father Mike uncapped his canteen, guzzled a long swig, and then sneezed. "I suggest that we stand ready at the crossroads of three actions. We must choose only one. The choices being this: do nothing, change our plans, or charge ahead. Let's pick number three. Charge!"

Rosswell nodded agreement. "You are one-hundred-percent right. We are moving forward into the unknown. The unknown is not a stranger to Reverend Searl and not a stranger to Father Mike, either. An encounter with both men happened before, and today I'm saying it's going to happen again right here in our presence."

Ollie said, "I'm marking my X in the skeptic's box."

As if answering the call from Ollie, a copperhead wriggled out from under a shady bush and aimed for the sunshine of a close-by bluff. Rosswell stopped in his tracks. The fat viper, measuring about forty inches, had a large, triangular head and small cat eyes. The brown body featured darker hourglass-shaped cross bands down the length of its body.

"What's the matter?" Ollie said. "You're safe. I told you before that copperheads give a warning strike before they actually bite you. And, even then the warning bite could be a dry bite, meaning they inject a relatively small amount of venom, if any at all. There you have it. Mathematically, you're safe." Rosswell squeaked out a laugh as the snake put distance between them.

Ollie pointed to the copperhead slithering down the path. "See? The snake is scared of us and is leaving. That's a good omen right there, mathematically speaking."

"No." Father Mike remained stone-faced. "The creature is merely seeking a warm and sunny spot. Second, the snake could very well be an omen. A harbinger of good or evil."

"Or," said Ollie, "an omen that could be a portent of prophetic significance."

Rosswell continued to watch the snake. He had reversed course immediately when he spotted the viper. The snake finally stopped in the sunshine at the edge of the outcropping. "No matter what you both say, according to me, the only way that critter could be classified is *alive*, which means it's violating my First Rule of Goodness in the Entire Universe."

"Which is?" the priest asked.

"The only good snake is a dead snake." He folded down one finger at a time. "I hate three kinds of snakes. Live snakes, dead snakes, and sticks that look like snakes."

Rosswell moved along and gave the creature a wide berth. Behind him, he heard a definitive hiss, as if the snake regretted missing the opportunity to possibly kill him.

CHAPTER 10

Day 2, continued
Trail of Tears State Park
Adam Cain speaks

Adam Cain pointed to the body, then motioned toward a cliff, and said to his sister, "Let's drag her to the edge of that bluff."

"I can't see the edge of the bluff or the river through all the brush and trees," his sister said. "It was easy back when our daddy killed our momma. We learned murder is easy. Murder is simple. You decide who needs killing, and then you use the simplest means available to dispatch the worthless slug." Martha Bailey spoke to her brother as though she were the elder sibling.

"Yeah, well now murder is more complicated," Adam admitted. "When we were kids, Momma was the innocent victim and Daddy was the worthless slug."

"Don't forget it," Martha spat back.

He could hear the shrillness edging into her voice. She was pissed, too. They'd argued many times about Daddy and Momma and who should've killed who. No need to re-hash it now.

He said, "Man has known this eternal truth since humans popped up on the earth. They've known it but they don't remember it." He remembered it every second of every day. It had saved his life several times. "Nowadays, however," he continued with his lecture, "you have to be fussy, what with the government going all nanny state and getting all uppity about breaking murder laws and such silly things. You can do a murder that's easy, but you must use an abundance of caution to assure yourself that you don't get locked up in a little bitty cell with the only toilet but a hole in the floor, which may or may not be the home of The Rat Family."

Martha shivered at the mention of rats.

"Isn't that simple? No. Apparently not." He answered his own rhetorical question as he looked at the mess. "The idiot I sent made a major screw up. The Raggedy Man couldn't find his butt under the noonday sun on the longest day of the year with two hands and a flashlight."

Martha said, "Sure. She shouldn't be here. No one will find her here. You can't trust anyone, much less idiots. You should've killed her yourself." She stuck the toe of her shoe under the corpse's chin and gave it a little kick. "Or you could've let me do it."

"You said your boyfriend was back and he was reliable," Adam said, first tilting his head left, then right as he observed the dead woman.

Did it make sense to the idiot—the one am going to kill soon—that the dead one would be on display here in the middle of the dark forest where no one could see anything? Step back five feet and she disappears into the underbrush. He shook his head. That's not what he wanted. If he wanted to HIDE a murder, he would've conked her on the head, wrapped her in chains, and then dunked her into the middle of the Mississippi River. "Why am I the only smart one around here?"

Martha laughed. "I'm smarter than you and my boyfriend, which admittedly isn't saying much." She poked again at the corpse with her booted toe.

"Umm. Maybe sometimes."

"All the time." Martha cocked her head as her brother had just done, but he had copied her. She had done that since she was a kid. She said that made her look like an intellectual, thinking hard. "That's why I'm telling you we best get moving." She lowered her voice. "People are going to be swarming around here soon. I can hear them coming. Hurry."

CHAPTER 11

Day 2, continued
Trail of Tears State Park

SHORTLY BEFORE TEN IN THE morning, Rosswell, Ollie, and Father Mike negotiated a switchback, which looped around a massive white oak tree. There they discovered Reverend Ed Searl. He was on his knees slumped over the body of a young woman. The minister looked up at the men as they approached. He sat back on his legs.

"She's dead," he said. He looked down at his hands smeared with blood. When he stood up his shirt and trousers looked as if some Carolina Wrens had dropped from the sky, brushed their feet through puddles of blood, and then dragged their tiny claws across his shirt and trousers.

"Are you all right, Ed?" Rosswell asked.

"I watched her die."

Rosswell touched the minister's arm and said, "Let's move over here, Reverend. Ollie, will you help him take a seat on that log?"

Once the man sat and without touching anything, Rosswell stepped close to the woman and knelt down. She was slender and tall with strawberry blonde hair. He didn't recognize her, but she reminded him of Tina. That fact alone released ice spiders in his gut, spewing venom everywhere inside him, especially onto his spine, where the awful critters danced up to his brain and then back down to his tailbone. If the woman had actually been his wife, he'd have died from grief the instant he realized it was Tina.

She lay on her left side with her left arm under her head as if she were sleeping. Her right arm was bent over her chest. A knife with an odd-looking hilt protruded out of her stomach. *Horrible way to die*, Rosswell said to himself. He noted that blood had pooled from the wound onto the ground and congealed. Notably, though putrid, the stink of death hung heavy.

After observing her now-peaceful form, he stated the obvious in a mournful whisper, "She's dead." All the men stayed silent for a few moments. Rosswell stood up and said, "If I haven't missed my guess, she's been killed somewhere else and then moved here."

Ollie said, "And you know this how?"

He pointed to the ground. "There's fresh dirt, see, where she'd been dragged here? And there are bits of leaves, mud, and twigs in her hair. She wouldn't have gotten that if she'd been killed here and just fell to earth. Yep, got all that from being dragged here." Rosswell walked over and squatted down close to Ed. "Is the area here the same as when you saw her, Ed?

"Yes. I mean . . . no. What you said. That's what happened." With eyes that looked past Rosswell, the minister said again, "I watched her die."

"Do you know her, Ed?" He noticed the minister's eyes flicker, searching for something, but then went blank.

Reverend Ed stood and walked a few steps past Rosswell, then turned around and returned to the place where he started. "I can't remember." He wiped a bloody hand across his forehead.

Rosswell put his arm around Ed's shoulder. "You mean you saw her die somewhere else?"

"Yes."

"Did you bring her here after she died?" Rosswell asked this although he didn't think Ed had dragged the woman from somewhere else. For one, there would have been more blood on Ed. For another, he couldn't imagine a man of the cloth killing anyone.

"No." Then as if he'd had an epiphany, Ed's eyes grew wide. He pointed at the body. "I do know her. Juliette! Juliette Fribeau. That's who she is."

Rosswell coughed to cover his surprise.

Father Mike angled forward to Ed. "Is she kin to Anna Fribeau, the woman whose funeral was at your church just the other day?"

"Yes. Sisters," muttered Ed. Now they're both dead." Ed teetered forward toward the priest.

"Here, sit back down, Ed."

"Fribeau? That name is common in Sainte Genevieve County," Rosswell said. "How well did you know them?"

"From church. They came to services and left right after. Rarely talked to anyone. But I think they wanted to meet the other people. Now she'll never talk to me again." Ed took a deep breath. "Juliette did tell me that she'd heard that I visited Trail of Tears State Park to meditate. She said she also visited the area on a strict schedule to exercise. She and Anna, her sister, often camped out here at the park, too, she told me. Primitive campers, as I remember." The man looked at the three men standing around him. With tears in his eyes, he said, "She told me 'Maybe one day I might see you out here.' I just never imagined it would be like this." He buried his face in his hands.

Father Mike said, "Do you know if they had any family?"

"I don't know. They hadn't been with us very long. I'd never heard that name around here before they came."

"Nor I," said Father Mike.

Turning to Ed, Rosswell said, "Ed, you said you watched her die?" Ed started to answer, but Rosswell held up his hand and stopped him. Again, Rosswell inspected the dead woman before he spoke to Ed. "Listen, Ed. Look at me. You didn't watch her die."

Ed looked around as if seeing his surroundings and the men for the first time. Then he looked over at the corpse on the forest floor, down to the bluff below. He glanced back and forth at the trio in confusion, as though trying to figure out why they were there.

"He doesn't look so good," the priest said.

"Might be shock. Sometimes happens when people come up on something like this," Rosswell said.

"Or if they realize they just killed somebody," Ollie replied.

"Nope," Rosswell said.

Father Mike said, "And how do you know Ed didn't kill the girl?"

"Not enough blood on him."

The priest knelt down next to the minister. "Perhaps we should get an ambulance here, Ed, to make sure you're OK."

Ed said, "I'm all right."

"You don't look good." Ollie said. "Besides, we need the police and the coroner here. Who's got a phone?"

"No." Rosswell yelled. "First things first. As his lawyer, I've got to make sure Ed understands the legal implications of what he's saying." He pointed to his companions, "And what is said here is said in the strictest confidence. Understand? Client-attorney privilege."

"I'm not your client," Ollie spat.

"As of right now, you are. As are you Father Mike. And you, Ed."

"What?" Ed said.

"Look at me and tell me, did you stab this woman?"

Ed stared at Rosswell dumbly.

"He's in shock," Ollie said, "Can't believe anything he says."

"Ed, did you kill her?"

"No. Of course not. I'm a minister of God. I don't believe in violence, much less killing, whether the victim is innocent or guilty."

"Okay. If you watched her die, then did you see who killed her?"

Ed didn't hesitate. "Satan."

Ollie snorted, then whispered, "Sounds like an insanity plea."

Rosswell ignored Ollie and continued to question Ed. "Again, you didn't carry her here either from wherever she died?"

"Yes." Ed scratched his head. "I mean, no, I didn't carry her here."

"Do you know who carried her here?"

"Yes. Satan."

Ollie shook his head. Father Mike crossed himself.

Rosswell pinched the bridge of his nose and closed his eyes to fight back a migraine that threatened to shut him down. Eventually, he said to no one in particular, "We've got a major problem. Ed says he watched her die. He says he didn't kill her. Then he says she died somewhere else. He denies carrying her here, but says the devil killed her and then brought her to this place."

"Yeah, that's gonna fly with the cops. Sure thing," Ollie smirked.

Father Mike said, "Let's just hope Ed is confused instead of telling the truth. Especially the part about Satan."

"Think about this," Ollie said. "As Rosswell pointed out, Ed isn't covered with enough blood on him to have done the deed. If he'd stabbed her and carried her here, he'd have more blood on him. Granted, I mean the young woman's not big by any means, but the reverend here is not a spry guy, so I doubt he has the strength to pick up a body somewhere else after she's been killed and transport her any length, either carrying her or dragging her. Now, as far as that devil nonsense goes, I don't believe that for one instant. With all that, I have to agree with you, Rosswell. Reverend Ed didn't kill her, and he didn't carry her here."

"Devil nonsense?" Father Mike retorted. "Don't forget Satan's miracles."

Ollie pressed his lips tight together, although Rosswell could tell something boiled in his brain. Probably a lot of nifty retorts.

Then the three men eyeballed the area again.

"You know, whoever killed her—if our reverend here didn't do it— may still be lurking about," Ollie said.

"Could be," Rosswell said. "I do believe the poor woman must've been killed shortly before she was dumped here."

Father Mike said, "I agree. The killer may be hiding in the woods looking at us right now." The priest pulled out his phone. "I'm calling the cops."

This time Rosswell said, "OK, I know that you all are aware that the authorities will bring a CSI team here to process the scene and I don't want the law enforcement big shots griping at us for messing up a crime scene. Everyone agreed?" Rosswell waited for any responses. The men nodded. "Go ahead, Ollie, call the cops."

"Damn, I don't have any reception. I'll go down to the parking lot. I don't want the cops griping at me for being tardy in reporting a murder, which is what this is."

"I don't have the slightest idea what the cops will do about Ed. Ed, when the cops come don't say anything to them. Nothing. Except, 'Talk to my lawyer.' Understand? By the way, do you want me to represent you?"

"Why?"

"Well, for one, we found you hunched over the deceased woman. For another, you are covered in blood, which I'm sure is her blood."

"But I didn't do anything."

"I believe you, but they probably won't. So, do you want me as your attorney?"

"Yes."

Father Mike, in the meantime had begun praying over the woman, offering prayers for her. "Eternal rest grant unto her, O Lord. And let perpetual light shine upon her."

Ed said, "Amen." Rosswell looked askance at him, wondering how often Unitarians responded to Catholic prayers.

Focusing on the necklace around the woman's neck, Rosswell said, "Okay, I have a hunch about this jewelry." He knelt next to the woman while the priest continued his prayers. Using a pen from his pocket, he gave a gentle tug at the black fabric cord of the necklace worn by the woman, vowing to drop it if there were a speck of resistance. Messing up the crime scene might not only damage Ed's case, the authorities would definitely frown on the touching or removal of anything. "Just as I thought."

A small gold, five-pointed star hung from the black braid.

Ollie whispered to Rosswell, "She's a Guardian."

Rosswell answered in a low tone. "Yep." He released the black braid and stood up. He jerked his head for Ollie to move away from the priest and Ed. Rosswell double-checked to make sure they wouldn't be overheard. "This was intentional. A typical set up. Somebody's trying to lure us here. It has all the fingerprints of Adam Cain or another anti-Guardian bad guy."

"I apologize for eavesdropping, but . . . a guardian?" Father Mike walked closer to Rosswell and Ollie. "What kind of guardian? And who is Adam Cain?"

Rosswell, noting in his brain that the priest must have super hearing the same as he did, said, "We'll tell you in a bit."

"Why not now?"

"Please." Rosswell held up both hands, palms toward the priest. "Trust me on this. There are things you must know before you can know what a guardian is, or who Adam Cain is."

Puzzled, Father Mike cocked his head to one side. "If you insist."

"I do."

Rosswell bent forward, close to the face of Ed and asked, "You doing OK Ed?" Ed at first shrugged, then ignored him. Rosswell swore to himself he saw flames of rage and pain burning in Ed's eyes. "Are you angry at someone? Or something?"

"She's dead." Ed lifted his head, raised both hands to the sky, and laid eyes first on Rosswell, then on Ollie, and finally on Father Mike. "I couldn't help it." Ed didn't otherwise move.

"What do you mean?" Rosswell was beginning to believe that there might have been a possibility Ed had killed the woman.

"She's dead," he repeated. Then as if the weapon protruding from the woman's stomach parachuted in from another dimension, his mouth fell open and his eyes grew wide. "I couldn't help it."

"Is that your knife?"

"That's not a knife." He closed his mouth before lowering his eyes to the ground with a sorrowful hesitation, as if losing sight of the weapon would be fatal to him. "Dirk."

Okay. Now we're getting somewhere. Rosswell asked Ed, "Who's Dirk?"

"No." Ollie coughed softly and looked toward Rosswell. "It's not the name of a man. Or for that matter, a woman. It's the name of what's sticking in the deceased. A dirk is a dagger fashioned after Scottish designs, the kind carried by Highland warriors once upon a time." Ollie spoke quietly and clearly, as if he were standing before the deceased in a funeral home. "Double-edged. Fancy handle." He pointed at Rosswell. "You probably knew that in the back of your mind, being a Scot and all."

Never heard of it. Rosswell cleared his throat "Of course I did. This is a stressful situation. I just wasn't thinking clearly." *The lady was killed with a knife of sorts. Probably not by a female. It takes a lot of power for a killer to break into someone's rib cage. Or, if I'm wrong about that, then it has to be a strong woman. Muscular. Weight lifter. Male or female. Has to be powerful.*

Staring downward, Rosswell once again stepped around the body, noting everything about the scene. Thoroughness was a virtue. Even so, only a few quick glances on his part convinced Rosswell that the prosecutor would push to make the case against Ed and send him away. He surmised that the dead woman must've been walking in the same direction the trio had been travelling, that is, from the parking lot, up the hill, then onto the bluff. She had no canteen or backpack, or at least none in the area. Her hair fell loose around her head. No braids, no barrettes, none of those rubber band thingies that women used to wad their hair into a bun and keep it on the top of their head.

All such things confused Rosswell. She'd dressed in well-worn hiking boots, new blue jeans, old denim work shirt with two front pockets, but no cap or hat and no sunglasses. The cap and glasses might have been lost in a struggle. Who would ever know?

Rosswell failed to spot any out-of-place thing rising to the oddity of Henry David Thoreau's "trout in the milk." On the ground away from the corpse and Ed, lay only the leavings you'd expect to find on a trail atop a bluff. Tree branches, rocks, leaves. Animal droppings. Arrowheads. Quartz. A coin. A couple of shoelaces. All normal stuff on a hiking path.

After motioning Father Mike and Ollie to allow him to continue questioning, Rosswell again knelt next to Ed. The minister's gaze flicked back and forth, eyes on duty, as if expecting a momentary attack.

"I couldn't help it," Ed said. "If the watchman sees the knife come, and blows not the trumpet, and the knife strikes, and takes any person, the watchman is spirited away in his iniquity. That means I'm guilty. I couldn't help it."

Rosswell said, "What couldn't you help?"

Ed didn't return Rosswell's gaze. Instead, he kept his watchman routine going. "My gun—" Ed first pointed left and then pointed right. "It was of no use."

"Are you the watchman?"

"Yes," Ed whispered. "And I have a gun."

CHAPTER 12

FATHER MIKE GAZED OUT OVER the river. Rosswell interrupted his reverie. "Father, did you reach 9-1-1?" The priest turned to face Rosswell and tried once more, without success. "Let me go down to the parking lot and call from there." He made for the nearby trail.

Rosswell, after glancing once more around the murder scene—and no evidence in sight suggested that it was anything but—and spying no pistol (or other firearm or weapon except the dirk), he asked Ed, "Where is your gun?"

"My gun?" Ed rubbed his forehead, as if he were trying to massage a migraine down to manageable pain levels. "Oh. Well. Somewhere. Not around here. On the path. Or bluff, maybe? Or somewhere. I'm not used to carrying a gun. I guess I lost it."

Rosswell scratched his cheek while he waited for Ed to say something else. When the minister didn't speak, Rosswell asked him, "Did you shoot someone?"

"Yes."

Rosswell leaned in. "Who did you shoot?" He didn't want to spook Ed.

The minister closed his eyes and again lifted his face to the sky. "The Hivite."

"Ed?"

Ed lowered his face and opened his eyes. "Yes?"

Rosswell spoke in a tone that was measured and clear. "I'm going to ask you some questions."

"Yes."

"Ed, how did you know the killer was the Hivite?"

"The black woman told me."

"What black woman?"

"The black woman at the hut."

"What hut?"

"The one where the black woman was."

"What was the black woman's name?"

"She was blank."

Rosswell mentally snapped his fingers. "Sonya Blanco?" When Ed didn't react, Rosswell turned and walked to where Ollie watched. He said, "I think Ed is in shock or getting that way or has injured his brain. He's trying to tell me about a black woman and I think he may be referring to Officer Blanco. I'm not sure."

"That's it," Ollie said. "We can't do anything for him. We need an ambulance. I hope that Father Mike reached the parking lot and 9-1-1."

"Yes, I hope they hurry. Let me ask just a couple more questions. Ed's going to have legal problems."

Ollie said, "He's not convulsing. Doesn't look like he has a fever. Or chills. I'll vote for Ed being safe enough to ask a couple more questions."

Rosswell knelt by Ed. "Was the Hivite a man?"

"Yes."

"Listen to me. Is the Hivite dead?"

"I don't know."

"Do you know where the Hivite went?"

"No."

"I don't see any blood except under the woman. Did you shoot the Hivite right around here?"

"No," Ed said, his face showing surprise. "I don't have a weapon. How could I shoot anyone anywhere?"

"Okay." Rosswell rose and again twisted around to face Ollie. "Yes, indeed. Ed has either gone into shock or will be soon."

"Again, yes," agreed Ollie. "We still need to get some more information." Ollie approached the minister and knelt close to him. "Look at me."

Ed, his face pale, directed his gaze at Ollie, but said nothing. The grimace on Ed's face showed pain. Mental or physical pain, Rosswell couldn't discern.

Ollie said to Reverend Ed, "Do you know who I am?"

The minister, instead of answering, leaned over to inspect the dead woman. "I let her die."

"Ed. Connect with me a moment. Do you remember this? You are a minister on the chaplain response team for first responders and law enforcement agents. Is that right?"

"Yes. We do good work."

Rosswell said, "If the face is pale, raise the tail. If the face is red, raise the head."

Ollie patted Rosswell on the back, showing he approved his wisdom. Rosswell shuddered at the unnecessary touch.

Ollie, giving a nod to Rosswell, said to Ed, "Listen to me. I'm going to lay you down. You're suffering from shock. Before I lay you down, tell me if you have any injuries."

"Are you a doctor?"

"No, but I took extensive first aid training."

Ed said, "I know training too. I know where all the tourniquets go. I know how to dial 9-1-1. Yes, of course. Go ahead. Do what you must do."

"Is your head hurting?"

"No."

"Can I check your head to make sure?"

"Yes."

"What about your neck?"

"No."

Ollie took Ed's pulse, inspected his eyes using the light from his phone's flashlight app, and felt his forehead and hands. "You're shivering and sweating a little. Do you know what that means?"

Ed said, "It's my wedding night."

Ollie grinned. "You got married? Who's the lucky woman?"

"No. I'm single."

Rosswell said, "He's disoriented. And his eyes are big. We need an ambulance."

"Does your back hurt? Do you hurt anywhere at all?"

"No." Ed stared down the bluff. He pointed. "I don't hurt down there, but someone does."

Rosswell followed Ed's finger, but didn't see anything except a glint of the morning sun reflecting off something near the bottom of the cliff. Maybe it was Ed's pistol. Or maybe a piece of jewelry. Or a coin or two. Rosswell said, "Father Mike has gone down to the parking lot to call the police and the ambulance. They should be here soon—I hope."

Ed nodded. "Sure." He continued staring down the bluff.

Ollie spoke, getting Ed's attention. "Can I check you for any possible broken bones, Ed?"

"I told you, I am not hurt anywhere. Except my heart. And my head."

Ollie asked, "Your heart?! Are you having any shortness of breath?"

"Yes, my heart. But it's not physical."

Ollie and Rosswell both scratched their heads.

"Stop asking me the same questions."

Ollie turned to Rosswell. "Skin is okay, pupils a little wide but okay, pulse and breathing okay. He's definitely confused and sweating a little. Right now I say the shock is mild. But it could get worse."

Rosswell patted Ed on the shoulder. "Do what Ollie tells you until we get you help."

Ollie maneuvered Ed until he lay on the ground. He then elevated the minister's feet about twelve inches above his head. "How's that?"

"I feel better."

Ed repeated his previous comment. "I couldn't help it."

"I'm going down to the parking lot to see if Father Mike had any luck getting hold of the cops and an ambulance—and a hearse for this poor girl. But, before I go, I want to tell you we've got trouble." Rosswell's legal radar had ramped up to full detection. "Ed, pay attention here. I'm going to tell you something that's more important than anything you've heard before." Rosswell knelt in front of Ed's head, drilling his stare into the minister's eyes. "Keep your mouth shut. Don't say anything to anyone about this." Ed didn't respond. "Ed, listen. Please. I'm going down to the parking lot right now to call Sheriff Talbot Reasoner myself. You know him, right? Do you know who he is?"

"Yes," said Ed. "Sheriff Talbot Reasoner. Sheriff of Cape County. I know him. Fine man."

Rosswell said, "I have to report all that's happened here. There will be a bunch of cops out here snooping everywhere soon. Don't you say anything to Sheriff Reasoner or anyone else about anything here. Understand? No one but me." After a deep breath, he said, "And you know Chief Max Chickering? Same goes for him."

"Don't talk to anyone but Rosswell," Ed said. "Not even to the chief of police."

"Do you know Brian Reeves?"

"The prosecuting attorney. Yes. I know him." Ed raised up on his elbow and stared at the woman's body. What he saw only he knew, but Rosswell sensed Ed was quickly fading. "A woman died and I might be blamed. The sheriff. The prosecutor. The chief of police. Fine men. All of them."

Rosswell groaned. "No, Ed, listen to me. As far as you are concerned, Talbot Reasoner is not a fine man. Brian Reeves is not a fine man. Max Chickering is not a fine man. They all are your enemy. They want to throw you in jail. Don't talk to them or anyone from their offices. Cops, prosecutors, none of them. Don't talk to anyone unless I'm by your side. This is very important, Ed. You must remember it."

"Is Sonya Blanco my enemy?" Ed asked Rosswell.

"Yes."

"All of them are my enemy?"

"Yes," Rosswell said without hesitation. "The only thing I have in mind for you is not being charged with this woman's murder. I know you didn't kill her."

"And Brian Reeves? What does he want for me?"

Ollie said, "Rosswell, the prosecutor goes to Ed's church."

Ignoring Ollie, Rosswell continued, "Ed, again, as I said, he wants you to be locked up the rest of your life. He's the prosecutor." Rosswell broke his own rules and held Ed's face in his hands. "Look at me." Ed stared into Rosswell's eyes. "You must do what I tell you, or you may never see sunshine again. Got that?"

"Surely they do more in a murder investigation than try to send innocent people to prison."

"Ed, do you want Rosswell to help you or not?" Ollie asked.

"Okay. I've got it. Now. Right. Don't talk to anyone but Rosswell," Ed said. "Otherwise, no sunshine. I got that."

Just then Rosswell whirled around when he picked up the sounds of someone hiking toward them from down the hill. He cocked his head like a cardinal listening for an earthworm in the ground. "Somebody's coming. Remember," Rosswell said over his shoulder. "No talking." The noise grew louder.

"Yes," said Ed. "No talking. Lots of quiet. Keep still."

"One more thing, Ed, besides the Hivite, did you see any other hikers since you've been here?"

"I saw a truck," Ed said.

Father Mike shouted just as he came into view. "I called the cops, but they said they already got a call about a murder. They're sending the cops and an ambulance, and the coroner."

"Who else would have known about this?"

Officer Sonya Blanco yelled, "Me."

The men jumped at the sound of another voice.

"Officer Blanco!" Rosswell snapped. "Are you trying to get shot? You scared the dickens out of me! There could be a murderer running loose in these woods."

"Unadulterated baloney. We both know you aren't scared. Second, I know how good your hearing is. If there was a murderer thrashing around in the woods, you would've heard them." Sonya appraised the situation eyeing each man closely.

"How did you know?"

"Candy."

Ollie rushed to Sonya's side. "Candy? Is she all right?"

"Candy's as right as a wet hen. Since you took off this morning with Rosswell and Father Mike here, and since she hasn't heard back from you, she got worried. That's when she called me." Her eyes narrowed. "I called the cops. You should have."

"I called the cops," Father Mike said.

Sonya showed Rosswell her phone. "I got this text a few minutes after I talked to Candy."

Rosswell read the text. "The numbers are the latitude and longitude for this spot?"

"Yes. I learned about that in the fifth grade. That's one of the things that made me want to be a cop. And the next text told me there was a body here." She showed him the second text.

Rosswell shifted around to Ed. "Don't say anything. Understand?"

"In answer to your question, I tried to call," Rosswell said. " No signal. We have a man going into shock. We got him stabilized and I was just heading down the hill when you and Father Mike showed up. Are you sure the cops are coming? I mean, the rest of the cops?"

"I called everyone."

"What about the medics?"

"Them, too." Sonya shook her head. "What a colossal mess."

"That's not fair," Rosswell said. "When we started up here, we simply came up here to find Ed. We certainly didn't expect to find a dead woman."

"Looks like you found him. And her," Sonya quipped. "A fine mess, Rosswell."

When it came to Sonya, a decision lay in Rosswell's future. After pondering everything she'd said, he decided right then to wait until later to inform her that she ranked as the only cop in the local cop shop who dressed her genius as downhome common sense. That compliment could come in handy in the future. But, for now, he stayed as wary of her as a roaring mouse is of a sleeping lion. She lived as a cop, and, on Rosswell's best days, she might admit he was her friend second. Or third or not at all.

Sonya said to Rosswell, "Why are your eyes all squinched up?"

"I'm frowning."

"Why?"

Rosswell said, "As my grandma used to say, 'Life is like licking honey off a thorn'."

Sonya didn't answer. Instead, she turned and walked over to the body. She bent down and studied the area around the dead woman, then stood and stepped around her. Three times she did this. As Rosswell had observed many times before, Sonya rarely missed anything at a crime scene. "Have you destroyed any evidence, Rosswell?"

"What? No . . . wait. We removed the reverend here away from her. But we touched nothing. Nothing at all."

Sonya stepped back toward the group of men. "Whatever causes a bad guy—

"Bad guy?"

"Or bad girl . . . to kill someone?" Sonya replied.

"Thank you. I never assume anything," Rosswell said.

"You're absolutely right, Rosswell. Never assume anything until we have all the facts." Sonya peered around Rosswell to Ed. "Reverend, the medics will be here shortly. We'll have them check you out. And I'm sure Sheriff Reasoner and Chief Chickering will want to question you."

"Thank you."

Just then, Ed turned toward the noise that was the sheriff and the chief marching side by side toward them.

He fainted dead away.

CHAPTER 13

Day 2, continued
Trail of Tears State Park

"**M**Y TWO MOST FAVORITE COPS in the whole wide world," Rosswell said by way of greeting. "Sheriff Talbot Unreasonable and Chief Max Chickenshit." Ollie coughed to cover his snort of laughter and the priest stuffed a fist to his mouth. The sheriff hustled over to the judge. Begrudging respect was something Rosswell yielded to Talbot. For a guy who'd been young when he became the sheriff by winning a contested race that ranged from nasty to mean, Talbot, on occasion, showed flashes of eerily sharp insight and an uncanny grasp of the way the human heart and human head worked together. Only last year, Talbot studied the habits of a dangerous robber on the run so thoroughly that he pinpointed not only the street, but the house where the perp would head for sanctuary. The sheriff even arranged for *Cape's First News* and Kelly Davenport—who mentioned the word *coincidence* several times in her coverage—to be wandering around in the exact place the bust went down.

Other times, Talbot Reasoner was merely stupid.

As in when he "accidentally" ran over a drunk's foot after a DWI arrest. The lawsuit was just gearing up and Rosswell kept mum on his predictions of the outcome.

"Is this a police convention?" Rosswell said to the chief and the sheriff. "Is this what I get when I ask for an ambulance?"

"You didn't call for an ambulance. You called 9-1-1."

"I didn't—"

"That was me," Father Mike said.

The sheriff removed a wide-brimmed Stetson perching on his head, stared inside the hat a long time before he finger-combed the sparse black hair on his skull. He replaced the hat, twisting it left and right until it sat tightly on his head, and then smoothed the brim with his fingers. "We came up here because *someone* called us. That's what happens when my ESP crashes on the way to work. I have to rely on electronic stuff. Phones. Computers. Radios. . . ."

Max added his two cents, "The sheriff called me and I hitched a ride since he initiated the major case squad."

"Activated." Talbot blew out a long breath.

Max's eyes widened. "What?"

"Chief, I *activated* the major case squad. I didn't *initiate* it. The correct term is in the rules."

The skinny cop thought about that for a few seconds, then answered the taller cop, "Sheriff, the term isn't in the rules. Don't you mean by-laws there?"

"Gentlemen," Father Mike said to the two cops, "more importantly here, we have a man going into shock, and we have a murder."

Both men stared at the priest. Rosswell decided that neither of them was a fan of Father Mike. However, they said nothing to confirm that.

"Back to the subject at hand." Rosswell said, "Sonya alerted everyone. But I never got through."

"Nope. Not true. At least one of your calls went through. Your number's still on the emergency list. See here?" He showed Rosswell a printout of his number calling the emergency number. *Now why did the sheriff think that was necessary?* "When the operator couldn't call you back, he called me. Then Father Mike here called, but Sonya had already called me. I fetched Max and here we are."

"Are you going to arrest me for failure to report a murder because I waited—" Rosswell checked his phone—"about nineteen minutes after we found the corpse? I was worried more about the living victim of this crime." Ed, seeming more alert, turned his attention to Rosswell, who put his hand on the minister's shoulder.

"Victim?" Talbot snorted. "How about perpetrator?"

Rosswell cleared his throat. "There's not a scintilla of evidence that Ed had anything to do with this woman's death."

"We," said the sheriff, "will just see about that."

"What," asked the chief, "exactly is a scintilla?"

Ollie risked an answer, and demonstrated by holding his thumb and forefinger millimeters apart. "A little teeny-tiny bitsy-witsy."

Chickering scowled at Ollie but said nothing.

"Why all the manpower?" Rosswell pointed to all the cops on the scene. "Is there a civil insurrection about to explode?"

"Judge," Sonya said, "you already know the answer to that. It always happens when there's a dead body. Like a fire call in the city. Two units head for the fire, each from a different station, so there won't be a thinning of coverage."

"You bet." Talbot snorted. "Besides, Rosswell, there are never small emergencies when you're involved."

"Of course." Rosswell rubbed his wrists as he'd seen prisoners do when their handcuffs were removed. "Just double checking."

Max sidled up next to Talbot. The chief motioned to someone Rosswell couldn't see. A couple of city cops arrived with a stack of blue opaque barrier sheets, setting them up to keep the public (namely the news people) from any further view of the corpse, although it appeared that no one had wandered about the scene who shouldn't have been there in the first place. Even now, if any pictures of the woman had been taken, they might be circling the globe, carried on the invisible wings of the Internet.

"Max, Talbot, Sonya," said Rosswell, while not quite bowing. "I apologize. I wasn't expecting to find a dead body. Futhermore, I haven't seen anyone suspicious in the area."

The blue plastic crinkled as it flapped in the soft wind. A faint odor of decay worked its way into Rosswell's nose. In the midst of the heat, that wasn't a surprise. The pollen and the smell prompted his lungs to burn and his nose to itch. He sneezed. The odor plus his claustrophobia would keep him away from the blue enclosure. And his disgust with an unknown assailant who'd killed the woman generated a gallon of acid in his stomach. If a century were granted for the quest, he'd still never figure out why these things happened. Possibly inbred human evil. It was the best answer around.

"Okay," said Talbot. "No one suspicious in the area. Except the preacher here."

"Yeah, okay." Max, his thin lips pressed together, drew out a Vicks® VapoInhaler™, snorting a couple of deep sniffs. "That's when you activated the major case squad. Right?" He screwed the lid back on the tube, stuffed it back in his pocket, and smacked his lips.

Rosswell couldn't decide which smelled worse: the pungency of the menthol, camphor, and eucalyptus concoction or the odor of the poor woman starting to ripen. He wondered, was Max's nose red from the inhaler, or from booze? Or some other drug? The chief was about Rosswell's age, but looked older. Max showed wear and tear, like a cheap tire with lots of miles, bumping along a bad road at an unsafe speed. All that bumping around on lumpy roads left him with a bad memory. Or maybe it was purely his inattention?

"Chief," Talbot said, "how many times do you have to ask this? We just finished discussing that."

"I've got a lot on my mind."

The sheriff paid no further attention to Max's mumblings or Rosswell's questions, instead scooted next to Ed, who'd regained his strength enough to stand and lean against the big oak tree. After reading the minister his Miranda warning, the sheriff said, "Now, big fella, tell me what's going on here."

Rosswell planted himself between the sheriff and Ed. "My client has nothing to say."

"Your client?" Talbot squinted at Rosswell. "What do you mean your client? You've been kicked off the bench." Talbot thumbed at the chief. "The chief here knows this, too."

Talbot's gleaming white teeth, Rosswell knew, were unlikely for anyone over thirty. Chiclets. Guess that's all the craze these days. Whitened, buffed, and polished. Perfect little white squares. Fake teeth, but otherwise perfect little white squares.

"I'm happy you all are here, but you're not talking to my client."

The chief straightened to his full height, which, to Rosswell, reminded him of a munchkin, only a bit taller. "We're supposed to be here."

"That's right," said Talbot. "Besides Sonya's call, I also got an anonymous one." He pointed to Rosswell's mobile device. "Check your phone."

Rosswell reviewed the status of his phone. "No service. That's obvious. Someone called you from here? But that someone was not me." Rosswell pointed his forefinger straight to the ground every time he said *here*. "And, furthermore, you don't know who it was who called you since it was an anonymous call. But you know it wasn't me." Rosswell scratched his cheeks, all the foreign stuff in the forest making his face itch, and blew out air with as much noise as he could produce. "And there's no way anyone could call from right *here*. Am I getting close?"

Talbot drew a toothpick from his pocket and nodded. "Correct."

Max Chickering said, "Not exactly. The anonymous call, in fact, was routed to 9-1-1." For a visual aid, he drew out his phone, waving it around as he turned a circle. "Anyway, even though no one can get a signal on any phone when standing here, we're sure the call must've gone through since we got it. Obvious. Although we don't know where the informant was when he called."

"Or she, called," Rosswell prompted.

Max said, "Yeah. Whatever."

"And," Talbot said, "the caller said he—or she—was leaving a surprise under the young lady here."

"He?" Rosswell shifted his gaze from Talbot to Max and then back again. "Both you all keep saying he. Do you already know that the perp is a male?"

As if by magic, the inhaler appeared in Max's hand. "We haven't heard the actual 9-1-1 recording yet."

"Correct," Talbot said. "He, or *she*."

"What's the surprise under the corpse?" asked Rosswell.

"Talbot, let me catch this one." Chickering appeared to be reading the fine print on his inhaler. Talbot raised no objections. He pointed to Rosswell. "Since you're the *killer's* lawyer—

Rosswell held up his hands. "Hold up there Chief Chickenshit. There is nothing to say that Reverend Ed, who is my client, is the killer, or that he had anything to do with this young woman's death."

The chief kept talking as if Rosswell hadn't spoken. "I'll tell you what's under the corpse. A phone. Leastways, that's the info we got. Won't know for sure until we look under her body."

"Father Mike, would you mind to keep an eye on Ed and make sure he doesn't talk to anyone? Including the medics? I see them coming now." The priest nodded. Rosswell motioned for Talbot and Max to follow him down the path away from the earshot of the reverend. "Come on," he said when the sheriff and the chief hesitated. "If Ed takes off, I know where we can get a blind three-legged dog to catch him. Besides, he's not going anywhere and you know it."

"This better be good," Talbot said.

Max laughed. "I need a little exercise. Sheriff, shall I include Sonya?" Talbot nodded. "Sonya, let's go."

Rosswell stopped and said in a low voice, "Gentlemen and ma'am, let me start by saying that you all know that Reverend Ed Searl did not kill that young woman."

Talbot brayed, "I know nothing of the sort. Your guy will fry!"

CHAPTER 14

Day 2, continued
Trail of Tears State Park

ROSSWELL SAID, "NO ONE EVER danced the hot squat in Missouri as far as I know. The state has killed bad guys and a couple of gals by hanging, gas, or bad drugs forced into their veins. Probably been a few bad guys got shot in the back when they threatened law enforcement agents. Saved a lot of time and money."

"But a young woman?" Talbot thumbed toward the corpse up the path. "Okay, so let's talk about the victim, not the killer. My sympathies lie with the dead girl. I doubt she's over eighteen. Someone killed that girl on this path. And since no one else is around except your so-called client who's splattered with blood—which I'm guessing is her blood—means your client is the most likely killer."

"Purely circumstantial. Reverend Searl is one of the most respected clergymen in this city. You already know that. His life has literally been an open book for every single day that he's been in Cape, which, I think, has been twenty years. Or more."

Sonya said, "Judge, this does look bad."

"Madam," said Rosswell, bowing low, "I politely refuse to believe that." He straightened and walked back to the other three men.

"Oh, for the love of little green apples! Don't go away mad, Ross! Just go away, " the chief called after him.

It's Roswell, dammit Chickenshit. Roswell knew the Chief was getting back at him by shortening his name to a nickname, something Rosswell hated. He chose to ignore the cop.

Ollie, having followed the trio from a short distance, overheard the conversation, cringed at the sound of the nickname. He cupped his hands around his mouth and bellowed, "Somewhere, there's a village missing a pair of their idiots!"

Talbot and Chickering walked back to the group. "Judge, is all that endorsement jabber for your client supposed to impress me?"

The chief added, "Preachers can be killers, just like atheists."

"You don't have much of a case right now, Rosswell," Sonya said. "Prior good character is not a defense to murder. Just because your guy was a good guy last night doesn't mean he couldn't have slipped off the narrow path this morning and cut this woman deep till she was dead."

"All that is supposition." Rosswell waved his hand, unwilling to grant even a tiny point. "My innocent client has not touched anything else, especially the murder weapon, which is still stuck in the poor woman in the same position it was in when it killed her. Nothing has Ed's fingerprints on it, I'll bet you. No. Wait. I don't have to bet. I can tell you for a fact that the—"

"Actually, that weapon is a dirk," Chief Chickering said, a grin splitting his face from one of his floppy ears to the other. "I've been studying up. I can tell by the handle. Most Scottish dirks have carved handles. And most of the handles are fancy."

Talbot, grinding away at the toothpick, stopped and stared at the chief for a few seconds. "Dirk? That sounds like some Hollywood pretty boy and not no deadly weapon."

Chickering bounced his head up and down once. "Look it up there on the Interwebs. You'll see I'm right."

"He's right, Sheriff," said Rosswell. "I'm a Scot and I was taught that at feet of *seanmhair.*"

Max squeaked, just a short one. One that sounded like the mouse who tripped the trap and had the bar break his neck. "The what?"

"*Seanmhair . . .* my grandma. Now, can we get on with this? Back to the phone, supposedly beneath the corpse. I can bet it also doesn't have Ed's prints on it."

"How do you know?" Talbot said.

"Because I know Ed."

Max said, "More than once it's happened that people who trusted each other have been surprised when one of them turns into a traitor. I've been studying about that, too."

"That's it," said Talbot. "Conversation is over. We're not getting on with anything. We're arresting Reverend Ed, and throwing him in jail. The prosecutor will file capital murder charges if I have anything to say about it."

"Brian Reeves? He's smarter than that," Rosswell said. "And, besides, cops don't tell prosecutors what to do. You never ever see a cop at a press conference saying that someone is innocent so they won't be prosecuted. The prosecutor makes up his own mind." He glanced at Sonya. "Or hers."

Sonya said, "I'm not the prosecutor."

"Then you need to go to law school and run for office." Rosswell nodded at her. "We need someone who has a brain."

Talbot leaned close to Rosswell and said in a whisper, "Brian Reeves will file whatever I tell him to file."

Max Chickering said, "Sheriff, I hope the judge here doesn't have a body camera on him."

Rosswell moved even closer to Talbot. "If you are in fact telling me you're blackmailing the prosecutor, I'll report you to the highway patrol and turn you in. And I'll turn in Brian to the legal ethics baboons who will take his law license away from him for not reporting that he corroborated with you—a felony that directly affects the integrity of the court system."

"Go right ahead. Report every cop and lawyer in the county, and even the state, and The of Land of the Free." Talbot barked a laugh and straightened. "I'll deny I ever said it. Besides that, no one will care. The prosecutor takes the easy way out. And he's careful never to leave any footprints showing illegal acts."

"Wait a minute." Rosswell pointed at each of the lawmen. "How about this? You all get all the evidence you need up here and I'll hustle Ed down to the cop shop, let the prosecutor interrogate him, and then we'll ask the judge for a personal recognizance bond and then he can go home."

Talbot bit the toothpick in two and said, "There's a word for that."

"What's the word?"

"No."

"You know he's not guilty of anything."

Max said, "We know you found Ed covered with the blood of a fresh corpse even though there's no one else around for miles. That's terrific circumstantial evidence. You're always telling us that circumstantial evidence can send someone to the death chamber. In fact, you told us once that the circumstantial evidence of footprints in the mud outweigh the sworn testimony of ten thousand archangels that no dog passed this way."

Rosswell hated the times when his own words were used against him. "You don't believe for a second he's guilty." He hoped his deflection made everyone's attention move away from him.

"I don't have to believe anything," Talbot said. "You've got a guy with a girl out here in the woods and the guy rears up a little frisky and the girl tells him to shove off and the guy goes ballistic and kills the girl. Happens all the time. Men are pigs. Men can't control themselves when they're turned down. There was a special about that on streaming television. I don't have to believe that's what happened, though. I leave that up to the court."

"How many times have you seen this?" Max again snorted a couple quick Vicks hits. "I've seen it a lot. Violence instead of sex. Or violence AND sex. Standard fare."

"Sonya," said Rosswell, waving his arm. "Give me your opinion."

"About what?"

"You heard them. Max and Talbot think Ed is guilty of murder."

"I never said that," said Talbot. "We'll leave all that up to the prosecutor, the judge, and the jury. I don't decide guilt or innocence. I bring in the bad guys and let the system work its magic."

Rosswell eyed Sonya. "You agree?"

"Of course I agree. Cops don't decide guilt or innocence."

"No," said Rosswell. "I mean do you agree that Ed is guilty?"

Sonya pointed to her ear. "You don't listen too good. I just answered that question."

Rosswell walked close to Max. "How about you?"

"I'm a city cop. Like Sonya. She and I are like highway patrol, FBI, deputies, IRS agents, or meter maids. We don't decide nothing about guilt or innocence. We let the system work."

Rosswell separated himself from the law enforcement trinity and strolled back to the priest, hoping to gain an appearance of nonchalance. "Okay, Father Mike. Stand by for the badges to carry Ed back into town. There's no way I can talk them out of it."

Father Mike said, "Let me help you, my friend," as he helped Ed stand. The minister stared straight ahead, again unfocused and blank. The priest walked in step with Ed's shaky gait over to the sheriff. "Ed is smelly and dirty. Let him have a shower, change of clothes, and something to eat and drink, before you start your interrogation."

"No can do. We will take him to the jail. His clothes will be tagged and bagged," Talbot retorted. "And, with all due respect, you take care of your parishioners and I'll take care of my prisoners. This is a worldly problem. Not a religious problem. You understand? Render unto Caesar and all that stuff."

"That," Rosswell said, "is not a good legal answer. You're opening yourself up to a civil lawsuit."

"Ross, you take care of your own business."

"My business is that my first name has no abbreviation because it's my family name. Rosswell. Use it correctly."

Talbot sniggered. "Right. I'll do that."

"Sheriff Reasoner, be humane." Father Mike patted Ed on the back. "Go with the sheriff. He won't hurt you. I promise you that." The priest threw a look of disdain that the sheriff missed. "I'll personally make sure he doesn't hurt you."

Max said, "Father Mike's right, Talbot. Last week he said in his homily that we are to love our fellow man. And woman. The least of our brothers and all that stuff."

"Sheriff," Sonya said, "I agree. Being humane doesn't cost anything."

Sheriff Talbot Reasoner's lips pulled up into a smirk, causing the ice spiders recently loosed into Rosswell's body to run up, down, and sideways on his spine.

"You all will need to come to the station, too, for your statements." The sheriff grabbed Ed by the arm. "Come on, preacher man." The sheriff's lips curled upward into a winning sneer.

"Stop," Rosswell commanded. "You can take him, but you can't speak with him without me present. I am his attorney and that is the law." Rosswell touched Ed's arm. "Ed, tell the sheriff here I am your attorney."

Ed shook his head yes.

"Tell them, Ed. Say 'yes'." Ed said yes. "OK, you heard that."

The sheriff rolled his eyes and proceeded down the hill with Ed in tow.

SOB thinks everyone is guilty. Rosswell only managed to stir up a dab of saving grace that Talbot surely cared about what his fellow cops thought.

He knew, too, that with Sonya and Max close, nothing bad would happen to Ed.

Nothing worse, that is, than being arrested for capital murder.

A murder the man didn't commit.

CHAPTER 15

Day 2, Continued
Trail of Tears State Park

THE CSIS, IN A SMALL bid toward decency to an otherwise deplorable defense attorney, allowed Rosswell to watch until they finished processing the scene. Of special interest were the phone and the dirk. "I'll need to know who owns those." Rosswell pointed to each in separate clear evidence bags.

"Couldn't tell you," one of the CSIs replied, as he passed Rosswell and kept on walking.

"Wait." Rosswell caught up to the man. "Sorry. I wasn't asking you as a law enforcement officer. Just thinking out loud as a defense attorney." The CSI sped up in an attempt to get further away from Rosswell. Snapping his fingers, Rosswell again caught up to the investigator. "Another quick question." *I'm beginning to sound like Columbo.* "Did you find fingerprints on the dirk?"

"You lawyers are all alike. Another quick question. Right. We'll turn over all our info to the prosecutor." The CSI, clothed in a HAZMAT suit that covered his entire body, waved a hand in dismissal, then clumped away. The man reminded Rosswell of a polar explorer of unknown gender tromping around. Eventually, all the badges packed up, the CSIs carried off the corpse, and everyone left the scene. Only Father Mike, Rosswell, and Ollie remained.

Rosswell said, "This situation is closing in on itself." Sighing, after a long pause to categorize the clouds in the sky, he continued in a monotone, "I'm afraid when everything collapses on to him, Ed will suffocate."

Slogging through the dense undergrowth to the edge of the cliff, Rosswell gazed where Ed had stood before he was dragged off to jail. Rosswell smelled the scent of new rain coming. There was a word for the pleasant smell, an aroma associated with the first rain after a long period of warm, dry weather. *Petrichor.* He loved the sound of the word. Ollie walked up beside him.

"I smell rain coming," he said.

"Petrichor," Rosswell said.

"I'm impressed," Ollie said, "that you know the word. But I bet you don't know the history of the word." Not waiting for an answer, Ollie continued. "When the Greek roots *petra* (rock) and *ichor* (blood of the Greek gods) were combined, it became the name of a natural aromatic oil predicting rain. You can still smell it after the rain stops. Mankind inherited an affection for the smell from ancestors who relied on rainy weather for their survival."

"Show off," Rosswell said.

The clouds gathered until they grew purple, as if bruised. Then without warning, fresh water slipped downward in sheets like glass, lit from behind by searing white flashes. Across the river, bolts of lightning zinged this way and that, morphing the air into a bitter soup of ozone and water, sterilized by the flash. Then the taste of the air turned electric, biting the inside of Rosswell's mouth.

"I think it's time to retreat to safety," the priest said.

"Agreed," Ollie said.

Then before Rosswell could turn away, a clap of thunder jolted him forward. The rocks beneath his feet slipped away then crumbled, tossing him into empty space. Instinctively, he grabbed at anything, hoping to stop the fall to his death. His hand latched on to the tendrils of a huge resurrection fern, a plant that could survive long droughts by curling up its fronds and faking death. In the barest blink of each eye, Rosswell knew that a fern did not contain enough strength to protect him from tumbling down the bluff. The fern gave way. A crushed skull and death, he knew, loomed close. Although Rosswell had only a microsecond to think about his fate, that microsecond stopped time when he saw the girl.

The little girl. There still existed that moment during the war in the Middle East when he'd stumbled upon her. She was swathed in a bomb carrier's protective gear. Without hesitation, he shot the girl. Later, the bomb squad told Rosswell that the child had been used. The entire set-up was a fake. He'd killed an innocent child.

Rosswell folded around a wrinkle in the air like a diver executing a complicated dive. In that instant, the girl was by his side.

"Daddy," she cried, "I'll save you!"

How, he didn't know, but he had time to ask, "Who are you?"

She clasped him in a soft bear hug and spoke, rather sang in musical tones "Feliciana was my mommy. And my name is Dina."

Then the blackness swallowed him.

CHAPTER 16

Day 2, Continued
Trail of Tears State Park

"**R**OSSWELL!"

Rosswell heard Ollie calling his name from a universe far, far away. Yet, when he opened his eyes, Ollie's face hovered over his, too close for comfort. "What? Quit yelling in my face." Rosswell rolled on his side, anything to remove himself from Ollie's nearness.

Why am I no longer in hell?

Ollie laughed, long and loud. "Rosswell is alive and still acting as cranky as a constipated baby."

Father Mike leaned over him. "How many fingers am I holding up?"

"Fifteen. Now, get the hell out of my way and let me up." He sat up and brushed himself off, which did nothing to make him cleaner. Everything he wore, including his skin, was sopping wet. Mud, bits of greenery, dead sticks, insects, and crushed flowers all stuck to him. The mud, in fact, was thick over his entire body, reminding him of a mummy wrapped for eternity. He had fallen into the only spring on the east side of the entire cliff.

Father Mike said, "How in God's name did you manage to survive that fall?" The priest stood and pointed at the cliff, a good fifteen feet above them. "And, to land in mud, at that?"

Rosswell tilted his head back and stared up to the top of the cliff. "I'm just lucky that way, I guess." He continued fruitlessly, to try and get the mud off his jeans. "It's not that far. I think I bumped against the side of the hill a couple of times, then grabbed a handful of ferns. That slowed me down. Then I curled up in a fetal position." He didn't tell them about his vision. Or the little girl. He sat up and looked around. A bed of resurrection fronds lay beneath him. And a puddle of mud, surrounded by dry, rocky ground. He stared at a huge rock. "I'm glad I found the mud instead of that boulder."

"You're banged and bruised, but you don't seem to have any broken bones," Ollie said.

"I know the name!" Rosswell shouted.

Ollie and the priest exchanged glances.

"You fell off a cliff and hit your head," the priest said. "We're getting you to a hospital."

Rosswell looked straight into the priest's eyes. "Wait!" Rosswell grabbed the priest's arm. "We need to tell you something. There's a worldwide organization called The Guardians of Dina. They rescue women and children from sex-slavers. We are totally against slavery."

"We?" asked Father Mike.

Ollie nodded. "Rosswell and me."

"We're getting you to a hospital," the priest reiterated.

"It wasn't that big a fall," Rosswell said. "And I'm not hurt."

"You're raving utter nonsense."

Ollie pecked Father Mike on the shoulder. "Actually, Rosswell isn't raving anything. Listen to him. He knows about the Guardians."

"Guardians?" Father Mike looked back at Rosswell. "Are you a member of this club?"

Rosswell wiped mud from his face. "I already told you that." He wiped mud from his teeth with a dirty finger. "Tina, too. She's a member, as is Candy." Rosswell spit a few times, cleansing his mouth of tiny rocks and thick mud. "And the bad guys are the Hivites."

"Sonya Blanco? Is she a member?"

"Not to my knowledge," Rosswell answered. "We don't publish a membership list."

"And you Guardians are fighting the Hivites because of something that happened four thousand years ago?"

"Yes. But we're also fighting them because of something that's happening right now." Rosswell sputtered and tried to spit out more mud.

Ollie broke into the conversation. "There are probably a hundred thousand victims of sex trafficking in the United States alone. Sex slavery is alive and well."

The priest's pale complexion grew red. "I feel angry when I think of the women who're being bought and sold. What do the Guardians do to combat this abomination?"

Rosswell said, "We kill them. The slavers, that is."

"You what?" Father Mike's face went from crimson to gray.

"We." Rosswell thumped his chest, pointed to Ollie, then thumped his chest again. "We are vigilantes."

"Vigilantes? The Guardians you're talking about are vigilantes? God have mercy." Father Mike backed away from Rosswell and Ollie, and made the Sign of the Cross, perhaps fearing something would jump from their mouths and infect him with evil. "Killing is a mortal sin."

"Yes, but self-defense isn't," Ollie pointed out.

"Keeping a woman in slavery for sexual exploitation is also a mortal sin," Rosswell said. "I'll take my chances. Protecting those who are enslaved are our responsibility. We are our brother's—and sister's—keepers. That's in the Bible. I hope God approves of our work."

Ollie jutted his chin towards Rosswell. "He always says that vigilantes must be right one hundred percent of the time. So far, we've been on the money every single time."

"I'm not going to kill *anyone* for *any* reason," said Father Mike. "And I won't lie to cover up a killing."

"I immediately recognized the necklace Ed found," said Rosswell. "It was a *soutache*, an old-fashioned decorative braid, sometimes used to cover a seam on a piece of clothing. The braid represents earth. The gold star represents heaven and signifies the Guardians of Dina. I don't know the girl but the Guardians must have claimed her as one of their own. When you become a Guardian, you wear one of those." He fished his out from under his shirt, as did Ollie. The priest scrutinized both of the gold stars hung on black ribbons.

Ollie said, "Rosswell is right. The woman—we'll assume her name is indeed Juliette Fribeau—belonged to the vigilante group that he and I long ago pledged allegiance to."

The priest backed further away. "Murder? Slavery? War? I won't help you kill anyone, in self-defense, or otherwise, even if they kill first."

"Father, we won't ask you to murder or shun the truth," said Rosswell. "Someone killed that girl because she was a Guardian of Dina. We intend to find whoever killed her, and we will, in turn, kill him, or her, or them. Guardians, unfortunately, have a high mortality rate," added Rosswell. "We are in a war. One we intend to win. And we don't take anyone's word that someone has killed another. We must witness this horror ourselves. If we catch them in the act, we kill them. Trust us on this."

"Judge . . . Ollie, I am *not* going to trust you on this."

Rosswell shrugged. "Suit yourself." He slowly got up and stretched. "Now, let's talk about something besides theology. Do you have any objections to posting Ed's bail?"

"What do you mean?"

"I want to post a bail bond for him. However, lawyers are strongly encouraged not to post bail for their clients. Ed has no money for that, I'm sure. I'm not sure his congregants would approve of him using church funds. Bail bonds are expensive."

"Judge, I don't have the money for it either."

"Let me finish. Therefore, I want to hand over the cash money so you can bond Ed out of jail. He will be charged with some degree of homicide. Probably capital murder. Prosecutors can lower charges, but the courts don't like them raising charges, so prosecutors start off with the highest charge possible. But no matter what Ed is charged with, it will be a whopper of a bail bond."

"Capital murder?" said Father Mike. "Any time you hear that on the news, it's usually followed by the information that the suspect won't be released from jail pending the trial."

"I'm hoping the judge in this case will listen to me when I argue for bail. I also hope that the prosecutor will go along with me."

"If I take your money and buy a bail bond, is that a crime?"

"I would lose my law license if I got caught. Somewhere along the line, there's probably a statute or two you and I would both be breaking."

"You want me to lie about it?" He stared straight ahead for a few seconds. "I told you I'm not lying for you, especially when the lie is also committing a crime."

Ollie stepped closer to the priest. "Listen, we're trying to keep an innocent man out of jail. We all know Ed didn't do this—"

Father Mike interrupted. "What if he did kill the girl? Do we still post his bail?"

"Yes," said Rosswell instantly. "Whether he's guilty or not guilty, I'll be his main lawyer, but will bring in an expert criminal lawyer as my co-counsel. I'm going to do everything I can for him, although I can't be caught messing around with posting his bail. I will help him even if he's guilty as sin."

"Why?"

Rosswell tilted his head and looked at Ollie. "A priest is asking me why I am helping a man who needs help? How many people confess the same sins over and over? A lot. You told me that one time. My reason for helping is, I'm a Good Samaritan. That's why."

Father Mike smiled. "Okay, I get it."

"Then you'll bail Ed out with my money?"

"Yes." Father Mike hung his head. "But I won't lie if someone asks me where the money came from."

"No problem. Bondsmen—or women—"

"That's really getting old Rosswell."

Rosswell waived Ollie off. "—don't really care where the money comes from. All they want is their money back with a bit of interest. I'll even go with you. Tell them I had to show you where their office was. If anyone does ask, I'll divert their attention to something else."

The priest nodded. "Okay."

"By the way, Father, you just heard me lie." It was Rosswell's turn to hang his head. "It wasn't a resurrection fern that saved my life."

Ollie narrowed his eyes. Father Mike's grew wide.

"What saved me was an angel. The very same angel that visited you and Ed."

"How do you know that?"

"Father, pay attention to the visitor who does not name himself. Or herself. Or . . . itself. The angel whispered it in my ear as I was falling from that cliff. The angel wrapped me in its arms and softened my landing. And that angel is the angel of learning. After God created the universe, He sent that very angel to teach humans to speak. Adam and Eve were his first students. Furthermore, that angel? Its name is Dina. The same name of the rape victim in the Hebrew scriptures, which is also the same name of my daughter who was never born."

CHAPTER 17

Day 2, continued
Common Pleas Courthouse

ARRIVING HOME AT THE CAREW residence, Rosswell whined to Tina, "I'm in a hurry. I'm supposed to meet the prosecutor."

"Shut up and let me clean you off enough to go inside. Besides, you can't be seen in public, much less at the courthouse, when you've fallen off a cliff and rolled in the mud."

Rosswell suffered through Tina hosing him down in the backyard before he was allowed to come into their house.

"You turned that nozzle to FINE NEEDLE!"

"Took that to get the dried mud off." She turned off the water. "Stay right there. I'll get you some towels."

Once Tina allowed her husband inside their house, he showered and dressed for a jaunt to courthouse park to chat up the prosecutor.

◆

Outside the courthouse, Rosswell discovered Brian Reeves, a tall, bald, bearded man with piercing blue-green eyes, lounging by the Union monument. It was a large fountain with a soldier facing, oddly enough, west, as if he were on guard for rampaging cowboys intending to invade the river city. Rosswell often thought that the soldier should've been facing south, keeping an eye out for Confederates, although now that he thought about it, the Confederate monument is located west of the Union monument.

Maybe it made sense after all.

When the prosecutor saw Rosswell, he quickly lit a cigar, and then yelled out, "Hey, pal!"

Rosswell had never classified their relationship as cozy. Yes, they'd been cordial with each other outside the courtroom and had never had a major dust-up during formal proceedings. In fact, Rosswell treasured a fond remembrance of Brian taking his side many years ago before the County Commission who thought that the hangman's noose displayed in the jury courtroom was nifty and should stay there. Rosswell, backed up by Brian, insisted that no one could get a fair trial in that courtroom. Rosswell and Brian won. The noose came down. Rosswell and Brian burned it in public. Still. That didn't mean they were pals.

"Good to see you again," Rosswell said, extending his hand, deciding not to discuss the pal problem. "I see you're growing your beard again."

"Same to you, Judge Carew, and yes, I am," he said, as he rubbed the hair on his chin. He grabbed Rosswell's hand. "I hope it's not long before the State of Missouri comes to its senses and puts you back on the bench. Someone needs to help straighten out our sentencing laws. They're so complicated. Sometimes they let the bad guys out before they've served their sentence." Brian looked up to study the clouds in the sky. "Or they get released if the software is screwed up, like it usually is. When the system depends on software, there are always glitches. Why don't they back up the records with written documentation? What do you think about that, Judge Carew?"

"Don't be in a rush to get me on the bench again because no one listens to me." Rosswell studied the prosecutor. He seemed sincere. However, he did find the conversation a bit odd.

Rosswell scratched his mustache, then subconsciously scratched his cheeks, checking for any fuzz and found none. "Is there some reason you shave your beard down to the skin every couple weeks?"

"It's a disguise thing and you just proved it works."

Rosswell purposely chewed on the inside of his lower lip for a few so he didn't blurt out something stupid really fast. "How did I prove the disguise thing?"

"With the court's indulgence, let me reveal to you that I don't want the criminals I prosecute to recognize me. If I prosecute a bad guy in January and get him sent off to jail for a couple months, I'll look different when he gets out. Not to mention I change suits and shirts every other month. The Salvation Army loves me and my gently used clothing."

He's off his rocker. Rosswell decided to keep things conciliatory. "Okay, that's got a ring of common sense to it, although I'm not sure how many of the defendants we've run through the system remember anything, much less what the prosecutor looks like."

"Judge Carew—I love the sound of that—I cut my beard six times a year." Brian rubbed the back of his nearly bald head. "Not only do I disguise myself a bit, but I simply enjoy the change, that's all. It's my own little ritual."

Since lawyers are trained to lie, Rosswell ascribed Brian's folksy demeanor to good acting. "Anyway, thanks, Mister Prosecutor. I'm quite happy doing what I'm doing at this time. I love being a detective and a defense lawyer. Furthermore, I do not intend to wear a black evening gown when I cross the threshold of any of these stuffy courtrooms around here. No one ever comes up with any new stories. It's boring work. You already know that."

"Oh, right." Brian, first dragged at least two lungsful of smoke from his stogie, then, slowly spewed a stink cloud toward the memorialized statue of the soldier. "I heard you've had one hell of a day today, Judge, and here it's not even—" he held his watch close to his face—"two o'clock." He pointed at the clock mounted in the courthouse cupola, which was off by only forty-five minutes. He blinked and looked at this watch again. "We won't go by old faithful stuck up there by itself, lying about the time."

"You know all about what happened on the bluff then?" Rosswell coughed. "I mean what allegedly happened."

"Yessir. Having a parson arrested for murder out at that Indian park doesn't happen all the time."

"Indian park? You mean Trail of Tears. Where thousands died, thanks to Andrew Jackson?"

Brian laughed. "I'm much too young to have been a part of that travesty. I'd love to be able to prosecute that rascal Andy Jack!"

"Then you know why I'm here talking to you."

"You want a cigar?" Brian pulled out what looked like the oldest cigar in the Western Hemisphere, wrapped in plastic with a claim in Spanish that it had come from Havana. Brian proffered the smoke to Rosswell, who refused it.

"No, thank you. Not right now. What I want now is to have Reverend Ed Searl released on his own recognizance. He's a Unitarian—"

Brian cut in, "I know who he is. I go to his church. Why would I agree to release him without a high bail? At this moment, I don't know how I'm going to charge him, but, damn it, Rosswell, he was caught red-handed with a freshly-killed woman. Could be capital murder." He inspected his own cigar, whose spark lay dying. Satisfied, he stuck it in his mouth and puffed the cigar back to life.

Rosswell lectured the prosecutor. "There are at least two legal elements involved in a murder case. A person commits the crime of murder in the first degree if he knowingly causes the death of another person after deliberation upon the matter." Rosswell stuck up two fingers on his left hand. "That first part—there's where you go wrong." He touched his left forefinger. "There's no evidence whatsoever that the minister knowingly caused the death of another person. Your case has already fallen apart."

"Bull." Brian, still unhappy with the state of the spark, ran his lighter around the lit end of his cigar, puffed contentedly for a while without speaking, and then scanned the ash, deciding that the end needed flicking. He sprinkled the ashes into the fountain. "Sorry, Judge. You can't *unknowingly* stick a dirk in someone. You've lost on that element. What's your second one?"

"Deliberation. Ed Searl didn't go after that girl. He went up to the bluffs to meditate. A part of his regular schedule. One of his favorite routines. He had no idea she was there. So he sure couldn't mull over killing her on his way up the bluffs, could he? So far, I have found no connection between Ed and the woman, nor Ed and the dirk."

Brian responded instantly. "I disagree."

"How so?"

The prosecutor held out his cigar again before he continued lecturing Rosswell on the law. "The length of deliberation required for murder in the first degree is cool reflection for any length of time, no matter how brief. That's been the law in Missouri since the days of French gentlemen dueling down there on the banks of the Mississippi."

"I know that. But you don't have any evidence that Ed stabbed that woman."

"Maybe. Maybe not. But he did have a gun on him when he was taken into custody. I'll tell you this. Maybe Ed fired that pistol within a couple of hours before he got arrested. If he did stick the dirk into that poor woman, there'll be residue on the knife."

Rosswell snorted. "Gunshot residue tests are notably unreliable."

"Possibly."

"Give me a fresh cigar." This time, when Brian tendered the smoke, Rosswell grabbed it and stuck it in his mouth. Brian gave Rosswell a thumbs-up. Rosswell pulled it out. Brian proceeded with the ritual of firing up a new cigar for himself.

"Are you telling me, Mister Prosecutor, that your evidence is that my client, who's never been arrested for so much as a parking ticket, climbed up the bluff, saw the girl, decided then and there he wanted to murder her because she didn't want to have sex, and, using the dirk he so conveniently brought with him, stabbed her to death after he shot a gun? Is that what you're trying to sell me?"

Brian clasped his hands behind his back while sliding his cigar back and forth in his mouth. "Judge, you were always fair, both to me and my assistants, as well as to the defense bar." He jerked the cigar from his mouth. "You followed the law and tempered it with common sense and, on occasion, mercy." The prosecutor again checked out the area to see if anyone was spying on him. "Tell you what I'm going to do. I'll wait three days before I decide what charges I want to file. Maybe longer. I'll give you time to rustle up your defenses. I'm not in a hurry here, and, the preacher man will be let out on his own recognizance."

"What? He won't have to post bail? When did that happen and why wasn't I notified? Was there a hearing?"

"Judge Carew, cool your jets."

Rosswell's love of trivia overpowered his common sense. "That phrase was first written in the *Wisconsin Rapids Daily Tribune* on January 29, 1973. 'If you want to cool your jets, just step outside, where it will be about ten degrees cooler under cloudy skies.'"

Brian squinted at Rosswell for a few seconds. "I just gave you the best news you're going to get in a million years and you want to play games?" Once more searching the area for eavesdroppers, Brian looked all around. No likely spies. "You now know I'm a member of Ed's church. You could have me kicked off this case in ten seconds. Do you want me off the case?"

"Right now, I'll reserve my options."

"Rosswell, don't get me kicked off. I'll make it worth your while. You and I won't bring up my church membership. Oh, and one more thing."

"What's that?"

"I know your guy didn't kill that girl."

CHAPTER 18

Day 5
The Hearing

THREE DAYS LATER AT THE BAIL hearing, Rosswell had argued that, "The weak facts in this case stick out like a skunk in a hot tub, Your Honor." Rosswell pled that Ed be released on his own recognizance.

"Mr. Reeves?" the judge asked.

"Your Honor, the prosecution believes that Ed Searl is not a flight risk. The state has no objection."

Ed had been released without bail on his promise to return to court.

After Ed signed the release papers for the court, Father Mike busted him out of jail.

CHAPTER 19

Day 6
The Purple Star

BEFORE SUNRISE THE NEXT DAY, Rosswell completed hasty telephone calls to Father Mike, Ferdinand, and Ed, strongly suggesting that they meet at Ollie's place as soon as possible. He then called Ollie to let him know they'd be meeting shortly. "And have some coffee ready . . . and maybe some muffins, eggs, bacon—"

Ollie hung up on him.

Rosswell turned to Tina. "I don't know who killed that poor girl, but I do know that Ed didn't. I'm going to hustle on over to The Purple Star. There I can chow down and chat up." Although Rosswell and Tina's office was only a couple of blocks away and afforded them a private conference, there was one fatal flaw. Sure, they had real Coca-Cola for Tina, and espresso for him, but it wasn't fresh and ready to go all the time. More importantly, there was no food. He knew, too, that if Ollie didn't prepare the coffee, Candy would, and she'd bring in a breakfast spread, no matter what Ollie said.

"I'm going to the conference, too," Tina said.

"You," Rosswell said, kissing his wife, "light up my life. Call Mrs. Bolzoni."

———◆———

A few minutes later, Rosswell and Tina arrived at The Purple Star. Father

Mike, who had earlier dropped by to pick up Reverend Ed, was already there. He greeted them and said that Ed was walking around the block to make up for missing his regular exercise regimen.

Just then, Ed walked in. His face dripped with sweat from the high heat and humidity. Ollie gave him a clean towel to sop up some of the perspiration.

"You look a might better, Reverend," Rosswell said.

"I feel more like myself today. Aside from being saddled with a murder charge." Ed walked over to the table. "I brought this for you."

It was the scrapbook.

Once everyone was settled in, sipping coffee and munching on doughnuts, Rosswell said, "I have thought about this case against Ed nonstop since it developed, and I hope to have everything tidied up before sundown."

"Yes, sir," Ollie said. "If you want to come to a quick resolution of a gnarly problem, call a big committee meeting. I should certainly hope you have it all figured out, Rosswell. Let's get on with it. Do you realize what this is costing me?" He pointed to a table weighed down with food and drink. "I want to help Ed, but I didn't take him to raise."

Rosswell clapped his hands. "The more I dissect it, the more I see weaknesses pop up like mushrooms in a manure pile after a summer thunderstorm. We'll shortly have this whole misunderstanding thrown into the Mississippi River and then everyone can go back to whatever they were doing before this poor young woman was so brutally killed."

"Except that poor woman," Ed said.

As though on cue, a deep tugboat whistle bleated mournfully from the river.

A sad tune for the murder of the unfortunate young woman.

———◆———

Everyone, especially Rosswell, appeared hungry, much to Ollie's obvious distress. Ravenous, in fact. The doughnuts soon disappeared. A rousing speech by Rosswell, that had overflowed with optimism started the meeting and the oration ended with, "Once the cops and the prosecutor hear Ed's facts, the whole thing will be dropped. I'm sure of it. We'll have the varmint who actually killed the girl trapped in the branches!" Rosswell regretted that he'd failed to bring a small American flag to wave.

"Don't start sawing till you've treed the coon," Ollie muttered.

"You know—" The antique overhead fluorescent lights launched into a fit of sputtering. Rosswell waited for it to stop, then said, "You know I'm right."

Ollie snorted. "Yeah, right. Well, tell you what. You're overconfident." Rubbing his shiny head, Ollie stood and stretched to his full height. "I'll tell you something else what needs to happen here. Father Mike and Reverend Ed should forget about those angelic visitations and antique scrapbooks. Trouble. Nothing but trouble."

In the dining area of the restaurant, Rosswell heard the clatter of patrons chowing down on the breakfast special of the day. He could smell the lunch roast beef being cooked and so tender it could be cut with a fork. It was one of Ollie's most popular dishes. Rosswell closed his eyes and inhaled a deep breath. He could hardly wait until breakfast was over so he could eat lunch.

I should be out there savoring a good meal instead of huddling in this storeroom trying to convince these people that everything is going to be okay. Especially since I'm not so sure of the outcome.

"First," Rosswell said, with far more enthusiasm than he felt, "I'll start with some background information. Then, of course, Father Mike and Ed both will have more to add."

Tina kissed Rosswell on the cheek, and then proceeded to eyeball everyone in the room. "Let me make something clear. I want to remind each of you again that anything said inside this room stays here. Nothing goes outside this room." Tina held up her hand in a Girl Scout salute. "Strictly confidential. That warning is required by the law governing private eye ethics."

"Hooray for Tina," Rosswell cheered. "I love you." Then he, in turn, kissed his wife on the cheek, smiled at her, and consulted his notes, which were entirely in his head. "I've had a thought or two about how to resolve all this. As I was pointing out, Father Mike and Reverend Ed could open an inter-faith food pantry or something, which would take their minds off other-worldly beings."

Ferdinand, who had slipped quietly in, coughed. "I agree."

Rosswell spotted what he thought were tears in the old man's eyes. Ferdinand sniffed, drew out a big red handkerchief, and blew his nose loudly, approaching what Rosswell thought could be the sound of Gabriel's trumpet at the end of time. Rosswell jolted and involuntarily raised his eyes to the ceiling, searching for the archangel.

Tina placed her hand on top of Ferdinand's. "Ferdinand, why are you crying?"

He dabbed at his eyes with the handkerchief. "M'lady, I fear for my minister's life." Ferdinand carefully folded the hankie and stuffed it back in his pocket.

Rosswell said, "God's watching out for him, I'm sure." *Those words*, he hoped, *would console the minister's friend.*

"God's not a part of this reality," countered Ferdinand, slapping Ed on the back.

Ed smiled at Ferdinand, who said, "Stephen Hawking said we didn't need God to explain the universe since the laws of physics clearly describe reasons for the spontaneous appearance of the universe."

Rosswell's eyes widened. He was astonished at Ferdinand's statement. "The laws of physics have causes and effects," he said. He thought a moment before continuing. "If there's a cause, there's an effect. If there's an effect, there's a cause. That means something had to start the creation of the universe. It didn't start itself. Or did nothing create everything?"

Ferdinand retorted, "I must inquire, is God the cause, or the effect? And, don't you dare say, 'Both!'"

"Could we slow down here?" Father Mike intervened as peacemaker. "Please, let's leave theology fights at the door. Instead, let's deal with the problems we have now, not discussions that sound like a bunch of old gray-haired men arguing about how many angels can dance on the head of a pin." Turning to Ed, he landed on earthly matters. "Are you happy with Rosswell as your lawyer?"

Tina's eyebrows shot up. "Reverend?" Ed waved his hand in front of his face, meaning, Rosswell supposed, that he didn't want to give up his free lawyer. Tina persisted, "There are superb criminal lawyers in this town. I'm sure Rosswell will help you find another one if you like. Besides, I'm sure your congregation will fill the offering plate to help pay for the attorney's services."

"I'm delighted with Rosswell and what he's doing for me."

When Ed finished, Father Mike said, "Before Ed took off to Trail of Tears State Park, he and I talked about the angel that earlier told me that I had to go on a forty day journey, similar to Elijah."

"I know that story," Ollie said. "That means you're off selling broom trees?"

Rosswell said, "Ollie, mind your manners and listen to the man."

The purple star on Ollie's bald head turned an odd color when he blushed. "Oh. Wait. Never mind. But I did read about Elijah in the Bible."

"You don't sell broom trees." Father Mike sighed. "You sleep under them. They're bitter bushes, not trees. It's part of life. Bitterness and defeat, although the journey leads you to the destination of victory."

"With no disrespect meant toward Rosswell, I'm afraid that Ed will be locked up the rest of his life. Let's get on with it." Ollie jumped up and rustled around in the storage room boxes until he found a long, thin rope. He sat and plopped it down on the table. "Let's cut to the chase. We need to free Ed. Not wait for him to be stuck in the state pen forever."

"He's sitting right here, Ollie. He's already free. Besides, how are you going to free him with a rope?"

"We'll pull the bars from the windows of the jail. I saw that in a cowboy movie."

Tina thumped Ollie's head several times. "You're headed for the edge, dear friend."

"Just trying to lighten things up a bit."

"Cool your jets." Rosswell smiled, but didn't share the source of the saying. "Put the rope back and sit down. If we're going to investigate this, the strangest case I've ever had, then we all need to talk this whole thing out and make sure all of us know everything that happened up to right this minute."

Ed said, "What do you want me to do?"

"Tell us what happened from the time Father Mike left your office when you all first talked about the angel incident until the moment we found you on the trail."

Rosswell and the others also sat, forming a semi-circle around Ed.

"No," Ed said. "I fear that the story must actually begin with Father Mike's visit to me."

"Ok, Father, you're on, so let's have the whole backstory. Then Ed can add his part."

CHAPTER 20

Day 6, continued
The Purple Star

"IT'S FINE BY ME," the priest said. Before he could utter a word, Candy flung open the door, positioned herself like the Evil Queen in the Snow White cartoon movie, only lacking a wooden box with a poison apple nestled inside. She snorted, then marched in, followed by Sonya. Tina, receiving some kind of female signal from Candy and Sonya, joined in as soon as she saw what was happening.

Lockstep, they're walking and thinking as one because they're female. Rosswell noted this only to himself—he was smarter than to *say* what he thought. The fires of righteous wrath, burning flames colored a cold blue made themselves visible in the eyes of all three women. Rosswell breathed deeply in order to work up the courage to face the women. *How in all God's creation do women do that? Is there some kind of conspiracy among the ladies who've been vexed beyond the limit by the stupidity of men? I'm guessing the answer is yes.*

Rosswell got up and sauntered over close to his wife. "Come on in, ladies and join us. Sit right here next to Tina. We could always use your perspectives."

Sonya said to Rosswell. "Since I am a representative of the police department, and you are probably discussing Ed's, case, I must leave if you tell me to."

Ed rose and bowed to Sonya. "Please, madam, stay."

"Rosswell?" she said.

"Actually, it is all right if you stay. I know that when we figure out who the actual killer is, you will share that with the chief and the sheriff."

"Judge Carew, you do know what the gossip is about you and your friends here, don't you?" Sonya said.

"Gossip? Me? And my friends here? Down at the cop shop? Do tell."

"Yes, yes, yes and yes," said Sonya. "No one downtown takes your stories seriously, nor do they trust the stories your friends here tell." She pointed to Ed and the priest.

"Seriously? My 'stories' are the truth. Ed didn't kill anyone. In fact, I don't think he's committed crimes of any kind. Ever. As far as taking my stories seriously? How's this? I know they didn't take me seriously, because if they had, Ed wouldn't have been arrested."

Tina patted her husband's hand. "They're not only talking about you, sweetie. They're talking about all of us—Ferdinand, Mrs. Bolzoni, Ollie, Father Mike, Reverend Ed, and me. They're saying you're delusional, and that all of us are nutso crazy."

Rosswell counted on his fingers. "That's seven people all having the same delusion. Which delusion exactly do we share?"

Tina spoke slow and succinctly. "The delusion that we all said that Ed is innocent because of what a spirit told Father Mike."

Ed spoke up. "Mrs. Carew, I assure you that I haven't agreed with Father Mike that an angel or spirit or something else spoke to him. Truth be known, I'm not sure he himself is convinced of that."

"There are many explanations," added Father Mike, "that aren't supernatural. I'm the one who had the visions, and I'm not sure what happened. I'm still trying to figure it all out."

Without knocking, Mrs. Bolzoni, holding Jonathan David Carew on her hips, flung open the door and power-walked into the tiny room. "I not deaf as the some of you thinks. I hear my name. Here I am working my headhit off for this Ollie so he can have meetings in the warehouse and talk about me."

Headhit? That's a new Mrs. Bolzoni word.

"We are always happy to see you," said Rosswell. "Please, come in." He knew better than to say otherwise.

"Mrs. Bolzoni," Sonya said. "Don't be upset. No one has said anything about you. We—all of us in this room—are trying to figure out what happened on that hill out at Trail of Tears."

"And you, Mrs. Bolzoni, are welcome to stay," said Ed.

"No," said Mrs. Bolzoni. "Then I will return to the house of the judge with this sweet baby."

On the way out, she slapped Ollie on the back of his head first, and then Rosswell. Neither man dared respond in any fashion, since they valued their lives. Shaking her head and giving Rosswell the tsk-tsk routine, she eye-surfed his body, head to sole, and sole to head. "I don't know the why of the reason the beautiful Tina picked you. You must have something what don't show." She turned and stomped to the door, but before she left, she shook her finger at Rosswell. "And one more thing you, Mister Judge Carew, must act more like this smart lady there." She saluted Sonya, marched through the door, and slammed it behind her. Her mutterings were heard all the way down the hall.

"Tina," said Rosswell when he felt that no one outside the room would hear him, "please tell me what a head hit is."

"It's Mrs. Bolzoni's first foray into cursing. A headhit is a butt. As in her phrase, 'The goat's headhit me.' She's saying that she's working her butt off."

Sonya waited a few moments to let the latest Mrs. Bolzoni word sink in before she said to Rosswell, "Why are you so confident that no charges will be filed? What do you know that I do not know?"

"The story that Ed is telling doesn't border on the ludicrous. It downright pumps its butt smack dab into the middle of the wild and crazy territory of ludicrous," Rosswell answered.

"And another thing . . ." Sonya silenced herself. "Wait. What? What are you saying?"

Rosswell said, "Did you not examine the corpse?"

"You know I did."

"Then you haven't talked to the CSIs. Did you notice that the woman lay on her left side, with her left arm under her head, her right arm bent, resting on her upper torso with her right hand sticking from beneath her sleeve, which revealed blood puddled inside her right sleeve?"

Sonya stared at the ceiling of the storage room, closed her eyes, and pointed here and there, obviously replaying in her mind the scene of her examination of the dead girl. Then her eyes opened and grew wide. She slapped her forehead with an open palm. "Of course!"

Ollie held up a hand. "Don't tell me." He lay down in the middle of the floor on his left side with his left arm under his head. It took him only a second after he placed his right arm resting on his hip that he jumped up and said, "Of course!"

Father Mike and Ed held their peace for a few moments, until Ed waved his hand at the priest and said, "I believe I speak for both of us. We are totally lost in this conversation."

The priest agreed.

"You all don't get it?" Rosswell stared at the two clergymen with his eyes wider than a new axe handle. "She was killed somewhere else. A corpse's blood pools at the lowest part of the body. That's plain old physics. If she had been killed where we found her and Ed, then her blood could not have pooled in her right arm since that was the highest point of the body as it lay when we found her."

Sonya said, "As I said, I'm here at the begrudging permission from the sheriff, who's running the major case squad. Anything I hear or see, or otherwise find out, I'm reporting to Talbot. Everyone got that?" Heads nodded all around. "If a single one of you don't want me here, then I'll leave immediately." Murmurs of agreement floated on the air. "Just remember that we discussed this. Twice."

CHAPTER 21

Day 6, continued
The Purple Star

IN THE MIDST OF THE conference, a minor confrontation blossomed. Before Father Mike could open his mouth, Sonya said, "Wait a minute. Go back and start right after that snake business."

Rosswell held up an open right hand. "Let me do that, Father Mike." The priest nodded. "After the copperhead incident, that is when we three—Father Mike, Ollie, and I—rounded the switchback and found Ed and the dead girl."

Ferdinand said, "That sounds straightforward enough."

"Nothing mysterious," Ed said. "When I came up on the girl, I nearly fainted. I knew her. Juliette Fribeau. She was the sister of Anna Fribeau, whom I'd just buried." He shook his head. "As far as I know, no one knows where she was before she was killed."

"What happened to Anna Fribeau?" Rosswell asked.

"A stray bullet."

"When and where?"

"About a week ago," Ed said. "She was walking alone at night along the waterfront and a stray bullet hit her. A stray bullet of all things." He shook his head. "At least that's what I remember you telling me, Sonya. Is that right?" Sonya nodded. "I'm just not used to living in a world where stray bullets happen along a peaceful river. There's no call for such things in this world."

"Correct so far," said Sonya to Ed. She looked around, then lowered her voice. "The police aren't really sure that it was a stray bullet, and neither am I."

Ed bowed his head and wiped tears from his eyes. He slowly looked up and said, "So sad. Two daughters, two sisters, two human beings dead in the same week. Anna dead and cremated, and then I find Juliette's body in the woods. No one knows where their parents are. Or even if their parents are still alive. And no one knows if they have any other family or where they might be. It's like they both showed up isolated and alone, and then died isolated and alone."

"Tell me, how did you know they were sisters?" Rosswell moved closer to Ed, although he made sure he didn't crowd the minister. *No need making the man nervous.* "Did someone in your congregation know them?"

"Not that I know of. They told me themselves about their kinship." Ed stared past Rosswell as if in a trance.

"Fair enough." Rosswell scratched his head. *Is Ed still a bit off? Maybe I should suggest a checkup.* "Let's get this straight. Were both Fribeau women members of your congregation? Did they arrive at the same time?"

"Anna and Juliette both attended services here at River City Unitarian. Started about two months ago. Sometimes one and sometimes the other and sometimes both of them. They rarely spoke to anyone. Simply came and left. I wouldn't call them friendly with the other people there, although none of us here prod and pry strangers who prefer to be left alone."

Rosswell said, "Didn't the two women fill out paperwork of some kind for membership?"

"Yes. I did have the presence of mind to bring that information with me. You'll notice they both say they are from Sainte Genevieve."

Ed handed the documents to Rosswell, who scanned them top to bottom, back and front. He muttered, Hmm, Fribeau. I know that name."

"Ladies and gentlemen, I'd like to ask for a short break. I want to talk to Reverend Ed and Father Mike about a couple of things. Alone." Rosswell pointed at Ollie. "Ollie here will provide you all with lunch. Bring what you order back here so we can talk while we eat."

Ollie shot straight up out of his seat. "I have a strong—"

"Yes," said Rosswell. "Ollie has a strong wish to make sure you all get a good meal, which I, by the way, am paying for. Get whatever you want."

Ollie swiped his hand over his hair-free head and exhaled. "Wonderful, wonderful."

Rosswell, along with Father Mike and Reverend Ed, headed for the front door. Before they could leave the building, Sonya pinched Rosswell's elbow. "A word, Rosswell."

"Go ahead gentlemen, I'll be right along."

Sonya checked the time on her phone. "I've got to go. I've got an appointment that can't wait. But, in a bit I'm going to call you with some important information. Top secret. You can't tell anyone what I tell you— including Tina. If you tell anyone, then I'll lose my job and any chance to have a career in law enforcement."

"Give me a dollar."

"What? Do you not understand that I have something extraordinarily important to tell you?"

"Yes, I do." Rosswell, paranoid as always, looked all around before he said, "That's why I said, 'Give me a dollar.' Just do it."

"Sometimes you are a complete weirdo, Rosswell." Sonya patted herself down until she discovered money in her left pocket. She dug it out. "Here. I've got seventy-six cents."

Rosswell accepted the change. "Good enough. That means you're my client. Anything you tell me is bona fide and protected under the lawyer-client privilege. By the same token, anything you learn here is confidential as well."

Sonya rolled her eyes

"Don't forget to call me," Rosswell said as Sonya bolted out the door.

Rosswell crossed Spanish Street and walked over to where Father Mike and Reverend Ed sat on a bench at the bottom of the courthouse hill. Rosswell handed the scrapbook to Ed.

"Something's bothering me, gentlemen," said Rosswell as he scanned the area to make sure no one was within earshot "You, Father Mike, had your first experience with the angel on this very hill, correct?" The priest nodded. "And you, Reverend Ed, where was your first encounter?"

"Judge Carew! How are you doing today?"

Rosswell turned around to face the voice. "Miss Jansen." The woman, a head shorter than Sonya, shook hands with Rosswell. "Do you know Father Mike and Reverend Ed? Gentlemen, JoEllen Jansen here is the probate clerk in the Common Pleas Courthouse."

JoEllen stuck out her hand to Father Mike. The moment he grasped her hand, she sucked in her breath and yelped like a new puppy. "Oh, I'm sorry, Father . . . I . . . uh . . . hurt my hand the other day. It's still tender."

Father Mike apologized and when she turned to offer her hand to Ed, he said, "Maybe we shouldn't shake hands. I certainly don't want to hurt you." JoEllen extended her hand, however. The second he touched her fingers, she screeched. Ed jerked back his hand, aghast at her reaction.

"JoEllen, are you all right?" *That's strange. When she shook my hand, she didn't wince in pain.* "Neither of these Godly gentlemen would hurt anyone if their lives depended on it."

JoEllen smiled. "It's okay, Judge. I already know that."

"You do?" Rosswell said.

Like Rosswell, JoEllen scrutinized the area for eavesdroppers. Finding none, she leaned in close to the three men and said in a low voice, "Neither of you hurt me. I've heard of you both and what Judge Carew is doing for you."

Rosswell said, "And how do you know this?"

JoEllen said, "An angel."

The three men fell to silence. Eventually, Rosswell, regaining his composure, said, "Wait, you've seen the angel, too?"

The woman smiled and nodded.

"And does the angel have a name?"

"Why, yes, yes she does, Judge. It's Dina."

"How did you come to know that name?"

"She . . . or . . . he, I'm not sure. . . ."

"Angels have no gender."

"Right, Father. The angel told me its name."

"I don't think so," Rosswell said.

"They, and you, Judge are coated with . . . a brilliance—that's the only word I know to describe it—and a knowledge others don't have. And through them, Dina wants us to visit someone."

Rosswell said, "And who might that be?"

"Do you remember Maman Fribeau?"

"Of course. She helped me save Tina." The memory rushed him back to a snug cabin high on a hill above the Mississippi River in Sainte Genevieve County. Tina had been kidnapped, and Rosswell had information that she might be in the Sainte Genevieve area. He'd gone to beg any information Maman might have about his then-fiancé. He and Ollie had earned an audience with Maman Fribeau, after giving her a bag of silver coins. *Wait. Maman must be related to the Fribeau sisters.*

Inside the log house, Maman—who knew about everything going on in the area—had held court in front of a huge fireplace where she rocked back and forth in a handmade bentwood rocking chair. Rosswell had said a silent prayer of thanksgiving that there was no fire as the temperature inside the tiny, dark house was stifling. He couldn't imagine the woman, in her shriveled body was cool, yet Rosswell had found no traces of sweat on her pale, translucent skin, which reminded him of a corpse.

When they had sat down across from her, he noticed she wore only a simple brown shift, which provided a perfect foundation to show off her striking hair. Snippets of silver curled out from beneath the pale blue kerchief tied behind her head. Rosswell still smelled the earthen aroma that enveloped the house. The odor was not spoiled, but pleasant. Like ground that had been refreshed by redemption and new life.

Maman had growled, "Many stand by Dina." Then she launched into an otherworldly chant as to why The Guardians of Dina existed. "Fight," she said, "fight against those who sell the bodies of women. Stop the sex slavery. We need more to help fight this horror!" Then her head fell onto her chest. Rosswell had thought maybe she had fainted. Finally, in a low voice, she chanted words that Rosswell couldn't decipher. He looked at Ollie and shrugged, as she continued. Ollie shrugged back. When she finished her song, Maman rummaged through a pocket on her dress and pulled out two small gold, five-pointed stars hanging from black braided ribbons.

"You." She tossed a necklace to Rosswell. "Much pain you have. *Soutache.* Wear this always." She stared at Ollie. "And you." She threw another at him.

Rosswell ran his fingers over the flat and narrow braid. He obeyed Maman and slipped the pendant over his head. Ollie did the same.

She pointed at them. "You . . . and you, are protectors, and now are Guardians."

The woman had dropped her head on her chest again and rocked and rocked. Her creaking chair, the only noise.

Eventually, Maman had raised her head and gave Rosswell what he needed to rescue Tina.

She pointed at Rosswell. "Now, it is best to be getting, you."

Rosswell pulled his pendant from beneath his shirt and rubbed his thumb across it. That meeting with Maman began his relationship with the Guardians of Dina, a shadowy and anonymous group whose real leadership remained unknown to him, even to this day. Their objective remained clear: Sex slavers are executed by vigilantes without trial.

"JoEllen," Rosswell said, "I have to ask. I heard Maman Fribeau had been murdered. Is that true?"

Instead of answering, she consulted her watch. "How about if we all meet tomorrow morning at the site where the body of the young woman was found? We'll talk more about Maman Fribeau then." She then drew a circle in the air. "Like the old song says, we need to keep the circle unbroken. We will all meet there."

Rosswell said, "Do you just want the three of us?

"No, the whole circle. Everyone that's involved. Except the cops. "

"That means the three of us, and Tina, Ferdinand, and Mrs. Bolzoni. I will have Tina secure a guardian for Jonathan David."

"I'll see you there."

"JoEllen, there's just one thing. Mrs. Bolzoni despises the French."

"Duly noted, but it shouldn't be a problem."

"We will have her there if you need her, but just be warned. She's likely to speak her mind about them. And it may not be pretty."

JoEllen nodded. "I know just the thing for her. I'll take care of it tomorrow."

"Ms. Jansen," said Father Mike, "I can't stress to you the importance of keeping all this quiet. Every. Single. Thing."

She answered with a smile. "Do you think anybody would believe any of this?"

To lighten the mood, Rosswell said, "JoEllen, you won't be conjuring up spirits tomorrow will you? You might accidentally call up Satan."

"There's no worry there, because the devil is already roaming the earth."

CHAPTER 22

Day 7
Holy Cross Church

THE NEXT MORNING, AFTER HEARING what he thought would be the last confession of the day, following seven o'clock Mass, Father Mike glanced out into the church. No one there. His reputation as the most conscientious priest around would suffer if he ignored someone needing help. Besides, sitting alone in the confessional always proved comforting to him. Solitude at this hour proved even more wonderful, since the sun shone through the huge stained glass windows bathing the inside of the church with a divine march of many colors. That quality, he mused, led many souls to seek out the pews for prayers.

Just as he was about to leave, he detected the silhouette of a man walking in a stately manner—head held high, straight back, hands clasped in prayer below his chin— toward a bank of prayer candles. The man stopped and lit one of the votive candles, then headed to the back of the church toward the confessional. Father Mike sat back down and waited for the man to enter the small room.

Instead of kneeling behind a screen, the man chose to sit facing the priest.

"Bless me, Father, for I have sinned."

To his astonishment, Father Mike recognized him instantly. Of course recognizing someone happened a lot in the confessional, but he never showed surprise, no matter who came to see him. There were times that people who didn't belong to his parish showed up. Occasionally, even people who were not Catholic sought him out.

This particular person astonished the priest. Nonetheless, he'd listen.

He asked the man sitting across from him, "Are you Catholic?"

"Yes. But I've been away from the Church for many years and I want to return because I must confess a mortal sin."

"Yes, of course. I'm happy to welcome you home." Father Mike blessed the man and then asked, "What is it you want to confess?"

The penitent cleared his throat before he spoke. "I killed a man." While he stared at the wall, a tear rolled down his cheek.

Father Mike had never heard a confession for murder. Most confessions were routine and dull. He folded his hands into a gesture of prayer, more so to keep his hands from shaking, closed his eyes, and sat quietly for a few moments. Eventually, after praying for guidance in a matter as serious as this, he asked the man, "When did you do this?"

The man didn't answer immediately. Rather he stuck his head out of the confessional, obviously to make certain that no one could hear him. He brought his head back in and sat straight in the seat for several beats before he answered. "In 2013." The man licked his lips. "August 11, 2013 to be exact." He reached for a clean handkerchief in his back pocket and wiped his face. "You know the seven murders that are documented in Ed's scrapbook?"

"Yes. Of course." Fear overtook the priest. *Do I have a serial killer in my confessional?* "Are those the murders you committed?"

"Father, please." There was a hitch in his voice. "I'm trying to tell you. This is difficult for me." The man wrung his hands.

"I understand. This is difficult for me, also. Take all the time you need. God hears and absolves anyone who is truly sorry for their sins. All I do is listen."

"I didn't kill seven people. Only one. I killed the killer of the seven people." Father tightened his shoulders and sat straighter. Bile rose in his throat. The man's breathing grew shallow and rapid. "This is what happened after I tracked down the killer. When I found him, I wrote down every speck of evidence that I thought a prosecutor might need to convict him before a jury. No good. Over the years, I ran my evidence by both defense lawyers and prosecutors. Every one of them said there wasn't enough evidence to convince a jury beyond a reasonable doubt. The killer was slick, and lucky, and cagey.

Still, I was totally convinced beyond even the slightest doubt. I knew he was going to kill again if I didn't stop him. I knew where he lived. I knew where he worked. I knew everything about him. I also knew that he had killed two others that weren't listed in the scrapbook. I knew beyond dispute that the maniac had killed seven people. All young women. Why, I don't know. You may remember that the media tagged this monster The Hivite Horror. The media never talked about the other two cases. I've tried telling the cops that the five cases are related to the other two cases, but they don't believe me. They think I'm delusional. Anyway, I discovered something about the killer that wasn't well known. The guy I killed was a dealer in human flesh. A slaver. Specifically, a sex-slaver. He was a major trafficker in human flesh. Slavery is alive and well I am sorry to say."

Father Mike pinched the bridge of his nose. "Are you telling me that you killed the Hivite Horror?"

The man shifted in his seat. "That's where I suspect I may have gone wrong."

Dear Lord. Father Mike feared what the man was going to say. He spoke softly in a gentle tone. "Wrong? You were wrong to take the law in your own hands. Do you clearly understand you were wrong? Even if you were right about the man being a serial killer, you were still wrong to kill him. Do you understand? Really understand?" The priest stopped himself before his lecture became harsh.

They both heard a noise in the sanctuary. Both looked out of the confessional. The penitent pointed toward the person. "Father, do you know that man out there?"

"It's okay. That's Alexander Comana. He's our janitor. He's been here forever."

"Oh, dear God." The man hung his head. "I killed his brother. Gregory Comana."

Father Mike's stomach lurched. A deep breath and a few swallows kept him from throwing up.

"However," the man said, "Gregory Comana was not the Hivite Horror." The man covered his eyes with his hands, sighed, and then continued. "I was wrong. Not only did I take the law into my own hands. I killed the wrong man." The man sobbed.

Father Mike looked outside the confessional. The janitor had left. "Please. Go on."

"That's it."

"And you know for sure you killed him?"

"Yes. One gunshot between the eyes."

In his mind, Father Mike replayed all the news reports of Gregory Comana's disappearance. One day after work, Gregory had gone home as usual to his cabin on the Mississippi River near Trail of Tears State Park. Later that day, someone reported that he had been killed in the doorway of his home, but then when the police arrived, no one was there. Subsequently, the police reported Gregory Comana missing. He was never found, dead or alive.

"According to the media, his body was never found, so how can I believe you when you say you shot him?"

"Father, you're not an investigator."

"Satisfy my curiosity. If you're confessing the sin of murder, I want to know all the facts."

"I disposed of the body. I wrapped him in chains and threw him in the Mississippi River."

A perpetual scent of incense hung in the air at Holy Cross parish church. The rich aroma calmed the priest and allowed him to think more clearly. "How do you know you killed the wrong man?"

"There was one thing in each of the Hivite murders early in this century that was never reported."

"Go on."

"Somewhere hidden on or around every corpse was a square red sticker. In the middle of the sticker was a gold, five-pointed star. No words. No slogans. No writing of any kind. That is the symbol of Communism. And I found out that the biggest consumers of sex slaves are the ruling classes of the socialist countries in the world. Russia. China. North Korea. Venezuela. And there are others."

Father Mike knew that by this stage of the confession, he should have blessed the man and sent him on his way. But, no. His curiosity overtook his good sense. "How do you know they are the biggest consumers? Are you telling me that someone keeps records of that kind of stuff?" The priest sat back in his seat. "I don't believe it."

"Father, the Guardians of Dina keep that info. And you know about that organization. Don't you?"

"Yes. I know about them and I know their claims." Father Mike raised his eyebrows and pressed his lips into a fine line. "Only you and I are here. The Guardians aren't here. Their claims are rather fantastic, but that has nothing to do with you."

"Exactly," said the man. "Now when the Juliette Fribeau murder happened out at Trail of Tears, I knew beyond doubt I'd killed the wrong man."

"What made you so sure?"

"Glued onto the cellphone under Juliette's body was a red sticker with a yellow star. Exactly like the other ones I'd seen on and around the prior murders. If I'd killed the right man then that sticker wouldn't have been there, because I was the only person in the universe who knew about the stickers."

"The only person in the universe, except the killer."

The man squirmed in his chair. "All right. Yeah. Me and the murderer."

"And what about the cops who investigated the murders?"

"I give up." The man threw up his hands. "Sure. Lots of people know. Some people, I mean. Not a lot."

Desperation in his voice, the man said, "I *thought* I was killing a serial killer. Oh, God, I'm going to hell."

Father Mike ignored the man's words. "How did you collect all the information?" He knew he was clearly overstepping his bounds in asking all the questions. There would be no way that he could ever tell anyone what he'd heard in the confessional. He would either, go to prison, or to his grave before he revealed what he heard during confession.

"When I would investigate one of these murders," the man continued, "I'd find witness testimony that described him. Where he hung out. What kind of work he did. One day early on in my investigation, I saw the killer in person and everything clicked. The guy was guilty in my mind. I followed him around for years before I finally decided to kill him. I was certain he was the killer."

"You said you threw him in the river wrapped in chains. Is that burying him in your mind?"

"No. In fact, no one knows but me that I killed Gregory. Obviously, people—his brother—knows he's missing, but only I know what really happened to him."

"This is a grievous sin. You have created much suffering for so many people. Someone is missing a son, a father, a brother, a husband. And they don't know—may never know—what happened to him." Father Mike bowed his head and said a silent prayer for Gregory, for his brother, Alexander, for the man in his confessional, and for himself. "You, too, have already suffered so much. Are you truly sorry for your sin?"

"Many times over."

"Say your Act of Contrition." When he'd completed the prayer and asked God for His forgiveness, the priest said, "I will give you a penance for your crime, but I believe your penance while still on this earth will be the constant haunting that you killed an innocent man. I believe the penance you deserve is this. Although I will forever keep your confession within, your penance is that you should reveal your murder to the police."

The man looked horrified. "But, Father...."

Father Mike raised his hand into a sign of blessing. "In the name of the Lord, I absolve you from your sins. Go in peace."

After the man left, the scent of his cigar lingered.

CHAPTER 23

TIMOTHY LOCKERBIE
Screaming like a banshee
Went on a killing spree
Cutting off the pearls
Chopping off the curls
Of all the pretty girls
But I've come back
To sweep up the slack
I'm not Tom all grim
I got bomb on a limb

I'd love to have all the classmates who sang that little ditty and made fun of me, see me now. I'd sing them a song they'd never forget. I'd sing them a special verse. Everyone who taunted me is dead. Dead. Dead. Gone. Murdered, they said in the newspapers. By an unknown killer. Oh, how I'd love to paste my picture on every grave of every bully who taunted me. Alas, that is impractical. And it might lead some smart cop right to my doorstep.

CHAPTER 24

Day 7
Trail of Tears State Park

"MAMAN, HERE ARE THE PEOPLE I need you to talk to." JoEllen introduced each one of them to the old lady the next morning at the Trail of Tears death scene. "We are here to learn from you."

"And you are the magic woman on the fortune telling table?" Mrs. Bolzoni snorted as soon as she saw Maman.

Rosswell had earlier hoped with all hope that Mrs. Bolzoni would behave herself. Her disgust boiled over at being in the presence of a person of French ancestry. Rosswell didn't want the women to distract from trying to figure out the real murderer. They should learn to live together. He wanted to say, "Can't we just all get along?" Of course, Rosswell wasn't about to say that out loud. Lest he be dead in an instant, either at the hands of Maman or Mrs. Bolzoni. Or both.

Rosswell said, "We need to level the playing field, allowing all of us to think outside the box when we reach out for one another." He hoped that he'd used all the proper clichés, but felt compelled to add more. "Therefore, going forward we should unpack the problem to discover all its moving parts so that the optics are visible."

Everyone stared at Rosswell. No one seemed to know what he was talking about, so he shut up.

JoEllen put an arm around Mrs. Bolzoni. "We are so happy you could make it this morning. Let me shake your hand."

Mrs. Bolzoni responded by removing her glasses. She wiped them clean with a tissue. "There is no call for me to being the hand shaking with another lady, for reason—"

When JoEllen grabbed Mrs. Bolzoni's hand, Rosswell himself detected a slight . . . *brilliance?*—It's the only word he could summon up to describe what he saw—surrounding both women. The women stood, hands locked together. Rosswell pinched his eyes into slits. *This has got to be an optical illusion.* None of the others appeared to notice it. *Father Mike and Reverend Ed look a tad brilliant, too. Okay, I'm losing my mind here. This must just be the slant of light. That's all.*

The women stepped back from one another. With fire in her voice, Mrs. Bolzoni pointed to Maman Fribeau. "You, you must be the psychiatric woman who tells all to my Ferdinand and takes his money."

Maman stomped up to Mrs. Bolzoni and stared at her, eye to eye. "Who is this, her?" She pointed a long finger at Mrs. Bolzoni. "She jabbers, leaving no room for using of the brain cells."

"You . . . frog!" Mrs. Bolzoni, rarely at a loss for words, blurted out the epithet.

JoEllen grasped the right hand of Maman Fribeau, who instantly emitted a dim brilliance, the same as Mrs. Bolzoni.

JoEllen said, "Mrs. Bolzoni and Maman, aren't you both happy to be here?"

The two women regarded each other, yet said nothing. Maman Fribeau tilted her head back and watched the sky. Mrs. Bolzoni flapped her hands in the direction of her French adversary. After several heartbeats, the brilliance enveloped each of them with a mellow, soft light, followed by a soft, delicate, and velvety harmony.

"Success," JoEllen whispered to Rosswell. "But not a big victory. The brilliance charm took, but it's not strong and it won't last for long. Work fast. They're both hard cases."

A charm? A brilliance charm? Oh dear.

"You mean hard-headed," whispered Rosswell to JoEllen, "and evidently very much alive. How old is she, anyway? JoEllen merely shrugged.

"Maman," Rosswell said, after licking his lips, "what do you want to tell me?" He shook both his hands, hoping to restore full circulation in his arms. The brilliance charm, he felt, worked *too well* on him. "Maman, now that I like everyone, what can we do to capture and convict the evil person who killed two members of your family?"

Maman, whose unwavering stare appeared stuck on the face of Mrs. Bolzoni, ripped herself away and wrenched around until she faced Rosswell. "The strength is small from this *bonne femme* who is small." Maman then glared at JoEllen. "But I let it stick for courthouse scribbler, her." Then she turned again to Rosswell. "Come. Find with me the silver."

Tina strode up to Mrs. Bolzoni, clasping her hands. "We will stand and watch."

Father Mike said, "As it says in the scriptures, 'Go, post a lookout, let him announce what he sees. Then the watcher called out: 'Upon a watchtower I stand, O Lord, continually by day, and at my post I am stationed throughout the night.'"

Ed added, "And I have heard that 'Evil is like those pernicious machineries which catch a man's coat-skirt or his hand, and draw in his arm, his leg, and his whole body to irresistible destruction.'"

Isaiah and Ralph Waldo Emerson. Spiritual and Literary quotes. Nice. But will it help us any? Simply thinking about it spurs a little migraine in the inner recesses of my mind.

Forcing himself back to the present and on to the subject, Rosswell said, "Silver? I recall spotting a glimmer of light when I walked the path the day of the murder. The light resembled a coin. At the time, it didn't strike me as important. A passing glimpse was the only thing I could afford. We were in a hurry." He squinted and gave the place a visual survey before pointing his forefinger. "I think it's that way."

JoEllen, Ed, and Father Mike followed at a respectful distance. Tina and Mrs. Bolzoni stood and watched at their post as Rosswell and Maman headed on the path in the direction he had pointed out.

When Rosswell and Maman reached the ground where the corpse had rested, he again discovered only the leavings you'd expect to find on a trail atop a bluff. Tree branches of varying size, big and little rocks, and leaves of all kinds. A pile of poop a bobcat recently deposited lay soft and fresh, close to the path. A large arrowhead. Actually, it was probably a spearhead. A shiny quartz rock. One brown and one black shoelace. A coin. All normal stuff on a hiking path in a forest.

Rosswell yelled, "A coin!"

The rest of the crew surrounded Rosswell and Maman.

"Maman. Look here." Rosswell showed her where the coin lay, then picked it up. After a close examination, he recognized it. "It's from the country of Vera Mardola."

Father Mike said, "Where is that?"

"It's an island nation in the Mediterranean," Rosswell said, as he turned over the coin. Next, he brought it close to his eyes and inspected the details, front and back. "I'm not believing what I'm seeing."

Ollie looked over Rosswell's shoulder. "What is it?"

"A *Kri-Kri.*"

Ferdinand and Ollie gasped.

Maman beamed a great smile.

CHAPTER 25

TINA CROSSED HER ARMS AND tapped her left foot in anticipation. "You all want to cut the drama and tell us what you found on the ground?"

If she's my private detective partner, I must always make sure she knows everything, every detail, in the cases we're working on. I'd hate to get killed and not leave enough for Tina to find my murderer.

"This," said Rosswell, holding up a coin slightly larger than a US silver dollar for all to see, "is a silver coin first minted in AD 1213 in the island nation of Vera Mardola."

Tina leaned forward, examining the coin. "This coin is at least 800 years old?"

"Yes, ma'am. Now, listen. The front side of the coin shows a *Kri-Kri*, which is a feral goat that lives in the Mediterranean area." He turned it over to show everyone the reverse. "The back side shows what we all know today is a *soutache* with a gold star attached, which is the sign of the Guardians of Dina. This coin looks like one of the first ones minted. The engraving is spectacular. If it is what I think it is, then I'm guessing it may be worth on today's market nearly ten thousand dollars."

Ferdinand grunted. "That's a bloody Chinese whisper."

Mrs. Bolzoni said, "I shall remember that. 'A Chinese whistled in his blood!' I like it!"

"No," said Ollie. "Mrs. Bolzoni, it's British slang that means something has been repeated so much that it's worthless info because it's been watered down. That's a bloody Chinese whisper."

"Yes, my love," Ferdinand cooed to Mrs. Bolzoni. "Ten thousand dollars would not come close to being the value of that coin. If it's the real thing."

Mrs. Bolzoni said, "A Chinese whistled in his blood?"

Ollie removed a small tube from his pocket and smeared a dab of Vaseline on his head. "That's right, Mrs. Bolzoni. You're absolutely correct." He began vigorously rubbing it into his skull with a clean McDonald's napkin. "A Chinese whistled in his blood."

"Yes, my love," Ferdinand said to Mrs. Bolzoni. "As usual, you are totally correct."

"This is yours." Rosswell handed the coin to Maman Fribeau who held it up to the sun.

"No." She deposited it gently back into Rosswell's palm. "You must keep it, you. You sell it for the expenses you have finding the killer of the women, kin of my blood. If you don't spend it gone, save it for the Guardians of Dina."

"Maman, I'm truly humbled. I will spend everything to catch that killer."

"Two of those women were granddaughters of my granddaughter." Maman shook her head and stared at the ground for a long time.

"Again, you humble me." Rosswell gave her a bow as he figured the math in his head. *She's got to be, what, two hundred years old? No. Maybe three? How is that possible? I give up.* "The killer will walk the earth no more when I find him. Or her. Or them."

Father Mike put a hand to his mouth and coughed.

Ollie said to the priest, "You're not scheduled for that tour of revenge."

"And," Ed said, "neither am I."

"And I," said Ferdinand, "make three."

Rosswell nodded his agreement to the trio. "We haven't forgotten that part of the bargain."

Maman Fribeau said, "My precious Juliette and Anna have gone before me which is not right, them." She closed her eyes tightly. Tears ran down her cheeks. She wheezed, finding it hard to breathe. In a whisper, she said, "The killer of my babies is still alive." She drew in another deep breath and her eyes flashed open. "And he is close to us." Maman Fribeau shrieked, up to the level of what Rosswell thought a banshee must sound like. Launching herself into a song he thought might be an ancient mourning dirge, she chanted loudly for several minutes.

After a final screech, Rosswell's ice spiders once more came out to skitter along his cold spine. Eight freezing feet. Per spider. Dancing along his spine.

"Bloody whisper!" Mrs. Bolzoni yelled. "The frog and I see the same thing. The evil demon man crosses the paths of the earth this way and that. I see him." She yelled even louder, "He must be stopped!" She pointed a forefinger at the horizon and drew a circle in the air around herself.

"Your name." Maman tapped Father Mike on the shoulder. "Père, who is like God, eh? Michael? That is what it means, *oui?*"

"Yes, in Hebrew, that's what it means. I am like God."

"Your God may be useful, him. Me, I don't need no god but what we call science. Even the ghosts follow the rules of the science. My ghosts fly and land and deposit things I must know in what we call The Warehouse. So this ghost must follow, too, eh?"

Father Mike presented his hands to Maman. Turned them over. Twice. "My hands are empty of an answer. I have no experience with these things." Father Mike wrinkled his forehead and then searched the faces of everyone else there, as if he needed confirmation. "Or, I guess I should say, I have some experience but it's brand new. There's no way I can tell you what's happening."

Maman tapped her closed lips and frowned. "Then let me ask you but one thing."

"Please do."

"Which personality of the evil one are we chasing?"

"Maman, that is easy." Father Mike held up a finger. "There is only one personality."

The ancient French woman walked up to the old Italian woman. Maman wrapped Mrs. Bolzoni in a great bear hug. "My little one, we have found the right holy man. And you brought him here, you!"

Mrs. Bolzoni, her voice cracking said, "It is much hot. Sweats. That is what falls down my cheeks. Sweats."

Maman turned again to Father Mike. "You. I need the saint. Bring me the one you call Alexander Comana."

"The janitor?"

Maman's laugh sounded more like a gurgle. "You have no janitor. You have a saint. And you the minister of your flock, you telling always to be saints and there one stands beneath your nose which you cannot see because you look flat across the horizon and not down where the common folk are."

Surprised at Maman's lashing, Father Mike said, "Perhaps an interview with Alexander is in order,"

"Yes," Mrs. Bolzoni said. "You, Father, the little frog woman says the janitor is the saint. Don't argue with her. She says. You go and do."

JoEllen whispered to Rosswell, "The brilliance charm is beginning to fade."

CHAPTER 26

Day 7, continued
Trail of Tears State Park

O LLIE CONSULTED HIS WATCH. "WHAT else am I supposed to do?"
Rosswell ticked off the names. "We have here, JoEllen, Mrs. Bolzoni, Ferdinand, Ollie, Rosswell, Tina. And me. That's an army. An army travels on its stomach." Rosswell listened for a while to the late night birds give way to the early morning birds before he saluted Ollie. "Give us a meal any time of day or night. You pay for it. We eat it. That's the deal."

"Unadulterated bullshit."

"That's exactly what your meals tasted like when I threw you in jail for the first time." Rosswell grabbed his stomach. "Please. I now recall some of your earlier attempts at cooking. You've caused me to eat a ton of Tums."

Ollie grabbed his wallet, drew out his Mensa membership card, and shoved it in Rosswell's face. "You know I'm smarter than anyone else around here. Give me an assignment worthy of my talents or the only place you'll see me is my restaurant."

"Give the bottom half of that card a row of tails and make something useful out of it. Namely, a comb."

"And why, Judge Rosswell Carew, would I need a comb since I have no hair?"

"Ollie, my sometimes friend, what we need is for you to comb through the facts we bring you."

The appeal to the research assistant worked its magic. Ollie puffed out his chest in the same manner that a Little Leaguer assumed when he banged a home run. "That's more like it. Thinking is my game." Ollie replaced the card into the depths of his wallet.

"Now, let me think." Rosswell, an inveterate pacer, began marching up and down the path in the woods, head down, hands clasped behind his back. *If only I had a deerstalker I'd look like Sherlock Holmes.* The morning coolness had left and the daytime heat ratcheted up. Rosswell felt he could think as easily in his air-conditioned office as he could on top of a cliff in a state park, where the humidity and the heat both measured in the high double digits. "We have had at least five murders over the years, and now the two Fribeau women makes seven. Seven unsolved murders without any clues. Five cold cases. All similar, but we have no suspects. Before the Fribeau sisters were killed—so say the cops—there were no possible Hivite murders. The one in 2013, they say was a copycat murder. I'm thinking that these two Fribeau murders, when I look at all of the previous ones as a whole, lead me to suspect our main enemy is in this area."

Ollie held up two fingers in a V-sign close to Rosswell to make certain Rosswell saw the signal. "Don't forget that there are *two* enemies, not one. Those two are slippery devils. We need a trap that is escape-proof."

"You're right and I haven't forgotten," Rosswell said.

Ferdinand nodded. "You refer to Adam Cain and Martha Bailey. But are we *sure* they are involved?"

"Yes, of course," Tina said. "All these strange things have their fingerprints on them." She chewed on a fingernail a bit before she spoke again. "Maybe not the angelic visitations. But the murders, yes, I'm betting on them."

"Who could ever forget those evil siblings?" Rosswell continued. "Everything I see leads me to them. These murders have all the earmarks of killings they've pulled off. Silly me. Since we haven't heard from them in a while, I was hoping they'd gone some other place befitting their morals. Russia or China maybe. In all, it seems they haven't left the country, so consider us under attack."

"Speaking of attack," JoEllen said, "I need Maman and Mrs. Bolzoni to help me scour the area for any psychic vibes. If Adam or Martha are as cruel and nasty as you all say, they could very well be radiating unpleasant energies in the area."

Okay? I've never seen any radiating energies in my entire life, but if the trio of sensitives want to traipse around Cape Girardeau trying to pick up signals from bad guys and girls, who am I to stop them? Certainly couldn't hurt anything. And who knows? They may accidentally stumble over some real evidence.

Rosswell hoped his thoughts couldn't be read by the threesome.

"JoEllen, you, Mrs. Bolzoni, and Maman Fribeau are welcome to search the area for any bad energy from Adam and Martha." *That is, if there is such a thing.* The women all nodded in agreement.

"I'm a great organizer," JoEllen said. "I'd be honored to have these two wonderful ladies helping me. The three of us together cannot fail. With Maman's extrasensory superhighway—"

"The Warehouse, that. It is The Warehouse," Maman interrupted.

"Yes, and our thoughts and messages we shall call 'Branching'." JoEllen eyed Maman and Mrs. Bolzoni probably to see if they had any objections. Neither woman balked at the name, so she continued. "One thought in my head, for example, reaches another mind, and that mind doubles the number of receivers and it happens again throughout the world, throughout the universe, all the way to infinity."

"How long does this take?" Rosswell scratched his emaciated mustache to keep him from laughing out loud. "Rough estimate. That's all I need."

"Faster than light," JoEllen answered instantly.

"Where do the bad people come into play?" Tina asked. "What you're telling us sounds dangerous, if it's not protected from evil. What protection is there for all of you—and us—when you're surfing the pathways of a psychic network?"

"Yes, JoEllen, you must the truth of the bad guys tell all," Mrs. Bolzoni said.

Maman Fribeau answered Tina. "There's much for JoEllen to say, her. Much of the evil which we must try to keep buried or it will us kill. *Oui.*"

"Great." Tina said.

JoEllen continued. "When I first started working here thirty years ago, people I met told me that up until the 1960s, the Common Pleas Courthouse used coal to heat the place. During the cold weather, a truck from the coal company came once a month or so, to dump coal into the basement where the slave prison was once located. I dreamed about that coal bin. In my dreams, I could go through the coal mounds into another room that was even bigger and brighter, and held a lot more coal. That room led to several other branches, all of which led to other tunnels between the coal bins. One branching came out on the river downtown. Another one, south on Lorimier Street. Yet another branch came out inside a huge warehouse that is still in business. There is no one who realizes that it's a secret operation. That one must have something to do with Maman."

Rosswell sighed in relief. "Fine. But you're speaking metaphorically. Or symbolically, right? You're not telling us that something is happening in the real world. Not in the physical world?"

Maman Fribeau guffawed loudly.

Tina asked her, "Aren't you the one who said you believed only what science could teach you about the physical world?"

"*Oui.* And The Branching, her, is a physical part of the real world."

Father Mike and Ed approached Rosswell. The priest said, "For the record, Ed and I have been chatting about this. We don't agree on everything, but we do insist that, just for this one investigation, we assume that everything JoEllen and the others are telling us about The Branching and the other psychic networks is true."

Ed snorted. "This is a bunch of hogwash. However, after discussing this with the good father here, I'm willing to accept The Branching as a working model of at least part of the universe. If we're all wrong, then we start over again."

Tina said, "I agree with everyone else. Rosswell?"

"Okay. But only temporarily. I want to see results before I cash my chips in. Ollie?"

The research assistant slapped his forehead, slumped his shoulders, and said, "I'm fixing to head back to town where I'll fry me up some chicken." He turned to stalk away.

"Ollie," Rosswell said, "you agreed that you would help Ed all you could. We need to make sure he is not found guilty of any crime whatsoever, much less capital murder."

Ollie whirled around and faced Rosswell. "And *how* will we know when we're successful?"

"Calm down, calm down. Your head is redder than a bloody tomato. We will know when the power of the state is no longer hanging its hatchet over Ed's neck."

Ollie, unsmiling, eyes squinted, and fists clenching, stomped up to Ed, shook his hand, and said, "In for a penny, in for a pound."

"Yes!" Mrs. Bolzoni yelled. "We must all pound the penny till it is flat and squashed out."

CHAPTER 27

The Raggedy Man

ANNA FRIBEAU. WHAT FUN SHE was to kill! And, although that idiot Ed Searl managed to order her cremated before I could leave my calling card, he inadvertently did me a favor by destroying any evidence. And then her sister, Juliette Fribeau. I surprised her and killed her before she realized she was being attacked. Every killer needs at least one or two 'Wham-bam, thank-you-ma'am' encounters. Sometimes I like to draw them out for days. Just like I'm going to do to Rosswell, Tina, and their kid. What's his name? Oh, yeah. Jonathan David. I can take a week killing the three of them. It will give them something to remember when they're dead.

Time to find Martha and Adam. After the plans? The execution. And then we have lots and lots and lots of fun.

My heart is ready.
My body always willing.
I love whiskey.
I love espresso.
I love meat.
I love risky.
I love tobacco.
I love sweet.
My soul is steady
Cause most of all, I love killing!

CHAPTER 28

Day 8
St. Mark's Hospital

THE NEXT AFTERNOON, ROSSWELL'S PHONE rang. He was trying to enjoy walking the grounds of the courthouse as a part of his daily exercise. Sonya Blanco. He tapped a fake button on the screen that beeped a fake beep, and answered the call. "I thought I was supposed to call you."

"Rosswell, shut up and listen. This is important."

"Spill it."

"No. Not on the phone. Meet me at the main entrance of Saint Mark's Hospital in fifteen minutes."

"Got it." Rosswell knew that Sonya, a generally humorless woman, never joked, especially when it involved anything about a police case. Sonya didn't socialize. She worked. If she wasn't working, Rosswell guessed she ate and slept.

Why the hospital? Cops were always going to hospitals. He hoped Sonya wasn't the patient. Had one of the bad guys hurt Sonya? A small trickle of fear and anxiety mixed in equal parts rolled down Rosswell's spine. He needed to get to her as soon as possible, but he didn't want to get another ticket.

Even without speeding, it took him only twelve minutes to arrive at the main entrance, which was on the ground floor. Lots of people around, although he couldn't spot Sonya. He called her three times but she didn't answer and the call did not go to voicemail. Rosswell stood in the hallway of the entrance until five minutes had passed. Surely, she had made it to the building by now. What if she hadn't gone to the main entrance? The hospital wasn't that big. Time to check outside. If she wasn't outside then he would check with admissions to ask if a cop had been hurt and admitted lately.

Leaving behind some of the noise and the faint smell of disinfectants and the aroma of sick people, he exited the front door into a quieter and kinder sort of noise floating in the semi-fresh air, heated by the sun and humidified by the river. He pressed buttons on his phone. The call to Ollie was answered on the first ring.

"Hello, Judge."

"Is Sonya Blanco at your restaurant?"

"No. She was here about twenty-two minutes ago looking for you. Told me she had guard duty at the hospital. Anyway. Have you gone there?"

"Guard duty. Must have to watch a bad guy receiving medical attention. That's where I am right now. The hospital. I'll snoop around a bit more. See if I can find her."

"I'll start raising your bail money. Goodbye." Ollie hung up.

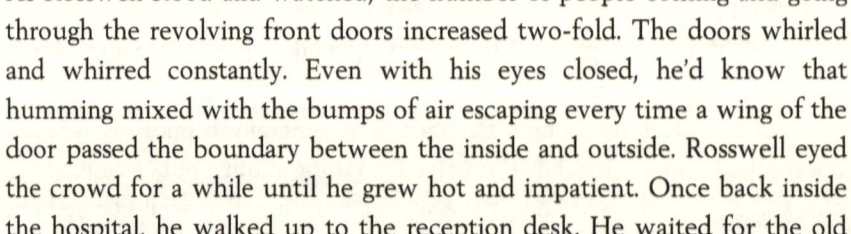

As Rosswell stood and watched, the number of people coming and going through the revolving front doors increased two-fold. The doors whirled and whirred constantly. Even with his eyes closed, he'd know that humming mixed with the bumps of air escaping every time a wing of the door passed the boundary between the inside and outside. Rosswell eyed the crowd for a while until he grew hot and impatient. Once back inside the hospital, he walked up to the reception desk. He waited for the old man in a faded blue coat and a green ball cap perched sideways on his head to acknowledge him. But he didn't.

"Sir, I need some information."

The skinny guy paid Rosswell no mind, intrigued by a solitaire game he played on the computer.

People still play solitaire? "Sir?"

The computer dinged.

"No use denying it. I'm good." Then as if seeing Rosswell for the first time, he adjusted his cap. Sprouts of white hair stuck out over each ear, giving every appearance of horns. "Boy howdy! That makes six in a row today."

"Six in a row. Wow. That's great. Yep, that's really great."

The guy, who looked like a senior citizen devil, glued his eyes to the monitor again and grinned each time he clicked the mouse. A new game danced onto the screen. Lucky seven. He cackled like a demon.

If this fellow weighed about ten pounds less, he'd launch himself into the air if he timed going through that revolving door just right. Bam! One of those doors slapping him in the ass would send him over the rainbow. Imagine that. A tired, old, faded Satan floating out above the trees until he lost momentum and plopped to the ground. I'd pay to see that.

"Sir, could I have your attention please for just one moment?"

The man glared at Rosswell.

"Would you mind paging Sonya Blanco, please?"

"Doctor who?"

"No, not Doctor Who. Officer Sonya Blanco." Rosswell slowly and clearly enunciated the word with his best Spanish pronunciation. "Blanco." The man batted his eyes, but still no sign of recognition as to what Rosswell wanted. Perhaps the Spanish pronunciation of Sonya's surname confused the erstwhile solitaire contender. Rosswell tried to Anglicize the words to their limits. "Blawn. Koe."

The old man's eyes lit up like the orange and black Halloween lights Tina draped around their front door every October. The curmudgeon licked the end of the pen, wrote the name on a slip of paper, and then keyed the microphone on the paging system. "Captain Blonde Hoe, please come to the reception desk." Returning to his solitaire game, he began clicking keys again. "There you go, young feller. That Navy lady will hear that page for sure."

Rosswell slapped his forehead. "Navy? She's not in the Navy. She's—"

"You said she was an officer."

"She's a *police* officer. I'm guessing it's beyond belief that you could page Police Officer Sonya Blanco?"

The guy cupped his hand behind an ear. "Beyond where?"

Rosswell saluted and said, "Best of luck with the game."

"Working on number seven!" He waved a fist pump in the air.

Rosswell leaned over the desk and whispered to the man before walking away. "I hope you have a computer and Internet access at home, buddy, because this job may not last long. Unless, of course, if you're a volunteer—God help us all who need information—you'll be here forever."

The geezer never turned around to acknowledge Rosswell's insult.

Rosswell checked his phone for the time since he never wore a watch. "Thirty minutes. Surely enough time for Sonya to get here to take up her guard duty." *Where would be the logical place for her to guard someone?* He headed for the emergency room. Surely a woman in a dark blue uniform wandering around all the medical people in white and green and (Rosswell's favorite color)—gray, the color of beans at a Mexican restaurant puked up on the floor—wouldn't be hard to spot.

CHAPTER 29

Day 8, continued
St. Mark's Hospital

THE INTAKE WOMAN BEHIND THE desk in the emergency room greeted Rosswell with a smile. If he was going to be admitted, he wanted a friendly greeting, and a clean place, which was quiet and peaceful. The girl's smile was nice, but the underlying aroma of the various discharges humans are prone to emit didn't assure Rosswell that the place was clean. And the banging and clanking emanating from the innards of the emergency waiting room didn't close the deal on the quiet and peaceful part. Nope. This was not a happy place.

"Hello," said the woman. "I'm sorry you're not feeling well. What are your symptoms?"

I doubt if she wants to hear about my long-running anxieties, playing on every channel in my brain since I came back from the war. Oh. And alcoholism. That's always a favorite, not to mention my leukemia in remission.

Rosswell drummed his fingers on the counter a moment before he answered, "Thank you, Ms. . . . uh . . . Miss . . . but I feel fine." He repressed the need to say the woman's name displayed on her nametag—*ETAOIN SHRDLU.* If he had more time, he'd have engaged her in conversation about where she hailed from. Of course, that could backfire on him. She could be just a plain old American citizen. "No, madam, I do not have an emergency. I'm looking for a police officer."

The woman closed her eyes and pressed the bridge of her nose. After a couple of seconds, she snapped her eyes open and glared at Rosswell with a *you're-one-of-those-aren't-you?* looks. Her smile failed at convincing him that she was happy about seeing him.

"Yes, sir, there are some police officers here. But not many." The last time Rosswell had heard a grown-up use that tone of voice was when he was in kindergarten, fumbling with finger paints. "That is because this, as you might know, is a hospital, not a police station." She stopped for a moment to allow him to absorb her words—and tone. He recognized the ploy from Tina's use of it. "But you're going to have to tell me your symptoms."

"Let me rephrase my request." Rosswell cleared his throat and straightened. "I'm looking for Sonya Blanco."

With her fingers poised over her computer's keyboard, she said, "What. Are. Your. Symptoms?" She spoke through clenched teeth.

"I have no symptoms."

"You're not sick?"

"No ma'am."

"Are you injured?"

"No ma'am."

Rosswell could see the gears in her head working furiously behind her eyes.

"Have you tried having the reception desk page the officer you're looking for?"

"*Que sera, sera.*" He shrugged. "I'm afraid that between my Spanish and the receptionist's love of solitaire, the Avenue de la Reception Desk is of no use."

The woman blinked rapidly. "Be seated over there." With an exaggerated swirl of her hand, she pointed out a 1950-style fiberglass chair in the far corner of the room. To Rosswell, the chair looked itchy. She said, "I'll find out if that person is in the hospital."

Rosswell shuffled to the chair and plopped down just in time to discover Ed meandering through the door toward the emergency room exit.

"Ed!" Rosswell jumped up and rushed over to him. He grabbed the minister's right hand and shook it as if Ed's appearance meant the difference between life and death. "I am so happy to see you."

"Judge, are you sick?" Ed's eyes were wide with concern and perhaps a little fear. "What are your symptoms?"

"No symptoms I'm feeling great. How are you doing after our adventure?"

"I'm telling you that I'm never going to Trail of Tears ever again."

"Listen," Rosswell said, grabbing Ed by his elbow, "we will get this whole mess straightened out soon. That I promise."

"I appreciate that beyond what mere words can convey. Trust me."

Rosswell pointed to the CLERGY badge that hung around Ed's neck. "Are you here on an official visit?"

"Just leaving. Had a few visits here. People in the hospital are always happy to see people from the outside."

"You're off duty now?"

"Reverends are never off duty, Rosswell."

"As are lawyers. Let me tell you a problem I'm having."

"What?" Ed sucked in his breath. "You are sick. Please, tell me your symptoms. Do you feel faint? Are you in pain?"

"Stop." Rosswell held up a hand. "Listen. I'm not sick. I'm looking for Sonya Blanco. She asked me to meet her here a while ago. I think she may be in the emergency area somewhere, but I can't get behind the security doors to look around."

"You told me not to trust her." Ed's brow furrowed. "You told me not to trust anyone in law enforcement. Not the sheriff, not the chief, not the prosecutor, not any cop, not even Sonya. Now you trust her?"

"With my life."

"What changed your mind?"

"Lots of things."

Ed pinched his lower lip.

"I need to talk to her, Ed, and we're wasting time."

"We? What do you expect me to do about this?"

"Give me your ID."

———◆———

Rosswell spruced up his hair and straightened his clothes before he opened the security door—with the code supplied by Ed—to the bowels of the emergency room. He made certain that Ed's tag faced front. People don't pay attention to the details of an identification badge. The only important assumption people glean when they see someone wearing a badge is that the person must be legitimate. And no threat. Rosswell learned that fact when he held court in Saint Louis County a couple of years ago. The security guard at the courthouse door took one quick glance at the black robe Rosswell carried on a hanger and waved him through the entrance without checking his identification. The black robe was Rosswell's badge. The security guard saw that and inquired no further.

The horseshoe-shaped emergency room had fourteen examination areas along its outside wall, each area accessed by opening a sliding glass door. Inside the horseshoe held stations for doctors and nurses and other services.

Rosswell scrunched his face into his best concerned clergy impression. As he passed each examination area, he peeked unobtrusively for Sonya. Nothing. He called her phone again. Nothing. Maybe Sonya wouldn't be as easy to spot in her uniform as he'd first thought.

After the third peek, a young man in blue scrubs stopped Rosswell. "May I help you find something?"

Like the way out? No thanks, Sonny.

"Yes, sir, I'd appreciate that. I'm looking for Cape Girardeau City Officer Sonya Blanco, who asked me for pastoral assistance. She called me down here, but I'm afraid that in all the rush I've forgotten the patient's name."

The blue-scrubbed kid's nametag gave no clue whether he was head janitor or junior surgeon. The guy appeared around twelve, maybe thirteen years old. He leaned close to Rosswell's identification badge. After studying it for several years, the kid's head bobbed up and he examined Rosswell's face.

Busted.

"You're Reverend Ed Searl?"

I wonder how many years I'll get for impersonating a preacher?

"That's me."

"Why did you shave your beard off?"

Rosswell rubbed his bare cheeks and chin. "I kept my mustache."

The kid leaned close to Rosswell's face. "Where?"

"Here." Rosswell ran his index fingers over his nearly invisible mustache since the stupid kid couldn't see the hair above his lip without help. "How do you like it?"

"Nice for sure." The kid snapped his fingers. "You preached my grandma's funeral. Remember that?"

"Of course I do." Rosswell laid a hand on the kid's shoulder. "That was a trying time for all concerned."

The kid smiled. "You're a great preacher."

"I prefer the term minister. It's less sermonizing."

"What? Oh." The kid frowned. "Nice for sure." He sounded doubtful.

"Do you know where Officer Blanco is?"

"I'll help you find her."

After searching six other examination areas, the kid found Sonya, guarding a young girl.

"Judge Carew?" Sonya pulled him away from the examination area. She whispered, "Juvenile. She's a runner. I don't want her winding up in the clutches of the slavers."

The helpful kid stared first at the nametag and then at Rosswell. "Judge Carew? I thought you were a preacher."

"I preach under an assumed name. It's a tax thing." Rosswell pointed to Sonya, who wore a puzzled look on her face. "The nice police lady here can vouch for me."

Sonya didn't hesitate. "That's right. He's good. Judge Rosswell Carew is fine and dandy."

"Whatever. Thanks, Officer Blanco. And you, also, Ross." The kid shrugged and left.

"My name is not Ross!" he called after the kid who'd apparently gone deaf since he walked away without a single sign of recognition.

"I've heard that your first name is really your last name and there's no abbreviation for that." A smile threatened Sonya's usual serious expression.

"It's a pet peeve. Anyway, do you have a prisoner in here I know?"

"No one you know. And she's not a prisoner. Cops have to guard people sometimes in hospitals. What I have to tell you has nothing to do with the hospital, or the girl I'm guarding."

"What then?"

Sonya motioned for a relief guard to spell her. She grabbed her small briefcase and said to Rosswell, "Come this way." He followed her to an empty examination room where she slid the door closed and yanked a crinkly drape to hide them. "I may know the identity of the owner of the phone found under the body of Juliette Fribeau."

CHAPTER 31

Day 8, continued
St. Mark's Hospital

"TIMOTHY LOCKERBIE? WHO IS HE? A maintenance man here at the hospital is the Hivite?"

"I don't know what to think." She stuffed the evidence envelope back into her brief case. "We do have a guy that we're trying to track down."

"Being?"

"Someone who calls himself The Raggedy Man. All we have is the alias. Most of the squawkers are afraid of him. Except that we had one female call him out. No one else will tell us anything."

"Squawkers?"

"Snitches."

"Is there any possibility that Lockerbie is The Raggedy Man?"

Sonya answered, "Anything is possible."

"I'll have Ollie check that out. What else?"

Sonya picked up her notebook again, licked a finger, and started leafing through the pages. She stopped. Went back a couple of pages and then went forward three pages. "Yeah. Here it is. That's where a big problem arises. Timothy Lockerbie had been serving a prison sentence in Texas for selling dope. The sentence began *after* the last Hivite murder. That means he could've had a window of opportunity. The Trail of Tears murder, however, happened one day *before* Timothy was scheduled to get out of prison. Unless he's got wings, he couldn't have gotten to Missouri and had enough time to kill Juliette Fribeau."

"And," Rosswell tapped his fingers on his leg. "Juliette's sister, Anna, was killed earlier by a day or so before Juliette. Timothy Lockerbie couldn't have killed her either." He scratched his head and hummed a few bars of *The Star-Spangled Banner.* He stopped humming mid-stream and said, "This is all too coincidental. There's just no way that a prime suspect in a cold case murder is going to travel from Texas to Missouri and plop down right in front of a detective who is looking for him."

"Agreed. There are a lot of job openings in Cape. Why did he pick one here in this hospital? And for me to be here at the same time he is? Too neat and handy."

"Too neat and handy, and there's no willing suspension of disbelief on my part."

Sonya stood and walked around the room. "You're correct, Judge. That's why I think someone is manipulating this guy, moving him toward you and me. We are targets. But I don't know why." She sat after her brief exercise. "Then who killed the Fribeau sisters?"

"Was a red card found under Anna?"

"No one knows. There wasn't one collected during the investigation of her murder. And she was cremated. Not much help there."

I've got to ask this even though it will get me in trouble. "Sonya, are you saying there was sloppy police work at the investigation of Anna's death?"

"I was there at the murder scene. She was killed by a shot to the head. What I'm saying is that the autopsy revealed nothing but how she died. We do still have the bullet in evidence, but that's it. And since she was cremated, basically, there's no evidence. No eyewitness testimony. No nothing."

"Was he in this area between 2006 and 2008?"

Sonya shook her head. "I don't think so. I need to do more checking, but I have to believe he was in Texas, locked up for dope. Or if he wasn't locked up, maybe he was running his dope ring and making a fortune. I mean, I've done everything I can to tie Timothy to the Hivite murders but I cannot place him in this area during that time. If he was here and if he committed any kind of a crime, there's no record of it because, I guess, he never got caught. He had no driver's license then and I don't think he has one now. If I had the manpower, I'd have him shadowed to see where he goes after he gets off work."

"Let me think." Rosswell tapped the fingers of one of his hands on the palm of his other hand. "I know." He stopped tapping his fingers. "Hire an extra cop."

"No money."

"Then remove one cop from parking meter patrol and have him follow this guy."

"There are no parking meters anymore in Cape. Listen, Judge, Timothy Lockerbie is one suspect who looks good for the killings, but there are too many holes in his background. What if we're watching him and the real killer gets away? We can't risk it. We just have to spread ourselves thin and hope for the best."

Rosswell nodded his agreement. "There are never enough cops."

She certainly is a Chatty Cathy today. Nervous. Something else is going on.

"Sonya, you've never discussed methods of law enforcement with me. What's the deal here? Why did you call me here to talk?"

She drew in a deep breath. "Simply put, I want to join the Guardians."

Rosswell swallowed. *Did I understand what she just said?* He glanced around. Satisfied again that no one was within earshot, he said, "*You* want to join the Guardians?"

"I *need* to. There's too much sex slavery going on in this country that's not being addressed by the law enforcement system." She closed her eyes, and massaged her temples. " There's more than even you know, that's going on around here."

"Your solution is to become a vigilante? That's an odd thing for a cop to do."

"Yes, it is. Why do you think it's bothering me so much? I've thought about this a lot."

"Who else have you discussed this with?"

"You mean besides you?"

"Right."

"You."

"Sonya, no, I mean who besides me have you talked to about this?"

"I'm trying to tell you. No one."

"There's one tiny problem." Rosswell got up and faced her. He let his words slip out slowly. "Right now, I . . . don't . . . trust you."

"Understandable, but there's more to me than just being a cop. I have a pistol and I know how to use it." Sonya readjusted her holster. "Vigilantes need someone good with firearms, and I am a sharpshooter."

"How does that make me want to trust you?"

"Judge, you don't have a choice. You told me about your weird phone messages, that certainly sounds like someone has a target on you and your family. They're trying to kill you. No one else can help you like I can."

Rosswell stood at a crossroads and he knew it. If he were going to allow Sonya Blanco entry into The Guardians of Dina, then he would be aiding and abetting her to become a vigilante. Sonya, of course, already had to know that. Besides, law enforcement agencies do not approve of their employees being vigilantes. It's a contradiction in terms.

A cop brings a bad guy to justice. A vigilante metes out justice to a bad guy.

If Sonya were fighting with me and not against me, I would have a powerful ally.

There really was no other decision he could make.

Rosswell closed his eyes. When he opened them, he said, "I'm putting my life—and my family—in your hands. If you're wearing a body cam and a wire, my life will be worth nothing. Since I'm willing to do what you ask me to do, knowing that I may die for doing it, I'll tell you this: You're in." Rosswell removed his own *soutache* and handed it to Sonya. "With this necklace, I give you membership in a special group that doesn't exist."

Sonya stood. "I put my life in your hands. I'll treat your life with the same dignity and care that I treat my own, which is awfully damned good if I do say so myself."

Rosswell and Sonya stood facing each other for what seemed to him (and, probably, to her) an uncomfortably long time until he broke the spell. "Well, the band and the caterer neither one showed up, so we had to cancel the reception."

Sonya's laughter rang out. She managed to offer her hand to Rosswell. "Shake, Judge."

Rosswell shook hands and then asked her, "Now, tell me about Ed and the hut or shack."

CHAPTER 32

Day 8, continued
Downtown Cape Girardeau
Tina Carew

TINA (THE SKEPTICAL NON-PSYCHIC), who was tagging along with JoEllen, Maman Fribeau, and Mrs. Bolzoni, all of whom claimed to be psychics, began to grow weary of the journey. Especially since it seemed to her to be . . . well . . . silly. And, for another thing, she'd not worn her comfortable shoes, the brown ones. The flats like nuns and nurses wore because they were on their feet a lot.

JoEllen positioned herself on the sidewalk, then pointed to the top of a building. "Something may be stirring up there." Outside an old three-story brick building on Water Street in downtown Cape, she halted, held up her hand as a signal to the other three to stop, and then once more pointed to the building. She looked like a Girl Scout leader selling cookies, cautioning her salesgirls that they were plunging into territory known for its extraordinarily high level of sales fueled by the overwhelming craving of human beings for mint-flavored chocolate. The main danger to the salesgirls would be the hordes trampling them to get to the cookies.

JoEllen continued, "Something in that building right there is speaking to me." Eyes shut so tight that tears began to drop down her cheeks, she continued. "Something in there is small but powerful. Computers. Computers with huge amounts of memory working toward a solution of a tangled equation derived from quantum physics."

Maman Fribeau sniffed loudly. "It's not magic gremlins, them, floating on supernatural waves. It's science! Quantum physics says particles can be two things at one time. Science. It's wonderful."

JoEllen said, "I won't disagree or agree with you, Maman, because I dom't know. Today is hot and humid. The info is not clear." Searching for information spread by psychic energy proved hard work for her as well as her cohorts. The afternoon sun, burning in a cloudless sky baked downtown Cape. "We'll take a break from walking. Let's stand in a circle. Close our eyes."

Everyone obeyed JoEllen's order except Tina, who said, "I have nothing when it comes to feeling the vibes of the universe or whatever it is you're looking for. If I were you all, I'd not expect anything from me. I won't play along, but I won't bother you either." She walked out of the light into the shadow cast by the floodwall along the river where the temperature may have been a couple of degrees cooler. "I'll stand by and watch." She also pondered the odd statement that JoEllen assumed that heat and humidity bungled up the psychic waves floating throughout the air. How that worked landed far beyond Tina's knowledge of the supernatural.

To pass the time, she shaded her eyes and surveyed the building, built a hundred or maybe a hundred and fifty years ago. Modern windows installed sometime in the recent past accented the building's age. According to the historical society plaque screwed to the front wall, the first business established there occupied the ground floor. Perhaps a hardware store. Or a dry goods store. The second floor had been a storage area and the third floor had been reserved for living quarters for the owner and his family. The whole building set on raised sandstone, which was an answer to the constant flooding of the downtown area. Before the floodwall was built in the 1960s, the high waters would creep up frequently into the commercial area. After the water receded, the downtown smelled bad and diseases were frequently spread by the stinking water. There was little light and not much fresh air in the part of the building surrounded by the sandstone walls, which were about six feet high. Tina assured herself that Rosswell would never enter that area, lest his claustrophobia grow in strength to the point where it could kill him by gnawing on his innards. Her husband, she further assured herself, would call it "an above-ground cellar." The last few decades had seen several people trying to dam the floodwaters of the river inching into downtown. Keeping water away from the sandstone part of the building never worked. The failure was now ignored since the floodwall kept the downtown mostly dry these days.

"That's fine by us," JoEllen said to Tina before turning to Mrs. Bolzoni and Maman Fribeau. "You all okay with that? With her not participating? Instead, standing over there?"

Mrs. Bolzoni said, "Okry-dokry," and Maman Fribeau, added, "*C'est bien.*"

Tina said, "If I do discover anything odd, I'll let you all know." There was nothing odd for her to report. The usual downtown noises—shouts, car horns, laughter, street bands—added to the usual downtown smells—bakeries churning out goodies, stale beer in the gutters, whiffs of tobacco smoke, the sweat of the tourists—kept things bland. Dull. Not odd.

A few pedestrians walked past the four women, yet all of the walkers avoided looking at them, and, if the passersby had said anything about them, apparently none of the women had heard it.

Tina, having lived with Rosswell long enough to learn when to cut to the chase, said, "Let's stop acting like a circle of psychics, which is what you all are, but let's not advertise it. Why don't we relax and start a chit-chat and stop being so obvious?"

JoEllen thrust her hands into the air and waved her fingers. "Can you feel it?"

"That's what I meant by being obvious."

Mrs. Bolzoni and Maman Fribeau nodded in unison. Tina, as promised, again tried keeping silent and not interfering with what she knew Rosswell would call a "kumbaya event."

"Also I'm hearing," Mrs. Bolzoni said. "There must be of them two. Yes. Two. Definitely. Talking to each other, they are. I hear it." She removed her eyeglasses and cleaned them. Before she put them back on, she wiped her face with her empty hand. "They talk of death of the judge and his family and of danger to all his friends."

"*Oui*," said Maman Fribeau. She grew silent for a bit, then tilted her head, and gasped. "Yes, they speak of the Judge Carew. Murder. Death. Killing."

"I also hear talk of killing him and his family," JoEllen said. "No. How horrible."

Maman pointed to the brick building. "Whose is this here? This place where the badness flows into the street there, making us all fearful."

"Follow me," JoEllen said, ducking into an alley.

Once there, she again did the normal search of the area to make certain no one was watching. She also cast a low-level weaving out on to The Branching, which was a net to catch anyone who was peeking into their plans. The weaving would alert JoEllen and her crew if a trespass happened, but the trespassers would never know that their presence was detected. A low-level weaving, while not all that powerful, still maintained enough energy to be one of the most useful tools in a psychic's quiver.

JoEllen said, "Let me call someone." She touched numbers on her phone and got an answer on the second ring. "Hey, it's me." After a pause, "Yeah. Fine. Listen, if I give you the info, could you tell me who owns a building in downtown Cape?" JoEllen listened for a few seconds then said, "Yes, here's the address." After giving the person on the other end of the line the info, she said, "Thanks. Got it."

Mrs. Bolzoni said, "Our excitement is big. Tell us."

JoEllen said, "The owner is a company called *Le Four Orange*. A French corporation."

"I can tell you right now," Tina breaking her promise of silence, said, "that those people are bad to the core. They've been a front for sex traffickers for three hundred years. It's an old French corporation that's kept its true purpose hidden all that time."

"Aha!" Maman said. "*Le Four Orange. Oui.* The orange oven. *Four* also means furnace or stove, in French, the language divine. And *orange* is the same word in the barbaric language English."

Mrs. Bolzoni snorted.

"The Orange Oven?" JoEllen said the words again. "What difference does the color of an oven have to do with anything?"

Tina, again breaking her pledge of silence, said, "The meaning is a play on words that is an example of meaningless French humor. Few people, even the French, think French humor is funny. What could be funnier than an orange furnace?"

JoEllen dismissed the question with a wave of her hand. "If you say so." She then asked all the others, one at a time, "Who is in that building? Anyone we know? Or should know? Anyone getting any hints?"

All the others answered with some version of "no." No one spoke, until at last Tina said, "We need to break this up and go our separate ways and think about this. I'm getting nothing but you all are receiving signals of some kind from who-knows-where. At least that's what you think you're getting. We need something concrete."

"I have something," said JoEllen. "I'm hearing something. A name. Maybe a family or a city, or a town. Yes. The town is the same as the family." She shut her eyes and pressed her forehead with both hands. Her eyes opened. "Lockerbie. Anyone know a family with the name of Lockerbie?"

"Me, I know how to find this one. The man who knows this is superstitious but speaks the truth."

"Thank you, Maman," said JoEllen.

"Yes, thanks. We'll wait at Ollie's place," said Tina. "Time for a break."

CHAPTER 33

THE RAGGEDY MAN

Many times The Raggedy Man
According to a detailed plan
Fried up brains in a cast iron pan
After cutting off the pearls
After chopping off the curls
Of all the pretty girls

CHAPTER 34

Day 8, continued
The Purple Star

Inside the Purple Star, Tina eyeballed the front door, guarding the place with one of her newer guns. It was a 380 Mustang, compact, light, easily carried, and readily concealed. Maman would soon return with someone who knew something. She hoped.

About an hour later, Maman marched into The Purple Star, dragging Alexander Comana in tow. She saluted Tina who had curled in a booth by herself, drinking a Coke. The midday rush hour had passed and the evening rush hour hadn't yet arrived. Tina enjoyed sitting alone, watching the few people around. No husband. No child. It was her time and her time alone. There were quiet conversations in all the occupied booths and tables. A louder burst of laughter occasionally interrupted the softer sounding chatter. Ollie's famous pies—served only for supper—cooked in the large ovens in the kitchen, sending out sweet aromas of apples, blueberries, coconut, and lots more, to every nook and cranny of the building. The best part of all, she thought, was watching the sun's rays hitting the downtown buildings, transforming the splashes of light into different shades of yellow, orange, and red as the sunset approached. Soon, the streetlights would blaze on, sending their sparkling rays out into the approaching darkness of night, which, as always, would try to drown the light.

Maman, as if showing off a prize catch, stood before Tina, Alexander by her side. She pointed a bony finger at him. "Here, this man is a good man who never lies. I have known him for many centuries." What passed for a smile appeared on her face, showing the teeth she still had were yellowed and crooked.

Centuries? Tina thought. *I hope she's joking. Or mistaken. Maybe she counts differently in French. I'll choose mistaken over a couple of people who are centuries old. That will keep my dreams more sane.*

Maman said, "I know him these many, many long years. And now I bring him to you."

Alexander smiled and bowed to Tina. "M'lady." His clothes were covered with soot and ashes. "I apologize, but I was cleaning the chimneys of the parish church and the rectory of the priests. The chimneys are hardly used any more for heating, but the birds nest there as well as bats and other creatures of God. We do not harm any creature of God. I thus try to keep every building clean for each of those animal companions who seek shelter. Unfortunately, some of my creature friends carry diseases harmful to man." Alexander searched Tina's face and then Maman's. Bowing he said, "Sorry. I must say, harmful to man and to woman."

"Nice to meet you," Tina said. "Let's go into the back where the rest of the gang is." She stood and took his hand. "You look starved."

Gently drawing his hand from Tina's grasp before they could start for the storage room—also known as the conference area—Alexander said, "Thank you, but I am fasting today so that I may ponder the endless wonders of the infinite universe of my eternal king."

"Then you?" Tina turned to Maman. "You must be ravenous by now. Ollie will prepare anything you like at no charge to you."

"I also fast," Maman said, shrugging. "I must not add any fat."

"Me, too," said Tina, "But I will eat."

Tina, Maman, and Alexander joined Mrs. Bolzoni and JoEllen in the conference/store room, where the two of them sat at a small table, with only a tiny lamp for light. Tina flipped the switch on the fluorescent lights, which sputtered and fizzed, winked, and then blinked, assuring her of a headache if she stayed too long. Fortunately, the lights blipped one last time and slid into a steady, peaceful, and low glow of white.

Tina said to Alexander, "Rosswell and I have been to Holy Cross before. In fact, I've seen you at your church but I've never met you until now." She offered her hand, which he did not take, bowing instead. "Maman says you know someone named Lockerbie. Is Lockerbie a man or a woman?"

"May I sit?" Alexander glanced at Maman, then back at Tina. "Standing all day on these old legs make them sore."

"Yes of course," Tina said. "Please make yourself comfortable. We're not much on ceremony here. Kind of relaxed. You know, like we keep the bowing and scraping to a minimum. Don't use a lot of titles. Things like that."

"I understand. Although I apologize if I ever misled Maman. I don't know anyone named Lockerbie. I do know in this country somewhere there is a town, however, named Lockerbie."

"In this country?" asked Tina. Alexander nodded agreement at Tina's question. She said, "You mean the United States?" Again, he nodded. "In Missouri?"

"No, m'lady," Alexander said, although he acted as if he couldn't hear Tina's teeth grinding. "Perhaps more than one."

Tina thought she didn't have all afternoon to play dentist. She'd pull a couple more teeth before she quit. "Then, what state is that town in?"

Alexander nodded. "Let me think." After staring at his shoes for a good bit, he looked up and said, "I now recall. In this country, there's a Lockerbie in Alabama, Florida, Louisiana, Minnesota, South Carolina, Texas." He pecked his head with a skeletal forefinger. "That's all I think. However, there is also one in Scotland, but I suspect that one isn't of concern."

Tina directed a question to Mrs. Bolzoni, Maman, and JoEllen, "Anyone of you all have any answers?" No one replied. Tina said, "I've got nothing. Lots of Lockerbie towns in the United States but I don't know what any of them have to do with what's going on here. Around here, I don't know anyone with that surname."

"I'm drawing the blankest of blanks," JoEllen said. "I admit it. We're at a dead end. Let's all stop for today. I'm exhausted."

Everyone took the hint, stood in unison and marched out of the storeroom into the restaurant.

CHAPTER 35

B EFORE ANYONE COULD LEAVE THE storage room to make their way out of the restaurant, Alexander said to all the ladies, "All I know is that someone in the 1980s filmed a movie in that town of Lockerbie, Texas. *The Raggedy Man.* It was about a woman and a man having an affair during a war." Alexander blushed. "Shameful."

Tina said, "We think there's a person or maybe more than one person who wants to hurt or even kill some of our friends. These bad people have some connection with the name Lockerbie."

Alexander brushed a smidgen of charcoal off his sleeve onto the floor. "I am both horrified and sorry, but who is it that you think is in harm's way?"

"My husband, Rosswell Carew. And our child, Jonathan David Carew. And me, Tina Carew. Maybe others. Sonya Blanco, who is a police officer here in Cape. She's out working somewhere. But Maman, there—" she indicated with her forefinger "—and JoEllen over there," she nodded and then with a thumb over her shoulder said, "—and Mrs. Bolzoni back there. All of us are friends. We all are . . . companions. A good term. It means one who breaks bread with another. We are a close-knit group. We love one another. If one of us gets hurt, we all get hurt. And we don't want anyone hurt."

Alexander said, "I know of some of those people that you name. But I don't know anyone who would want to hurt them."

No one spoke. After everyone looked at everyone else and no one had anything more to say, they started for the exit again.

When the crew reached the door, JoEllen clapped her hands. "Wait. Let's try something else. Let's not leave till we try one more thing." JoEllen motioned everyone to sit back down and she then sat, turning in her chair to ask Alexander, "Do you know anyone around here who is called The Raggedy Man?"

Alexander did not rush into an answer. After a bit of silence, he said, "No, I do not. If I did, I'd tell the police because they might stop my brother from getting murdered."

"What?" JoEllen sprang from her chair. She moved one chair out of the way so she could move her chair closer to Alexander. "Who is your brother? Where is he now? We need to make sure he's safe."

"Alas, he's long been lying in the grave and his soul stands before God."

"You're saying your brother is dead?" JoEllen smacked both hands on her head, a sign of despair. "This is awful!"

"Yes, Gregory, my brother. He died a while back. Back in 2013."

JoEllen said, "How did he die?"

Alexander smoothed his work clothes, although it did nothing to rid them of the many wrinkles. "There is no doubt that my brother knew better. Gregory summoned up the devil." Alexander's eyes filled with tears. "Gregory was no good but I loved him. He was my brother even though he never followed the laws of God. Or man. You don't hate your brother because he's bad. You must be like God who loves us even though we're bad. Thus I loved my brother as God loves him although he summoned up the enemy of God."

Tina asked him, "What did he do that was bad?"

JoEllen said, "He just now told us that Gregory Comana summoned up Satan."

"I'd like a few more details," said Tina.

"Satan, indeed," Alexander said. "Let me tell you more details. Do you remember the Hivite Horror? The five girls that were killed in 2006, 2007, and 2008?"

"Gregory Comana was the Hivite Horror?" said JoEllen. "I think we all remember those horrible murders. People in a hundred mile radius locked their doors at night and during the day and they put up spotlights around their house for when it got dark. It was scary for a long time. Alexander, did your brother commit those murders? Is that what you're telling us?"

"Oh, no. But Gregory was fascinated by the murders. He studied all of them. Everything that was on the Internet or in the newspapers or magazines, he read. Everything he collected and then printed. After that, he arranged everything chronologically and put it all together."

Tina said, "What do you mean 'put it all together'?"

"Oh, what do you call it?" Alexander tapped his head again. Then snapped his fingers. "Scrapbook."

The silence that fell in the room raised a cloud of astonishment thick enough to slice and dice.

After several fast heartbeats, Mrs. Bolzoni said, "Your brother with the scrappings he made into this book, what happened to this book?" She scratched herself on the head rapidly and with one finger, as if she already had the answer in her brain. Perhaps she feared the answer might escape her.

Alexander swung his hands back and forth. "Let me back up a bit." He took a deep breath. "Gregory was not right in the head. When he started collecting all the information on the murders, he left himself open to Satan. As you know, Satan refuses no invitations. Gregory was beyond control. And I do not know that he was murdered. I know only that he disappeared that night and has been seen no more. But I feel he was murdered so I will speak that way. The night he was killed, he told me he had killed a girl that very day. What an awful and strange coincidence."

"Maybe it wasn't a coincidence," Tina said. "What year was this?"

"2013."

"What date?"

"Sunday, August 11, 2013."

"Alexander," Tina said, "do you know the name of the girl you think he killed?"

"Stop!" Maman yelled and then began weeping, a profound and deep flood of tears. She held both her hands over her face until she could speak. "Do not insist that Alexander answer this question. Alexander Comana, him, and Maman Fribeau, me, know who Gregory Comana killed before he disappeared." Maman again sobbed for bit. Then she said, "I tell you all this, my friends. Alexander and I are bonded comrades. This is how I became the friend of Alexander. Gregory Comana, Alexander's brother, killed . . . Bernadette Fribeau . . . in the year of 2013." Maman sobbed before she could go on. Then she said, "Alexander has promised to help me until we both die because of his brother's actions in killing one of my great-nieces. I have lost a total of three female descendants since the beginning of this century. Many babies they would have had if they had not been killed. Now. Maybe. No more Fribeaus?"

Tina, uncertain whether any of the customers sitting in the main part of the Purple Star might be able to hear what was said in the conference area, opened the room's door and peered out. The small gaggle of patrons paid scant attention to the group's conversation, preferring their phones and laptops to listening in on what real people were discussing. Satisfied of their privacy, she quietly shut the door and regained her seat.

Alexander drew up his legs and hugged himself, moving his face away from the view of everyone else in the room. He spoke in a whisper when he bowed his head and said, "This all is true."

"This is nothing for you to be ashamed of," said JoEllen. "No man can control the actions of another man. Or woman, for that matter."

"Maman," said Tina, "what is it that you want Alexander to do right now?"

"Only this one thing." She held her hands and bowed her head after the fashion of a nun at prayer, although Maman had never prayed once during her long life. "Nothing else but what I want. Find the killer. Discover the murderer. Alexander and I both know that Gregory killed Bernadette, but even I say to you that Gregory was confused. He killed only one woman and that girl was my beloved Bernadette Fribeau. Alexander told me that his brother Gregory was possessed by Satan and that's what caused him to kill Bernadette. I don't believe, me, in that fairy tale of the devil." Maman raised both hands high above her head like a charismatic praising the spirit and said loudly, "I do believe that Gregory Comana, Alexander's brother, killed Bernadette Fribeau, my niece. Now we must find the killer of Anna Fribeau and Juliette Fribeau. Innocent blood cries out." This time she fell silent and stayed silent.

Tina peeked out the door again. The smell of the pies now being served made her mouth water. The supper special, roast beef and new potatoes and fresh green beans, also made her want to stop all the heartbreaking detective work for a while so she could eat her fill. In the main part of the restaurant, the customers, startled awake from their electronic trance by the loud words in the conference area sat with mouths agape, now openly staring at the door, behind which lay a motley group discussing murder and the devil.

Alexander said, "Maman and I are allies in that we both know that my brother, my awful and immoral brother, whom I loved, was guilty of killing Maman's sweet girl, Bernadette. But Gregory was not the Hivite Horror."

"True, that." Maman put her arm around Alexander. "We find, us, the Hivite Horror! *Oui?*"

"*Oui.*" Alexander smiled through his own tears.

JoEllen asked him, "Did you see the scrapbook the night Gregory disappeared?"

"No. Someone had broken into Gregory's cabin out near Trail of Tears. The person who broke in killed him I must assume. We do not know what happened to Gregory's body, if he indeed was murdered. And no more was seen of the scrapbook. No one of good morals would want that scrapbook." Alexander sniffled and wiped away a fresh tear. "I have only this question. Are there clues of my brother's murder in that scrapbook?"

JoEllen said, "Someone preserved that scrapbook and it is now in the possession of Ed. That is, if the cops haven't confiscated it."

"I know this for the facts," Mrs. Bolzoni said. "Ed has the scrappings."

"Nonetheless, that's still a good question, Alexander," said Tina. "And Mrs. Bolzoni is right. Ed has the scrapbook because it's not evidence of any crime. So far as we know right now. Therefore, JoEllen is right. Then let me assure you that Rosswell and I intend to answer all the questions in the cold case."

"M'lady, the trail has indeed grown cold, but where do these people come from who hate you and want to kill you?"

"We're drawing attention to ourselves so we need to speak more softly." Tina pointed to the door, then gathered her cohorts closer to her. "I have a bit of history you all need to know."

JoEllen said, "As the old proverb goes, if you live in the past, you lose an eye. If you forget the past, you lose both eyes."

"You have to know this past before you can understand the future," Tina said. "Let me give you a brief rundown on who is after us and by us, I mean all the Guardians of Dina. There were five members of this crime family. We know of four adult children. Two still living, namely, Martha Bailey and Adam Cain. Two have died. Fortunately, Nathaniel Dahlbert is gone. He was horrible. Joshua Granbarco, a good man and Ollie's friend, is gone. One of the few good men in that family. All of them were borne by one Gertrude Bailey, a caring and gentle mother. Gertrude is gone also."

From his shirt, Alexander withdrew his sign of the Guardians of Dina. "And, except for the good ones, if there are any, all of that family hates the Guardians."

Tina nodded before she continued. "You rarely find so much evil in one family. Even in a family that is mostly evil, I've always seen many good people in a bad family. Not this family. Few, if any at all, who are left alive now, have any kind of conscience. They are bereft of any moral compass. Everyday living in such a family as this, is misery. Every day, each member of the family wonders if they would ever see the next morning or if they'd be murdered."

JoEllen said, "About this Adam Cain. Are you saying it's like Adam and Eve, Cain and Abel? That's where Adam Cain gets his name?"

Tina said, "Adam Cain always said that Cain was Adam's favorite son."

"Not true," said JoEllen. "Cain gave a sacrifice of leftover plants to God. Abel offered a first-born animal. God wanted the best blood, not the leavings from the last harvest."

"Right," Tina said. "A steak always beats a salad."

JoEllen asked, "Is there one father? Or many?"

"Only one, oddly enough. Dennis West, the long-time lover of Gertrude Bailey. Did I say lover? The poor wretched woman was the victim of a serial rapist. The family history has it that Dennis is a slaver. He deals in sex toys for rich people. And the toys are human beings. I suspect the mother was at one time a young girl he captured and fell in love with. No, not love. Nothing pure and sweet like love. Obsession. Evil and horrid-like obsession. Dennis West is a depraved man, devoid of any human feeling or emotion."

"Where," JoEllen said, "is Dennis West right now?"

Tina shook her head. "Not in this part of the world. He could be anywhere. Anywhere and recruiting more evil minions."

CHAPTER 36

Day 8, continued
St. Mark's Hospital, earlier that day

DEEP INSIDE THE EMERGENCY AREA of Saint Mark's Hospital, Sonya released her hand from Rosswell's grip. "Now that I'm a Guardian of Dina, I'll tell you about Ed and the hut or shack. But I prefer to call it a cabin." She began walking out of the hospital, almost at a trot. Rosswell asked no questions, just followed her at a brisk pace.

When she reached the underground parking lot, she arrowed for her car, hopped in, and Rosswell made for the passenger side. The parking lot was somewhat cooler and darker, making it a bit easier to breathe in the heat of the day. There were no cars nearby, making it a good place to chat about secret things. She turned on the car and kicked the air conditioner to high.

Rosswell turned toward Sonya. "OK, so tell me the story about this cabin."

"I believe you know Alexander Comana." Sonya adjusted the fan. "He's a fellow who's been a janitor at Holy Cross church for decades."

"Yes. Even though I'm a lapsed Catholic I still hang around Father Mike's church on occasion, like if there's food or other important things I need to see about. I mean, as in detective stuff." Rosswell hated talking about his lapsed condition. Maybe he'd best go to confession and get himself right again.

Sonya cleared her throat. "Alexander Comana is a true saint. But he has a brother who's no good. Or, I should say, he *had* a brother—Gregory Comana—until a while back. He was a true agent of evil."

Rosswell snapped his fingers. "I remember now. Heard that on *Cape's First News* when it happened. Gregory lived in a cabin out in the woods on a bluff close to Trail of Tears. And one day he up and disappeared. It's been eight or ten years and no one's ever seen him or found a body."

"Bingo," she said.

"What does Ed have to do with that?" *He's never once mentioned anything to me about Gregory Comana. Was he lying in any part of that information he gave me? I hate it when clients withhold information.* "Are you saying that Reverend Ed Searl is a suspect in that disappearance?"

"I don't want to say this." Sonya shook her head and breathed in deeply before she continued. "I, and I alone, suspect Ed may have had something to do with the disappearance. Only I think it was a murder. No one else investigating it agrees with me. No. That's not right. No one is investigating it any longer. And the higher-ups won't open a new investigation unless someone shows up with new evidence." She bit her lip and when she glanced at Rosswell, her puffy and bloodshot eyes told him she'd not been sleeping well.

"Why do you suspect Ed?" *May as well get some free information, just in case Ed needs me as his lawyer on a second murder charge.* "Is there any evidence at all, even if it's old evidence?"

Sonya said, "No. I was the first one on the scene. It was an anonymous tip phoned in. Whoever reported it said that the door to Gregory's cabin was standing open and he was lying on the doorstep, dead."

"Someone phoned in a false report, right?"

"Right. I got there and Ed was standing outside. Actually, Ed was standing on what turned out to be the neighbor's driveway. The sun was going down but there was still plenty of light when it happened. When I went back, I could tell where the boundary lines to the neighboring property were. Anyway, the night of the disappearance, I walked over to Ed and chatted awhile. Never gave him the Miranda warnings because he said he'd just arrived. I asked him if he'd seen Gregory. He said he hadn't seen him in quite a while."

"Did you ask Ed why he was at the scene?"

It's getting cold in here. The air conditioning on her car is exceptionally efficient. If I say anything, it could break her chain of thought. I don't want to snap any weak links.

Sonya said, "No, but it wouldn't have been difficult for anyone to figure out why I would be asking a lot of questions about Gregory. Ed is a smart guy. He knew why I was there."

"Did you tell him that someone had called in a murder report?"

"No."

"So you let him go?"

Sonya turned the thermostat up a little. She must have been chilly herself. "I didn't let him go because I hadn't detained him. But I did make a big mistake."

"Let me guess. That's where Reverend Ed got the scrapbook?"

Sonya turned in her seat to glare at Rosswell. "Now wait a minute, Judge. Am I still your client? And we still have the attorney-client privilege?"

"Yes, ma'am. Until one of us revokes that relationship, I'm still your lawyer." *This is a nice car for a police detective. I don't see anything that looks like a radio. There must be something she uses for communication besides a phone. But I'm not seeing it. And I'll bet myself a dollar she's recording me right now.* "But I can never ever tell anyone about what you tell me when I'm your lawyer."

"What if I hire another lawyer?"

"Then you will have two lawyers. Unless, that is, you or I revoke the relationship. Preferably in writing."

Sonya drummed her fingers on the steering wheel, probably deciding how much faith she would put in Rosswell. "Yes, Ed had a scrapbook. The same one I saw in the storeroom conference at Ollie's restaurant."

"Do you think he has a second or third scrapbook, perhaps?"

"Not a clue."

"What date did all this happen?"

"I'd have to check my records to make sure, but it was hot and it was in the year 2013. Probably August."

"And you're thinking that the scrapbook you saw back then was the same one Ed has now?"

"I certainly do."

"Well, then Sonya, what was your mistake?"

"I should've confiscated the scrapbook."

"Did you look through it at the scene of the crime? Or, I should say, supposed crime."

"Thoroughly."

"And did you look through it at the conference we had?"

"Again, thoroughly."

"Did that scrapbook have any evidence pertaining to Gregory's murder either now or in 2013?"

"Not that I saw."

"There was no evidence of any kind of crime in that scrapbook other than what was reported by someone else. Gregory never put anything in the scrapbook to indicate that he had committed a crime of any kind."

"Yes," said Sonya. "That statement is one hundred percent correct."

"Then you didn't do anything wrong." Rosswell gave her a thumbs up. "Although I'm still not sure why everyone thinks Alexander's brother was such a bad guy."

"Let me make this clear in my own head." She nodded and pursed her lips for a few seconds. "Here's my theory. Gregory Comana was the Hivite. He was in this area during all of the times there was a murder attributed to the Hivite Horror. Now, there are more murders that the cops think are copycat murders—the murders of the Fribeau women. Anna Fribeau first and then Juliette Fribeau at the park. Those killings happened after Gregory was murdered."

"You're assuming Gregory was murdered," Rosswell said.

Sonya said nothing, merely nodded.

Rosswell removed his tri-focal glasses, patted his face with a paper towel he found in his back pocket, then replaced his eyeglasses. "Gregory could not have killed either or both of the Fribeau women since he was dead."

"Thank you, Captain Obvious. Although, now I'm thinking I was too hasty back in 2013. Shortly before Gregory got killed or got disappeared or whatever happened to him, Bernadette got killed. No clues."

"It's true."

"You're right, Judge."

"Gregory Comana could have killed Bernadette."

"Maybe, maybe not."

"Sonya, stop being coy and tell me your point."

"Maman has had three kinfolks killed. The two murders of Juliette and Anna were what every other cop is saying. Copycat murders. I think whoever killed the women, probably killed Gregory, who had killed Bernadette. I can tell you I could never believe Alexander would ever kill anyone, ever!"

"I'm getting dizzy," Rosswell nodded. "Sounds logical to me."

"That's where I'm stuck. Who killed Gregory? Maybe that scrapbook wasn't made by Gregory. Maybe the real Hivite Horror killer made that scrapbook. I'm almost convinced that the Hivite and Gregory were buddies or at least acquainted. They had a falling out and the asshole killed Gregory."

"Have you interviewed Alexander?"

Sonya said, "Alexander, the brother of Gregory?"

Rosswell said, "Yes, who else? We've been talking about them both."

"Just making sure. It never hurts to be clear. And the answer is, no."

"Anything else you need to tell me?"

"Yes. One more thing. The fingerprints on the phone under the body of Juliette Fribeau belong to Pastor Ed Searl. That makes your client good for one murder. And that means this client"—Sonya pointed to herself—"is no longer your client. As far as the outside world is concerned."

"Pinky Pledge." Rosswell extended the little finger of his right hand to Sonya. "You're still my client as far as the outside world is concerned."

"This is the first time I've done this since the fifth grade." Her right pinky grabbed his and they shook.

Rosswell said, "That's the reason Pinky Pledges are sacred. They're rare. And serious."

"Meaning?"

"I need to examine the evidence you have that makes you think you found Ed's fingerprints."

CHAPTER 37

Timothy Lockerbie

I WAS IN *THAT* MODE when I met Anna Fribeau.

In Sainte Genevieve, it was a nice day in the middle of June. Hot, but pleasant, since the humidity was low. The old buildings were made of red bricks or vertical logs or plaster smeared all over the outside walls. I walked around among all the old buildings until I met her. And the moment I met her, I knew I needed to have her that night. I talked her into taking me back to Cape Girardeau with her. She was easy.

When I'm in *that* mode, I can persuade anyone to do anything.

After I sexually assaulted her—oh, come on, Timothy Lockerbie! You raped her! Then I strangled her. It wasn't premeditated. It was spur-of-the-moment. I'd decided to go out looking that day but I hadn't decided to sexually assault anyone and I hadn't decided to kill anyone so it wasn't premeditated, when I found her up in Sainte Genevieve and drove back with her to Cape. It was a risk I could take. She liked me and wasn't scared of me. I talked nice to her and never made any funny moves all the way down.

I decided to kill her when we got to town. I'd been in *that* mode for a long time. When I'm in *that* mode, I can think and plan clearly. When she wanted me to go into her apartment, I decided to kill her.

It smelled like lilacs in her apartment and she lit some purple candles. And I think incense.

I made her undress in her bathroom. Took her back in the bedroom. Tied her up. And I thought, *I have to kill her.*

Sometimes I wonder, why did I decide to kill her? Or any of them? I'd say at the time that I had never planned to kill any of them, but they just seemed like they needed killing. I don't know why, some of them I killed and then some of them I didn't. Should they live or die? Never made a lick of difference to me.

There was no gun on me when I met Anna. So I strangled her. It took a long time. She'd pass out and then I'd take my hands from around her neck and she'd breathe. I did that for several hours until she died. At least I think she died. When I woke up, I was passed out in the band shell at the courthouse. I couldn't remember where her apartment was. So she was either dead or alive, and it didn't matter to me. I hitchhiked back to Sainte Gen.

I once told one of my cellmates all about my killings. He asked me if murders made me happy or sad. I said there's no happy or sad when I'm in *that* mode. It's just do. Do this or don't do this. No emotion either way.

When I told him everything, I sang him a pretty song.

He choked on his supper that night and died.

I'm efficient when I'm in *that* mode.

CHAPTER 38

A T THE STROKE OF MIDNIGHT, the priest sat in his car and punched a number. One second after the first ring, the minister answered. "What's up, Father Mike?"

"Last night I fell asleep around six after a heavy supper and then woke up just before twelve. And I feel rested."

"You called me at midnight because you had a good sleep?"

"Yes. There's a cobweb or two in my brain but otherwise it's clear. Not only am I rested, I feel summoned."

The minister made no response. Father Mike heard Reverend Ed breathing noisily After a few beats, Father Mike said, "Ed? You still there?"

"Yes. Tell you what, let's you and me take a stroll down on the riverfront. I'll tell you my side of the story."

"In the middle of the night?"

"Well, you called me and now that I'm fully awake, why not?"

The priest hesitated. The good father wasn't afraid of the dark, although he never intentionally walked around in unlit places. Too many things for him to run into. And too many things to run into him.

Sensing Father Mike's hesitation, Ed said, "There are plenty of street lamps on both sides of the floodwall. The city council had a bunch installed down there after the mayor tripped in the dark a few months ago. Did you miss that? Her Honor moves quickly on public safety problems."

"I was simply checking your resolve, Ed. I'm way ahead of you. I'm sitting in my car with the engine running. See you at the regular place."

In the light of the full moon, Father Mike and Ed strolled down the middle of Broadway toward the riverfront. The area was devoid of vehicles and people. Just as they crossed the railroad tracks that ran parallel to the floodgate at the riverfront, a short freight train from the north screamed past them. The lights on the poles next to the tracks blinked when the train cars tripped a switch on an optical scanner.

"So much for thinking trains had to obey a speed limit in the city," Father Mike said as they maneuvered their way over the cobblestones of the riverfront. "Let's walk over here to the streetlamp, if you don't mind."

Once there, both men swatted at the moths swarming the light. "Looks like we aren't the only ones searching for light," Ed said.

Father Mike nodded. "Ed, when you were summoned did you receive anything else?"

"Yes. A word."

Shocked, Father Mike sucked in his breath and blew it out. After a minute, he reached into his pocket for his notebook and tore out a piece of paper. "Here." He gave it and a ballpoint pen to Ed. "Write down the word and fold the paper." He turned his back to Ed who pressed the paper to Father Mike's back and wrote.

"There," said Ed. "Now you do the same."

Father Mike repeated the actions.

Then, each man unfolded his slip of paper.

Both men had written the same word: BOMB.

Ed said, "What do you think this means? Do you know anything about bombs? Are we supposed to stop a bomb from going off somewhere?"

"I haven't a clue about any of it."

"What are we supposed to do?"

Father Mike brushed his forehead, as if that would clear any remaining cobwebs from his brain. "If we were supposed to stop a murder, we saw how badly that turned out. I don't think we're going to be any more successful at stopping a bomb."

"It wasn't you. I was the one who was the failure."

Without speaking for a few minutes, they stood on the shore and watched the glow of bioluminescent algae sloshing in the river.

Ed said, "Fireflies of the brown water." As an afterthought, he added, "You know, algae are pretty low on the ladder of life. Even so, I wonder if they're sending us a message."

Father Mike, entranced by the display, said, "The Lord works in mysterious ways." The glow winked on and off. "Still not as beautiful as lightning bugs blanketing a hayfield just after sundown."

Both watched in silence. Finally, Father Mike raised one foot then the other. His feet hurt from walking on the bumpy pavement. "Maybe we should ask Rosswell what to do."

"Rosswell? He thinks we're both nuts." The minister picked up a couple of pebbles and skipped them across the water. The darkness kept him from counting the number of skips. "Maybe we are. Or maybe we're sharing a hallucination?"

"Maman Fribeau and Mrs. Bolzoni both think the visitation is explained by science. They're both atheists, if my guess is right." Father Mike also picked up a handful of pebbles and threw them one at a time into the river. "JoEllen is convinced it's all supernatural. Then there's Sonya. She's agnostic about all this. She won't make up her mind until there's evidence to weigh in."

"I know. Instead of Rosswell, maybe Sonya is the one we need to chat with."

"Better idea yet. Except we might get tossed in jail for dreaming up a conspiracy." Just then a bunch of women, all drunk, walked out of a tavern across the street from the floodwall. "Speaking of algae, liquor is right down there with it. Gives both of us lots of work."

The group staggered along the sidewalk for a block, wobbling back and forth. When they reached the floodgate, they walked through it, and all of them silenced themselves to stare at the dark waters. One of them rushed back to vomit in the middle of the street. Her friends taunted and jeered and then the whole herd of them moved on, hopefully to go drink coffee somewhere.

As they passed Father Mike and Ed, one of the women in the group stopped, whirled around. She bowed to them. "The good time of night to thee, good sirs."

Ed returned the bow. "Good even to thee, pretty lady."

She answered, "O, speak again, bright angel! For thou art as glorious to this night, being o'er my head as is a winged messenger of heaven!"

The whole group whooped and laughed and then began waving their arms and running away. The two men watched until all the women disappeared.

After stepping a few more feet, Father Mike said, "I suspect a Shakespeare class from the university is out celebrating the end of finals or last rehearsal, or something. We need to be careful we don't step in the evidence of their overindulgence."

"And they quote a boy's lovesick plea to what he thinks might be an angel on a balcony. When you look around, Father Mike, if you but half-close your eyes and have a few drinks, the area takes on the appearance of a tiny subset of New Orleans. Fortunately, we don't have as many muggings in the middle of the street as does the Crescent City. I also suspect that we have more drunken students quoting lines from Romeo and Juliet than does New Orleans. Just a guess."

"I'll take your word for it," Father Mike said. "To change the subject. You promised to tell me your side of the story without any gloss."

"First," Ed said pointing, "here is where Anna Fribeau was gunned down. By a stray bullet. A horrible accident. I don't believe any of it, though. I believe she was picked to die by the same person, or persons, who killed her sister. Someone, for whatever reason, wants to wipe out the entire Fribeau clan, including Maman Fribeau."

Father Mike stared down at the street. After a moment or two, he could find nothing physically significant about where the woman had lost her life. He then crossed himself and said a silent prayer. Ed stood by and bowed his head. "You know, Ed, I'm on the verge of volunteering my services to Rosswell and Tina to see that all the killers are brought to justice."

"Yes. You may need to do that. You have been summoned."

Ed folded his hands in the fashion of a man praying. "I have also been summoned, or so it seems to me." He bowed his head. "When you called, I awoke from the soundest six hours of sleep I've had in my whole adult life. I call it the sleep of summons. I wonder if I'm supposed to be well-rested when the angel appears again."

"Angel?" Father Mike looked sidelong at his friend. Despite all the minor discomforts of the night, he tried to sound as serious as he could muster when he said, "You think an angel has summoned us?"

"Actually, Dina. Not the poor woman in the scriptures who was raped by the Hivite, but the angel Dina, who taught Adam and Eve to speak."

Then the priest said, "We agree that we have somehow attracted the notice of a supernatural being, meaning an angel. What did we do to deserve this notice?"

"You don't have *to do* something to alert an angel to your presence. You have *to be* something. Not do something. In other words, angels are not attracted by action, but by a state of being."

"What must *we* be to attract an angel?"

"My guess is that our relationship to the people involved in the Hivite murders long ago sealed our fate to be involved in the recent killings. Then, again, maybe it's nothing more than a delusion that we share, although two or more sharing a delusion is exceptionally rare. I don't know, but I shy away from giving the visitations, as you call them, any kind of supernatural origin. If it is a supernatural visitation, I am still confused as to why we were picked."

Father Mike said, "If you don't admit to a supernatural origin, do you admit that there is certainly something out there that we can't explain?"

Ed scratched his right ear. "I do admit that. It scares me. I wish the thing would go away, no matter what it is. I like the ordinary. Not the extraordinary."

"So do I. I feel we're in serious trouble, and it's not going away."

"I agree." Ed said. "What shall we do?"

Father Mike touched his friend's arm.

"That's what we're here to decide."

CHAPTER 39

Day 10
After midnight
Riverfront

T HE RIVERFRONT, LIT BY STREETLAMPS shining a bright orange light, generated the illusion of receiving the first rays of dawn, although full darkness still reigned in the sky above.

Neither Father Mike nor Reverend Ed spoke for the time that it took a fast-moving barge pushed by a tugboat, probably headed for Memphis or Vicksburg or New Orleans, to plow downstream past them. Its spotlight swept the route before it, searching for dangers on the water.

After the vessel disappeared, Father Mike stuck his foot into a pile of bleached tree branches on the shore. In the midst of all the wood lay a skull, probably from an unfortunate cow who'd drowned in a flood up north. The priest picked it up and said, "Alas, poor Yorick! I knew him."

"Well, then," laughed Ed, spreading his arms out wide, "if we are to be deluged by Shakespeare tonight, then, 'We all are men, in our own natures frail, and capable of our flesh; few are angels.'"

"'There is nothing either good or bad but thinking makes it so.'" Father Mike set the skull down, then turned it over with the toe of his black tennis shoe. He had stopped wearing all black priest clothes the year after ordination when he nearly passed out one August night while walking for his daily exercise.

Ed pointed to a group a short distance away. A few old men lounging in plastic chairs sat, their fishing poles dangling in front of them. Except for snagging a cold beer every so often from a ratty ice chest, the men moved little and spoke even less. If any of them caught a fish, he silently reeled it in and then threw it back without comment. However, one of the men pointed to the sky and remarked, "I'll be damned. There's a bald eagle night hunting. I didn't think their eyes were good enough to allow that." The man's amazement earned him only a couple of grunts from his buddies.

Father Mike punched Reverend Ed to get his attention. "My Granny Smothers always said, 'All you can expect from a hog is a grunt.'"

Ed leaned close to the priest and whispered, "We in the clergy are supposed to be compassionate. But I'll have to agree with Granny Smothers on this one."

They both suppressed a laugh.

Occasionally, one of the fishermen would spit tobacco into the river, which raised no mention from the other men. Another barge's whistle issued a long and low mournful sound, meant to let everyone within hearing distance know that a vessel claimed the right of way. The nasty water churned up by the tugboat lifted fish and other aromatic pieces of unrecognizable organic matter into the air, where they attracted ravenous nocturnal gulls who launched a full-assault on each other, fighting for a post-midnight snack. During the daytime hours, bald eagles and Cooper's hawks gliding high in the sky above the boats, caught the rising streams of warm air, lifting the birds higher, allowing them to scout the skies. Not too many hours in the distance, a full sunrise would bathe the whole Mississippi River Valley with burning light. But for a while longer, the darkness— although not cool—would keep the sun's rays from heating the air.

"Boys, where are all your friends?" One of the fishermen—a tall guy who weighed about three hundred pounds, and whose red beard and stringy hair stood out in the light of the full moon—had spoken to the clergymen.

"All these—" Father Mike spread his arms wide—"are our friends. Fowl and human."

"And," said Ed, "as well as all things that crawl and fish that swim."

The fat man stared at them. In the near dark, it was difficult making out his reaction. All he did was add, "Need to be careful about the offspring of the dark." He turned back to his fishing.

Father Mike said, "Good fishing to ye fishers of the night," and nodded to Ed, who joined him as they sauntered away from the fishermen. When they were out of earshot, Father Mike said to Ed, "A lot of things stink around here."

"I agree if you mean the river. But what did you have in mind specifically?"

Father Mike said, "I've never seen so many people fishing in the middle of the night. Ordinarily there might be one or two fellows night fishing, but not a whole string of them. Or maybe there wasn't anything good on television tonight. Or do people watch television anymore?"

"Habits change," Ed said. "Nothing stays the same. When I was a kid, all the cops were friendly. Not now. They're trying to put me away for life."

Father Mike cleared his throat and wiped his hands on his shirt. "Listen. Sonya Blanco called me about you. She wanted to know how she should handle something." Before Ed could answer, Father Mike pointed to the ground. "Watch your step."

The two men continued carefully over the cobblestones, both fearing a face-first fall into the uneven, and very hard, cobblestones.

Ed said, "A cop calls a priest asking for advice? That's a new one."

"It happens more than you think. Anyway, she's matched the prints on the gun found under the girl's body we found at Trail of Tears."

"I know. They're mine."

"That doesn't surprise me. You hinted as much at the time we found you with the body. You're lucky that she was killed by stabbing and not with the gun they found under her."

"Truer words were never spoken." Ed patted his pants pocket. "The prints on that gun are the same on the gun I have on me now."

"You have another gun?"

"Can't be too careful, my friend."

"You're a pacifist, Ed, and you've never had a gun that I know of. Why would you have a gun tonight?"

"Self-defense."

"Take that load of crap down the road and sell it because I'm not buying."

Ed chuckled. "Rosswell bought the gun for me. Glock 43, complete with a Crimson Trace laser. Total point and click interface. The only way I could miss is to stick the barrel in the ground before I pull the trigger."

"You've been doing your research."

"Indeed," said Ed.

Father Mike pointed where he thought the handgun showed a lump in Ed's pocket. "That's not the weapon the cops found under Juliette's body."

"No, it's not." Ed withdrew the Glock. "Never been fired. In fact, the second time I ever touched this weapon was when I put it in my pocket before I came down here to see you."

"How did your prints get on the gun under Juliette's body?"

Ed sighed, then said,- "I handed it to the murderer."

After what Father Mike had been through the last few days, his surprise threshold had shot up considerably. He was ready for anything, because practically nothing surprised him anymore. "Who is the murderer?"

"Before I answer the question, I must know if that priest-penitent thing works between you and me? I'm not a Catholic, and you're not my priest. That wouldn't seem to work between us."

"I'll make it work. When it comes to theology, at the time of death, everything is permissible."

"Time of death? I'm not dying. Yet. Meaning?"

Father Mike turned and stood directly in front of Ed. Staring the Unitarian minister in the eye, the priest said, "You've known me too long to think that I would ever divulge a single confidential thing you told me. If you shoplifted a candy bar or killed the Pope, and you confessed to me, I'd never reveal it. On pain of imprisonment. On pain of death. In fact, I'd not tell on you even if you never told me anything."

"We are that close?"

"What do you think?"

Ed said, "Thank you. I knew that already. I wanted to hear it again tonight. Let me tell you, Father Michael Smothers . . . vice-versa."

"Yes, Reverend Ed Searl. . . and vice-versa."

They started their stroll again after shaking hands. They reached a bench, conveniently lit by one of the street lamps.

Father Mike pulled a cigar from his pocket. He lit it before handing an unlit one to Ed. "Let's sit and smoke and think and talk."

"Let's." Reverend Ed lit his stogie and they both sat.

After a while with only the background noises for company, Father Mike said, "Quiet helps thinking."

"Brings one nearer to God."

"Amen."

After a few more puffs of his cigar, Ed said, "The night when everyone thought I was a goner, I got a call before I left from a person who said there was information floating about that a woman would soon be killed and that I should stop it."

"Who called you?"

Ed ignored the question. "I asked the caller why I should be the one who drew the assignment of stopping a murder. I was, and always will be, as you've already pointed out, a pacifist. Anti-violence all the way. Besides that, I'm not a cop. I don't meddle in things I haven't been asked to meddle in, unless the people involved ask me to meddle. In answer to your question, I certainly did not know who the caller was."

"Let me guess. The caller couldn't give you a reason why you should stop the murder so he called off the mission."

"Wrong. He was adamant that I help him stop it."

"What did he want you to do?"

Ed sighed. "He wanted *me* to kill a murderer."

CHAPTER 40

Day 10, continued
After midnight
Riverfront

Father Mike stubbed out his cigar. "And how were you supposed to kill this murderer?" He stood and stretched.

The odd coloring of the streetlights warped the clergymen's appearances into a bad dream of pale ghosts, wandering around in the dark. Yet it didn't keep the pair from talking about deep feelings gnawing at their souls and dark things fluttering in the night.

Reverend Ed also extinguished his smoke and stood. "He said the person who was going to kill someone at Trail of Tears had murdered before."

Each of them threw their dead cigar into the water.

Father Mike swiveled toward Ed and asked, "May I meddle in your business a moment?"

Ed stepped closer to him and said, "You may."

Father Mike walked a couple of steps toward the water to study the darkness of the river before he asked his question. "Suppose this man who called you told you never to tell anyone about what he said, would you be bound not to reveal the secret to a third party?"

Ed never hesitated. "Maybe. Maybe not. We have no rules about that." It was apparent to the priest that Ed had been thinking about such a question for quite a while. "The discretion is left to me. I'd never protect a sex abuser, especially if it was against a minor. Or sex slavery. I'd report that to the cops in an instant. In this particular instance, though, I decided I would go to jail before I'd tell anyone what the guilty party told me—"

"I understand."

"—except you. I am going to tell you. And I claim your Roman Catholic seal of confession to keep it between us."

Both men turned to the sound of yipping in the distance. Canines of some sort ran in a pack along the river's edge. Pointed upright ears, long snouts, and bushy tails hanging low. Their coat color was a light gray.

Father Mike said, "A pack of coyotes, gaunt and wormy animals."

"Will they attack us?"

"Not unless they all have rabies. If they do decide to attack, they'll meet up with the enemy who has a gun."

Reverend Ed patted the gun in his pocket. "Navajos say that coyotes were present at creation, and that they taught people and healed them as well, although they could never be trusted. Always wanted to fool people."

The animals disappeared into the gloom, barely raising the attention of any human in the area. An agreement—a truce—between man and trickster floated in the air.

The priest returned to the subject of privilege. "You want to violate your promise not to reveal this person to me? You're implicating me in hiding a killer. We could both go to jail."

CHAPTER 41

Day 10, continued
After midnight
Riverfront

"AS I WAS SAYING," ED continued after a few moments of silence, "I know who killed Juliette Fribeau. I got a call to meet my informant out at Trail of Tears. There, we schemed to capture the killer and bring him to justice. As you know, I failed horribly."

The explanation of a major failing sounded worse to the priest when made during the blackest part of a hot night on the banks of the Mississippi River. "Who killed her?"

"The man who called me to help him. He killed her. He calls himself Timothy Lockerbie. Whether that's his real name or not, I don't know, because he also calls himself The Raggedy Man. What a stupid nickname for a bad guy. He told me that until a few days ago, he was imprisoned in a jail in Lockerbie, Texas. There was a glitch in the sheriff's software and he got out two days early. At least forty-eight hours early. Recall now that Juliette Fribeau's sister, Anna, was killed earlier by a day or so before Juliette was. In other words, the deaths were about forty-eight hours apart. That's why I suspect Timothy killed Anna, too."

Father Mike held up a hand. "You're going awfully fast here. Let me recap. Timothy accidentally gets out of jail two days early in Texas, comes up here, kills Anna Fribeau, and then about two days later, kills Juliette at Trail of Tears. I can't make it sound sensible even when I try. Why did he do this? Did he say?"

"There's the weakness in my theory. I don't know why some guy from Texas would come up here and kill two women."

"Contract killing maybe? That's what it is in the movies and novels. Bad guys hang out around the release door of prisons waiting for a newly freed convict who has no money. The bad guys know the con will do anything for money."

"Possible," agreed Ed. "Possible, but doubtful. I doubt the bad guys would want to waste their money on a con. What would stop the con from just taking the money and disappearing? What if the con messed up and the bad guy got nothing in return? He'd have to kill the con and then start recruiting another killer all over again. A lot of work for no benefit. Plus, real and experienced contract killers rarely stumble and fall as badly as Timothy Lockerbie did. The killing of Juliette was a horrible nightmare. Timothy will glow forever with the stink of the jail cell. And, of all things, he killed her with a dirk."

"Ed, you sure know a lot about contract killing and stuff. How did you come by all this knowledge?"

Ed chuckled. "I read a lot of mystery novels."

Hmm. That's convenient. Father Mike said, "Where, when, and how do you fit in all this?"

"This all started for me when Timothy called me. He introduced himself on the phone and said he was a friend of Juliette's. He also knew that I was her minister. How, I don't know. It didn't occur to me at the time to ask him. He sounded desperate and said someone was going to kill her. He even told me when, where, and how. Now I know most of it was a lie. Except for the dirk."

"Again, Ed, you're spouting things that are ludicrous. You'll never convince a judge and jury of your story. Nobody would believe your version of what happened." Father Mike drew in a deep breath when he felt himself blush, although he was comforted by the fact no one could see his red face in the dark. "I'm sorry. I didn't mean to sound so harsh. I meant to throw the cold water of reality in the mix so you could see the obstacles you face."

"You're not being harsh if you're telling the truth, and you can stop worrying that anyone won't believe my story. That's because this story will never be heard by anyone except you. And Timothy Lockerbie, the person I helped."

Father Mike said, "Stop right there. Why didn't you call the cops at that moment?"

"Two reasons. He had asked me to talk to him in confidence. Plus, I thought I could stop the murder."

"Why did you even go meet this guy? He was obviously nuts."

"I didn't want Juliette to get hurt."

"Then why didn't you tell her to go to the cops? Or at least stay home?" Father Mike felt himself growing angry at Ed, an emotion he knew would cloud his thinking, which, at this moment, needed to be clear and sound.

"After Anna's death, I believed that Juliette went to the park to mourn and be away from people. No one's found her campsite. At least not that I know of. But she was a primitive camper. She never left a trace of staying in the woods."

"Why would you trust anything that a stranger like Timothy Lockerbie said?"

"Have you seen the man? No, of course not. You didn't know he existed until now. He's clean cut. Handsome. Soft spoken. He *looked* nice, but now I know he's not even close to being nice."

"Looks deceive."

"Also, he told me about Juliette's habits. He convinced me that he was her friend. He buttressed everything he said about her by telling me things that she had already told me. I did try to reach her, but failed in that, too. Her sister was dead and I didn't know anyone else we had as a mutual friend. Then Timothy comes along and tells me the story of her being in danger and everything he told me sounded true. Especially after her sister had just been killed by an unexplainable stray bullet. He convinced me that he was a good guy, even though he'd been imprisoned. He wanted to help her but was scared the cops would concoct a probation violation he'd committed and make it stick. Then he'd get sent back to prison. That's why he came to me."

"This makes no logical sense."

"We've left logical sense a long time back. Timothy is a persuasive person who could sell saltwater to Hawaiians. And I'll be the first to admit that I'm gullible. If someone tells me a story where a third party wants to help and the tale-teller is not getting anything out of the deal, I have a tendency to believe him. Or her."

Father Mike nodded. "I get it. When we devote our lives to helping others, we sometimes encounter pitfalls. And sometimes, like now, deadly pitfalls."

Ed hung his head. "I know. I know. God help me, I know."

He looks like he's headed over the edge again. Time to be gentler. Feeding the wind always gets you in trouble.

"Thank you for admitting that." Father Mike softly thumped his chest with his fist when he said, "Priests—including this one—aren't a whole lot different from you in that respect. Now, let's talk about where you met Timothy out at the park. He hands you a gun. What did you do next?"

Ed cried out. He stood to face the place of the coming dawn where he raised both hands and screamed a long, plaintive cry. Falling to his knees, he beat his fists on the cobblestones while sobbing loudly. A covey of quail that had settled in for the night took flight at Ed's wailing. Some of the night fishermen took a gander at the mourning minister, although none of them showed any concern at the screams.

"Ed, stop!" Father Mike grabbed him and forced him to stand. He'd witnessed one time that a slap in the face stopped a breakdown. He just couldn't bring himself to hurt his friend. "You cannot blame yourself for Juliette's death."

"Don't you understand? I was supposed to protect her. I failed. I killed her."

Father Mike knew he had to assuage the minister before he went into shock as he had up on the bluff. "No one is blaming you."

"Why did I agree to such a stupid plan?"

"Was it your plan?"

"No. Not my idea at all."

"Whose idea was it?"

"Timothy Lockerbie's."

"Exactly. Therefore, you aren't at fault." He held Ed by the shoulders. "Take some deep breaths." Ed did, and after three or four breaths, he calmed. Father Mike removed his hands from his friend and continued to question him. "You're standing on the bluff waiting for Juliette. What happened next?"

Ed wiped his face with his hands before blowing his nose on a clean handkerchief. "Juliette came jogging down the path and I stopped her. I thought I had saved her life. There was a killer loose, all right, but I had unknowingly been working with him. Before I realized who the real killer was, Timothy ran at her and stabbed her with the dirk. I was in shock. I couldn't move. It took me a moment to realize what he'd done. Then he turned toward me. His eyes were wide. He looked like a crazed man. Drool ran down his chin. Then, of all things, he giggled. Can you believe that? He giggled and said, 'She's gone! Another one down!' All I could do was stand there. I lost my mind. In a panic, I dropped the pistol. I remember nothing until you, Rosswell, and Ollie found me." Ed shook his head. "There's nothing I can do to redeem myself."

"Maybe there is. Let's go back to one of the benches and sit for a while so you can get yourself together. We'll wait for the dawn."

I need to treat him with the proverbial kid gloves. He's a strong man but witnessing a murder can strike down the strongest among us.

"Let's take our time," Father Mike said.

Reverend Ed said, "Yes, it's always darkest and treacherous before the sun rises."

CHAPTER 42

Day 10, continued
After midnight
Riverfront

ONCE ED AND FATHER MIKE settled themselves on the park bench again, the priest spoke first. "There's one more thing we need to discuss."

Squinting toward the east, Father Mike couldn't make out the sun even hinting that it would soon light this part of the world. He checked his watch. Dawn was still far off. Instead of the night growing smaller, the night seemed to expand. After a while, the sun would burst up and spill light over the land. Right then, though, he couldn't imagine that the old cliché of things looking better in the light rang true. In fact, the closer it got to dawn, the more agitated he grew. "I need to know where it came from."

The minister yawned. "Excuse me. It? You mean the scrapbook?"

"Exactly. Where did you get it?"

Ed sketched the happenings the night Gregory Comana disappeared.

Then Father Mike said, "I need more details filled in. Gregory Comana, you say, lived next door to the house where you were that night?"

"Correct."

"And whose house was that?"

"It belonged to Brian Reeves."

No surprise there. "You went to visit the prosecutor also?"

I'm assuming that everything Brian Reeves confessed to me was true—people don't confess lies, do they? Who would a liar be fooling? Anyway, if it was all or mostly true, then I'm now wondering if he confessed the murder to Ed as well as me? And if Brian did, was it the same victim as when he came to me? Has Brian killed more than one person?

"I mean, I know you visited Brian," said Father Mike. "And what did the prosecutor say when you visited him?"

"I visited him a lot of times. We talked about everything. Brian did many favors for me completely voluntarily. We frequently visited with one another at each other's house. We ate out together. Neither one of us is married. Nothing odd there. He's a big help to me at the church. Never complains. Always on time. Neat as a pin. Organized. I haven't heard a single complaint about him. He's never done anything bad to me. Other than charging me with murder."

Father Mike couldn't help but chuckle. "Good thing you have a sense of humor. I'm not a lawyer, so you need to ask Rosswell if what I tell you is right or wrong. I don't think any charges have actually been filed yet."

"Filing charges?" Ed said, "I don't need to ask Rosswell or any other lawyer. That's a mere technicality."

"You may want to rethink that. Everything in the law is a technicality. Back on the subject, that night, what were you doing for Brian? Or what was he doing for you?"

"Gregory was an inquisitive young man, but he was a boy who had committed every crime he thought he could get away with."

"Including murder?"

"I don't know for sure," said Ed. "I doubt he murdered anyone. The problem was that Gregory was fascinated with the Hivite Horror. And, whether or not he knew it, he was living next door to him. But Gregory was not a killer."

"Yes," said Father Mike. "Like you, I never saw Gregory as a killer."

"Right. They lived next door to Timothy Lockerbie before he went to prison in Texas. I don't think anyone knew at that time that Timothy was a murderer. That man has no conscience. He can kill someone, then go to a party, and have fun. Now that I know he has no concern for human life and now that I remember things he said to me, I am creeped out."

"It seems rather coincidental that Timothy and Gregory lived close to each other." The priest scratched his chin. "Something's bothering me. Are those houses rentals, or did Gregory and Timothy own them?"

Ed said. "Rentals."

"How do you know?"

"Once Brian told me that Gregory couldn't pay his rent. Gregory didn't want to tell Alexander because he was afraid it would make his brother think less of him. I told Brian, 'Lots of people can't pay their rent at one time or another. Gregory has temporary money problems. He will work it out. I'm sure his brother will not think less of him.'"

Father Mike said, "Oh, absolutely not. Most saints can't pay their rent." The priest thought a moment and said, "Why am I suspicious that all these people lived so close together? Surely they knew each other. What was going on?"

"Father Mike, you need to get out and about. These people may not have even known who their neighbors were. People out in the country are now introverts and introverts don't neighbor with each other as they did in the twentieth century and earlier. Today, rural society is a bunch of people living in their own electronic cocoons. They don't want to socialize or hear about the troubles their neighbors are having. They want to watch movies on television. Or surf the Internet."

The priest considered this. "Yes. You're right. Electrons are supplanting religion."

Ed said, "Alexander is a living saint, but Gregory was no saint, believe me. Anyway, back to the rent problem. Brian asked me if our church could pay his rent for one month only. I said it could and sent a check to the landlord."

"Who was the landlord?"

"The owner is a company called *Le Four Orange*. A French corporation. They have a lot of rental property up and down the Mississippi River, in several states."

"A French corporation?" Father Mike shook his head. "Doesn't ring a bell."

Ed said, "Nor with me. Nonetheless, the discovery of the scrapbook didn't happen until later."

"This Lockerbie fellow," Father Mike said. "When did you first come in contact with him?"

"It must have been before 2013 because it was after that year that he took off for Texas and somewhere along the line he was arrested for dope pushing. I'm still not sure who he hung around with in Texas."

"There are loose ends floating in the wind."

"Yes, there are, Father Mike, but it's all coming together."

"I can do nothing less than agree with you, my friend."

CHAPTER 43

Day 10, continued
Early morning
The Carew home

WHEN THE DOORBELL RANG, ROSSWELL tapped the AtTheDoor app on his phone.

The app displayed Mrs. Bolzoni and Ferdinand. "Greetings. Come on in." Rosswell opened the door, then stepped back, while sipping his morning espresso. It would be a long night he'd guessed around sundown yesterday. That's why he filled a big hot chocolate mug with the bitter brew. The whole house smelled like coffee.

Ferdinand followed Mrs. Bolzoni inside. He turned back and poked his head out the door and stared around. Finally, he shut the door and said, "You must know that Mrs. Bolzoni and I would move heaven, earth, and the space in between if need be to help you and Tina."

"Yes, we both know that and I appreciate your coming on such short notice. I don't know how long we'll be gone. We need some fresh air and exercise. It's quiet and dark and not so hot now. Perfect time for low-impact exercise. Anyway, you all know where everything is. Help yourself if you're hungry or thirsty or need to sleep. I doubt if we will be gone long."

Ferdinand said, "We should be admitted to the least bit of knowledge on why you are doing this. It is, you must know, unusual, coming here in the very early morning so you and your lady can walk around the neighborhood in the dark."

Mrs. Bolzoni, in a rare display of affection for Rosswell, patted his arm. "This much you know of. And that is we love Tina and your baby son Jonathan David." She smiled and nodded and said no more. Ferdinand cleared his throat, then tapped her on the shoulder. "Oh," she said. "And yes. Much we think of you also Mister Judge Carew." She nodded again. "I must not forget of the judge who loves his baby and his baby momma." A wide grin spread over her face, her thick eyeglasses pushed up by her cheeks. "We will do anything for you after the summons."

"Summons?" Rosswell said, "Mrs. Bolzoni, what did you say about a summons?"

Now what does she mean? Is someone suing someone? Or maybe it's a crime. What's going on?

"Tell me what kind of summons you're talking about," said Rosswell.

Ferdinand tried to shush Mrs. Bolzoni who resisted and shrugged his arm away. "Don't shush me. I know when summoned I am."

In the background, Rosswell heard his child whimpering, as if he was having a bad dream. Luckily, the bad dream—if that's what it was—didn't wake the boy.

"Ferdinand," said Rosswell. "Listen, please don't stop her. I need to know."

"Alas," Ferdinand said. "I have heard you do not believe in The Branching."

"Psychic networks," Rosswell said. "Thoughts bouncing around the infinite universe from sender to receiver is a bit of a stretch. Let's say . . . that I will keep an open mind."

"That's all we ask," Ferdinand said as he shook Rosswell's hand. "Maman and the Guardians of Dina communicate on a psychic web, which they dubbed The Warehouse. JoEllen and her crew raised up The Branching for the allies of the Guardians. And then, of course, Mother is the evil network for the slave traders."

"Sounds complicated to me." Rosswell scratched his mustache. "The first thing I want to know is how do the thought waves or whatever they are keep from running into one another or jumping on to a network that they're foreign to? Are there gatekeepers somewhere?"

"Alas." Ferdinand wheezed as he spoke. "I'm not certain of anything along those lines. I just use what is. Without explanation. As do all the rest of the sensitives around here." He paused to cough a couple of times. "I know that the closer you are to a person, physically and psychically, that you can send and receive easily. I can't receive the thoughts from the bad folk. I may get a touch of angst, which I think it's them trying to contact me. Nothing dramatic or clear. It's a bit of jumble, truth be known." Ferdinand pounded himself on the chest twice. "Last time I filch one of Ed's cigars."

"Thank you for your truthfulness. And, stolen tobacco is harder on you than honest tobacco."

Ferdinand's story sounds like a load of crap to me. Except for the cigar part.

Rosswell said, "Tina's waiting for me outside. Did you see her as you came in?"

Ferdinand and Mrs. Bolzoni stared at each other for a second.

"No," said Ferdinand.

"I have not seen her until the last week one day." Mrs. Bolzoni smiled.

"See you later." Rosswell gave them both a salute and walked out the door.

"Rosswell," said someone in a stage whisper. He recognized it. Tina.

"I see you behind the hedge. Come on. Let's go for a walk." He motioned to her to join him on the sidewalk by the street.

In a couple of seconds, Tina caught up with him. "While you were in there chit-chatting with the babysitters, I was out here detecting because, you know, we are detectives. You'll never guess what I saw."

"I give up." They walked a few steps before Rosswell said, "Tell me."

"There are all kinds of people walking around downtown." She pointed. "Look at them. It's dark but see how many are out? The businesses are all closed. They're just walking around with no apparent purpose. Yet . . . no one seems worried or panicky or, for that matter, they're not particularly happy or joyfully celebrating. Kind of neutral. Not like zombies hungry for human brains. They're more kind of like people who aren't affected by anything. Emotionless."

Rosswell said, "Streets still warm from the day's blasting sun, now full of blasé people making not a sound."

Tina said, "How poetic. Who said that?"

"Me."

The number of people milling around, comparatively speaking, astounded him. However, if the whole crowd had been in Times Square in New York City, no one would've noticed their presence. Rosswell remembered a couple of springs ago when it was mild and sunny with low humidity and a gentle breeze on a day in May. The streets were full of people walking about aimlessly then. That had been in the daylight. Not the dark of night.

Processing what Tina told him, Rosswell jerked to a stop and stared at the crowds. "You're absolutely right. Is this a late-night holiday of some kind?"

"No," said Tina. "JoEllen called me earlier and said there would be a summons tonight."

"Ha," Rosswell snorted. "You've told me time and time again that you don't believe in such a thing." Rosswell's phone buzzed. "Ollie, what's happening? What? Let me put you on speaker. I'm with Tina. She needs to hear this."

Rosswell pressed a button and Ollie spoke.

"Candy and I are at The Purple Star. We're open for business."

Rosswell said, "It's the middle of the night. You opened a tad early. Either that, or you never closed last night."

Tina said, "Ollie? Can you hear me? What's all that noise?"

"We're having the best day in the history of this restaurant. Rosswell, I'll forgive you for all the stupid things you ever did to me, including the many times your stupidity nearly got me killed, and since I'm in such a generous mood, you and Tina come down here and eat a totally free meal."

"What?" yelled Rosswell. "What stupid things?" Silence. "Talk to me, you coward!"

Tina said, "He hung up on you."

"I really miss dial tones. I never know when someone cuts me off."

CHAPTER 44

Day 10, continued
Early morning
Riverfront
JoEllen

JOELLEN JANSEN, WHO LIVED FIFTEEN minutes from the courthouse, arrived there sixteen minutes after she felt the summons, which woke her from a sound sleep. She parked, and then jogged to the fountain in the park adjoining the building. The building, the park, and the area around the courthouse were not only deserted, but also dimly lit by weak lights. When she passed under one into the pool of another provided by the next light, her shadow bounced around as if it couldn't decide whether to stay attached to her feet or make a run for its little dark life. All the fun stuff was going on downtown at the foot of the hill. She scrutinized her surroundings, looking for company. After a moment, she heard a short blast from a hi/lo siren. JoEllen walked toward the sound after Sonya waved to her from a parked cop car near the courthouse. JoEllen approached and pointed at the crowd down the hill. "What is going on around here?"

Sonya scooted out of the car. "About an hour ago, I was on routine patrol when I started hearing radio chatter around midnight. Crowds downtown, but no businesses were open. Not even the bars. Well, except for Ollie. His business is open and jam-packed."

"A riot?"

"Hardly. Peaceful as a bunch of Canadians smoking pot."

"Ah, that tells me a lot," JoEllen said. "You know what this is, don't you?"

"I'm a cop. I'll wait until all the evidence is gathered before I make a decision about what's going on."

"I repeat, you know what this is. There's a summons of some kind. I'm not sure from whom or how long it will last. We're supposed to gather down here and . . . do . . . something. Not for sure what. From the whiffs of thoughts from the bad guys that I've been getting for the last few days, they've discovered something or found something or figured something out. I don't know what, but it can't be good for our side."

Sonya laughed. "That's a bunch of crazy, all that weirdo business. There's nothing worth calling evidence in any of that psychic stuff."

JoEllen said, "It's not psychic stuff. It's quantum entanglement. Albert Einstein called it, 'spooky action at a distance'."

"Okay, quantum stuff. Right. I haven't quite finished my doctorate in physics. I'll stick with Albert and call it 'spooky action at a distance' and let it be. Besides, what does this 'quantum entanglement' mean? Like a boyfriend you're tired of and you can't get rid of him and everywhere you go, he goes? Is that what you mean?"

"That," said JoEllen, "is exactly what I mean. It's physics. When two particles interact physically, they become entangled. From then on, whenever one particle does something, the other one does it also. It's identical twins, but you never know which is which until you get one by himself and ask questions. Then the difference is between one twin and what he knows and the other twin and what he knows. That difference is the psychic message you get. That's the simplest I can make it. The real explanation is several thousands of words long."

"And you understand all of that?"

"Not a bit. What I told you is all I know. Plus, I know that it works."

Sonya asked JoEllen, "That means I'll never get rid of a pesky boyfriend?"

"Do you have one you want to get rid of?"

Sonya leaned over to whisper to JoEllen, even though no one was visible in the vicinity. "If I had a boyfriend or, better yet, a husband, I wouldn't be volunteering for twelve and fourteen hour shifts."

"Gotcha." JoEllen started to grasp Sonya's hand in a shake but drew it back and yipped.

"JoEllen, did someone hear that? Is that what scared you?"

"No, that didn't scare me. You shocked me. Psychic energy jumped between us. And, yes, someone must have heard what I said. That's what caused the spark."

Sonya cocked her head, as if listening, then assumed her cop demeanor. "Tell me about what else you think is happening."

JoEllen motioned for them to walk to a bench and sit. "Remember when we were getting those vibes from that building downtown a couple of days ago? I know what that is."

Below the hill on the streets, people continued milling about. Why wasn't there music? Would anyone dance if there were music? JoEllen didn't know. She needed to find Rosswell.

"Sonya, face it. We are in danger. There are people in that building who would like to kill us. You, me. Not to mention Maman Fribeau, Mrs. Bolzoni, Candy, Ollie, Alexander, Ferdinand, Tina, Jonathan David, and Rosswell, and now probably Reverend Ed and Father Mike.

"But Ed Searl is a suspect in the murder."

JoEllen continued, "Ed is totally innocent and you know it as well as I do. Juliette Fribeau did not die at his hands. Someone else killed the woman while he was up there on that trail."

Sonya reached for her notebook and turned a few pages. She stopped at a blank page and began writing. "Let me get this straight. If he's innocent, then he's in danger, too. Is that what you're telling me?"

"Yes, and I'll tell you something else. Reverend Ed and Father Mike are interconnected psychically. They may not know it but they are. However, I think they do know it. They don't want it made public because no one wants to think their spiritual leaders are spiritualists who talk to angels."

"Spiritual leaders are spiritualists?" Sonya tapped her forehead. "This brain here is working overtime trying to keep up with your explanations. None of this stuff would be allowed into evidence during a trial. You already know that though, don't you?"

"You can bet your life I know that," JoEllen said. "That's why I'm trying to get some real evidence about this mess. Trust me when I tell you that we are all connected by a network. You, too. Some of us have greater psychic power than other sensitives. Some are lesser and some are greater."

"Who controls all these psychic networks?"

"That's where the problem lies. The bad guys are gaining ground. It's getting harder to move information over our networks because their network is frequently able to block us at every turn. We can't figure it out."

Sonya said, "We?"

"Maman and me."

"Maman told me she is an atheist who claims all this is scientifically-based, not spiritually-based."

"She's half-right."

"JoEllen, talk straight for once."

"Maman and I are having a disagreement about exactly where the network is located. I'm trying to convince her that it's in a box somewhere on Earth and I mean right here in downtown Cape. She says the network is flying faster than light around the universe as photons or something."

Sonya closed her eyes and frowned. She whispered, "What possible difference does it make?" She opened her eyes and shook her head.

JoEllen said, "You're right. Something's happening no matter the cause."

Sonya said, "Then it's time to gather up everyone. Right?"

"Absolutely. First of all, we need to talk to Rosswell."

"Then let's go. We're headed to Ollie's where I'm sure we'll find the whole gang."

Both women jumped up and headed for the cop car.

Before JoEllen could fasten her safety belt, she froze for a moment, holding her hand behind her ear, increasing the volume of sound waves reaching her head. She turned around to stare down the hill at the train tracks running on the street side of the floodwall. "Did you hear that?" A light engine (what the industry calls a locomotive and one car)—the same one Father Mike and Reverend Ed had seen—hulked along the tracks, heedless of traffic, human, or car. "That train is only an engine and a caboose. Or maybe with a second car." About every quarter mile, the motion-activated lights installed along the tracks blinked on and off, maintaining records of the location and the status of each car, reporting the information to a central computer.

Sonya asked, "What is it?"

"They're moving it in the freight car."

"Moving what?"

"There's an optical scanner reporting information to a computer, I think. I'm not for sure what info it's collecting."

Sonya said, "Tell me something you know for sure."

The train groaned to a dead stop at the foot of Broadway, the street that led to the open floodwall where Father Mike and Reverend Ed conferred about the state of the universe.

JoEllen unbuckled her seat belt, and threw open the cop car door.

She knew exactly what it was. She could hear it ticking.

"It's going to blow up."

CHAPTER 45

Day 10, continued
Early morning
Riverfront

JOELLEN AND SONYA ZIG-ZAGGED ON foot like bolts of low lightning into The Purple Star. Candy greeted them and Ollie asked them what they wanted to eat. The place resembled an overstuffed can of sardines, packed as it was with customers. A line of people waiting to be seated, snaked out the front door and down the block. Although JoEllen tried to make it obvious to the crowd that she was heading for the conference room (and not for a vacant table) and, furthermore, that she kept Sonya in her cop uniform close beside her (making some folks think JoEllen was under arrest), there was still murmuring about line-jumping and needing a police escort.

"Where are they?" yelled JoEllen when she opened the door to the storeroom, only to find it empty. She stated the obvious. "No one's here." She felt as though she'd run off the road of reason and was doomed to drive off the cliff of sanity if she didn't find her companions.

Ollie said, "Where are who?"

JoEllen made a face at Ollie. "The rest of the group. The Guardians. Our companions. Where are they?" Breathing hurt her now. She closed her eyes and counted to twenty-five. It helped. With a bit more calmness, she said, "Don't be coy, Baldie."

"Baldie?" For emphasis, Ollie rubbed his head. "That's low."

Sonya said, "Ollie, Baldie is a mere statement of fact and not an insult. Where is everyone? Answer the question. There are lives on the line."

"They're outside, wandering around, enjoying the night. Like a whole bunch of people. Yeah, and I've heard that lives on the line hogwash before. It's a classic Rosswell come-on."

"As always," Candy said, "all the lollygaggers will soon be in the storeroom. Then I'll bring some food for all y'all. Don't trip going back there. You might get stomped in the crowd."

"No," said JoEllen, shaking her head.

"No?" Candy repeated. "Why not?"

"Something is about to happen. Or not. If it doesn't happen, we'll be back to eat your food. Come on, Sonya." She waved the cop onward and outward.

Sonya squinted sideways at Candy, shrugged, and headed out the door, barely a step behind JoEllen.

On the sidewalk in front of The Purple Star, Maman Fribeau and Alexander Comana sprinted. Or as close to sprinting as the two ancient friends could make it. They needed to be somewhere and didn't mind pushing people aside. Both swerved to a stop in front of Sonya and JoEllen before they collided in one big mess.

Alexander bowed to the three women. "Sorry, m'ladies, and regrets are given for nearly running into all of you. We are in a quandary." As usual, the janitor was covered with soot. The four of them ducked into the restaurant but stayed next to the door.

"The saint tells the truth, him." Maman Fribeau pointed to Alexander. "Except I do not accept the superstition of making them people saints."

"Although," Alexander said, pointing to Maman and smiling broadly, "I never lose hope in converting my friend the Maman."

Yes, thought JoEllen, *we have heard these stories before. Alexander and Maman please, now is not the time for arguing for the existence of God. We are in dire straits here. I've heard all your arguments.*

"Thank you, both," JoEllen said aloud. "We want to help you. What is your problem?"

"She can help," Maman said, grasping Sonya's hand. "Follow us."

Alexander said, "Allow me to go first." He trotted out of the restaurant onto the street and veered for the railroad track. Before he could run across it, he turned north, on Water Street, and scurried to the open floodgate at the foot of Broadway. He rushed through the opening, screaming loudly, "Father Mike! Reverend Ed! Be sober and watch, because your adversary the devil, the roaring lion, goes about seeking whom he may devour! Now he strides for you! Put on the whole armor of God!"

Even through the gloom of the night, the brilliance surrounding the two men gave them the appearance of moving into forever.

Everyone saw it.

That's because everyone in the group was wrapped in the brilliance.

Sonya made for her car.

JoEllen whispered, "It's started."

CHAPTER 46

Day 10, continued
Early morning
Riverfront

"IF PEACE AND CALM ARE floating in the air," asked JoEllen of anyone who would listen, "then why am I not happy? Nothing's happened yet. There's been no resolution."

No one answered her as all of the companions gathered near the floodwall gate. The prior anxiety they'd all felt around midnight drained. None of them were nervous or upset. Dawn would soon arrive from the east, across the river, in Illinois. Then calm would reign when everyone would flock to the shore and watch the sunrise.

No fires polluted the air. No bad smells floated over downtown, except the ordinary putrid odor of the river. Quiet hung in the dampness of the air. Father Mike leaned up against the floodwall and noticed the high humidity had caused the structure to sweat. Although the streets in downtown Cape were almost full of people wandering around without any apparent purpose, none of them disrupted anything, or littered, or started any fights, or talked loudly. All were sober. In fact, not only was there no alcohol, no other drugs were in evidence. No one smoked pot. Meth was absent. Opiates were nowhere to be found. Even now, no one knew why all the folks gathered there had flocked to that place at that time.

Cops (besides Sonya) had earlier flooded the place. Sheriff Talbot Reasoner and Chief Max Chickering themselves had stood at the corner of

Broadway and Water, surveying the open floodgate, the riverfront, all the streets downtown, and everything else they could see.

Talbot had said, "There's nothing here. No problems." He doffed his Stetson and wiped his brow with a shirtsleeve. "Someone called me and said I should activate the Major Case Squad. There's no major case. In fact, there's no minor case. Truth be told, there's no case period. It's not illegal for people to walk around. I'm going home. These last few days have been exhausting on me."

"I agree." Max, his thin lips pressed together, drew out the Vicks. "This weather is making my allergies do the boogaloo." He hitched up his belt. "I reckon a slice or two of Ollie's apple pie with black coffee will give me a little more energy. You run along, Sheriff. I'll handle it if anything happens." He put his inhaler back in his pocket, blew his nose on a large checkered handkerchief, then folded the snot over in quarters, before returning the handkerchief to his pocket. "It looks mighty peaceful."

After a long while of people dawdling, still, nothing had happened. The area still sounded unusually quiet. Most of the law enforcement officers returned to routine patrol. Sure, earlier there had been drunks carousing in the streets and old men fishing along the banks of the river. Now, however, the entire riverfront had emptied of human and animal life. No more coyotes. No more eagles. No more critters of any kind.

Father Mike said, "Rosswell, Tina, and Brian Reeves are the only ones not here. Ed, you call Brian and I'll call Rosswell." Both got voicemail. "Let's walk to Rosswell's place."

Father Mike assured Reverend Ed that the people who surrounded them were not merely companions. "The companions understand the phenomenon that will certainly follow."

Ed said, "Can they sketch a picture of how it would look?"

"I doubt it."

"Then they don't understand it."

Father Mike asked Alexander Comana, "My friend, what is happening?"

"We'll all explode and then fall arse over teakettle—begging your forgiveness, padre—into a pile of atoms is what is happening."

Reverend Ed asked JoEllen, "If our janitor friend here is correct, do you have any idea how we can avoid disintegration?"

"Yes, you and Father Mike must never separate before this is over," JoEllen said. "You and Father Mike are the only ones here who can stop this. That's why the angel's visitation came to you both at the same time."

Father Mike said, "And what did we do to deserve a visitation?"

JoEllen shook her head. "That I cannot tell you."

Maman approached the priest and the minister. "You are *conduits*'—she pronounced it like the French . . . *cahn-dwee* . . . "—the two of you. Out there in infinity something hovers around you two that affects you and the universe the same. Thought is both a particle and a wave or both or neither."

"Maman," said Father Mike, rubbing his temples, wishing for an Excedrin to ease the pain of an oncoming migraine, "I don't want that job, mostly because I don't understand the job description."

"Too bad, you," said Maman. She poked Father Mike in the chest. "And there's no retirement plan. At least not in this world."

Alexander said, "There's no way out of it. Fight or die."

"You two," Maman said, pointing to Father Mike and Reverend Ed, "must fight. And maybe you will live or, don't fight and for sure you die. That's the choice."

"That's not much of a choice." Father Mike closed his eyes, took a deep breath, made the sign of the Cross, and said, "What do we do next?"

Maman pointed down the street toward Rosswell and Tina. They stood outside their office door, waving flashlights, shouting, urging the companions to hurry to their building.

A rumbling echo vibrated the railroad tracks. Something big coming from the north growled.

The ground shook.

CHAPTER 47

Rosswell eyed Sonya as she wheeled her cruiser next to a parked car in front of his office. She left her car running, blue lights flashing.

As they say on television, Sonya exited her vehicle.

Rosswell gave her a brief salute, which she ignored.

"Do you have a gun?" she asked Rosswell.

"Yes, ma'am. I have a .38 Special. It's in a holster covered by my shirt."

Tina said to Sonya, "You know that he always carries his pistol. Why are you asking?"

"Judge Carew," said Sonya, "relax. Stand down. Whatever you want me to say in your police procedure drama."

"Yes, ma'am," he stood down—meaning he relaxed. Rosswell said to Sonya's passenger, "I'm always armed. Granted, not too often that you see people wandering the streets this late, but it's a calm night. A nice night.

Sonya," Rosswell said, "I never want to be on the wrong side of the law. And I never want you to be on the wrong side of the law either. Your driving habits could be tidied up a bit."

"Double parking," she said to her passenger, the prosecuting attorney of Cape Girardeau County.

"Is it okay for me to get out?" Brian Reeves asked Sonya.

Sonya nodded.

Rosswell was the first through the door into the office.

Like an ice cube melting in the noonday sun of a summer day, the crowd downtown thinned, people walked off, presumably either to their homes, or to their cars and trucks. Traffic on the streets had also thinned. Soon the streets appeared as any other predawn morning. Some cars moving here and there. A pickup truck rumbling along. A motorcycle vibrating down hills. More normal. Still dark. Still hot. Yes, a bit more normal.

"I know people who can fix a ticket," Brian Reeves assured Sonya. "Thanks for picking me up." He yawned. "An odd thing happened yesterday evening. I fell asleep at home around five in the afternoon and didn't wake up until you called me." As though he couldn't believe what he'd just said, Brian checked his wristwatch. "I've never done that before in my life. Must be getting old. But I feel great."

Rosswell gathered all the companions around him inside his office building. "We have problems. Major problems."

Brian said, "Like what? What do we do and when do we do it?"

Tina said, "We don't know what. Or what to do, which means that we don't know when to do whatever it is we don't know what to do."

Ed stepped forward and held up a forefinger, cleared his throat, and said, "Father Mike and I have been talking."

All eyes turned to the two clergymen.

Father Mike said, "All of us here now know about the visitation of the angel. For the past few days, we've gone over every detail with each of you." He paused and looked into the eyes of every person there. "Some of you believe it was an angel. Some of you don't. But Ed and I both now agree that it was an angel."

Rosswell said, "Regardless of what any of us believe or don't believe, if we've got problems, we need a plan."

Ed said, "We were summoned down here. Father Mike and I got here first. We're all here now and we need to gather by the railroad tracks."

Father Mike said, "Agreed. Not *on* the tracks. *By* the tracks. We don't want anyone run over by a train. Even if it were straight up noon, trains cannot stop quickly. It's physics."

The two clergymen led the group to the railroad tracks.

JoEllen scanned the tracks for a train. Finding none, she bent low and touched one of the metal ribbons, listening and feeling for the loud rumble she'd heard earlier. "A train is far up the tracks. Up north. It's headed this way. It's slowed down, but it's still headed this way."

She gasped.

"There's a bomb on the train."

CHAPTER 48

Day 10, continued
Early morning
Riverfront
Adam Cain

O N THE SECOND FLOOR OF the old brick building, which served as the headquarters of the local nest of enemies chasing the Guardians, Adam Cain slumped in a high back chair, eyes wide open, his nerves humming with the buzz of an electric fence. He frowned and stayed far away from his sister, Martha Bailey and her good-looking boyfriend, Timothy Lockerbie. On the other side of the room, Martha and Timothy cuddled on a couch positioned under a large window, facing Illinois. A joint lying in an ashtray on a low coffee table burned, curling acrid smoke into the air. The fumes reminded Adam of the scent of burning alfalfa in a field he'd torched long ago. A farmer had dissed him about something. Adam couldn't remember the insult, only that he'd been insulted by a man of the soil. He retaliated by setting the farmer's crop afire. Although he couldn't remember what the farmer had done to him, the smell hadn't been forgotten.

Martha had earlier baked a large pan of triple fudge brownies for their post-midnight snack. She displayed the sugar goodies along with a bottle of cheap wine and a pile of joints on the coffee table.

Adam slipped a vinyl on the stereo, *Smooth Jazz Ballads & Love Songs* by saxophonist Alfonzo Blackwell. Adam's sister might be somewhat controllable, but in Adam's hardheaded brain, Timothy could be classified as either a sociopath or a psychopath or suffered from an anti-social personality disorder or he was just simply crazy as a bedbug on meth, or all four. Adam hadn't kept up with the latest politically correct terms to refer to insane people. Anyway, all Adam knew for sure was that the guy had no conscience. Timothy Lockerbie could kill someone then go out for pizza. That was what attracted Adam to Timothy.

Now, tonight, if Timothy or Martha made a move that Adam didn't like, he'd shoot them center mass in an instant. He'd never had problems killing people who threatened him. He'd done it before many times and he could do it again one more time.

Something besides people bothered Adam now.

"What's wrong with this box?" Adam asked, pointing to his desk.

Martha laughed. "Box? If you're talking about the computer, then there's not a thing wrong with it."

Timothy said nothing but sniffed and turned on the TV to watch old reruns of The Lawrence Welk Show, all the while singing an impromptu ditty. Fetching more cookies and another glass of wine, he flopped down on the couch, chewing his cookies and imbibing his wine in between puffs on the joint. He'd been lost to reality a few hours earlier and stayed that way now.

"Nothing wrong with it? Yeah?" said Adam. "Then what's this message for?"

Martha said, "What message?"

"The one that says, 'Countdown initiated.Bomb' and the clock beneath it running down to zero."

Martha scrambled toward the monitor. "Holy horsefly!"

"What? A horsefly?"

"No, you idiot. That's just something I heard that old lady say. She works at The Purple Star and talks funny."

"What the hell are you talking about?"

"Look, you two idiots, this box, as you call it, is connected to the whole world. The Hivites are going to destroy the Guardians. Something has started ticking down. It can't be good. Not if there's a bomb."

"What kind of experiments?" Adam asked Martha.

" Martha held her head in her hands, sobbing. "I hope it's not painful for us."

Adam said, "What are we supposed to do?"

"Maybe we should hope for a restful night and a peaceful death."

"Wow," moaned Timothy as he stood on the couch with both hands and his face pressed to the window. "Cool."

"Aren't you going to say 'far out, man'?" Adam launched himself for the window. If things looked that bad, he could always jump from the window. That was only two stories high. He'd probably survive. Adam felt of the revolver in the holster at his side. Yes. Shooting himself in the mouth would be the quick way to go. "What're you looking at?"

Martha said, "It's over Timothy's shoulder. Outside. Dawn. But not dawn. Something bad wrong that's lit up to beat the band of seventy-six trombones." She hitched her breath and moaned. "The sky is on fire."

A tiny but brilliant yellow light, only a dot, shone in the eastern sky.

Adam said, "It's the sunrise, you dopeheads."

Timothy launched into his singing voice when he wheeled around to gape at Adam. "No, it's something way more powerful than a sunrise." The pothead had trilled up and down the scale effortlessly.

"See there?" Martha said to both of them as she again pointed at the window toward the growing light. "Can you not see that?"

Timothy cackled. "Time for the train. Today is the day the Hivites abolish the Guardians." He rubbed his hands together, laughing, making his new ditty sound like something that just hit the charts.

Time for the chorus.

I'm driving this time.

No way to run off the tracks.

He continued singing and cackling for three or four more choruses.

Adam turned to Martha and said, "If that lunatic gets on that train, we're all dead. I'm going to kill him first."

"No, you don't get to," sang Timothy.

Two rapid shots later, both siblings lay dead.

Raggedy Man, Raggedy Man, what's the score?

Mother daughter slaughter and two more,

Fribeau their name and murder the game.

Raggedy man, Raggedy man, what's the score?

Four before, plus two on the floor.

Six there be, more to see.

CHAPTER 49

Day 10, continued
Dawn is coming

AFTER GAINING THEIR ATTENTION WITH a finger whistle, Rosswell hustled all the companions to the riverfront. The jabbering, while plentiful, didn't rank up there as loud. Only a tad above immediately noticeable. The group around him stared at each other while they talked, although the light was feeble. The stares followed one right after the other, questioning in their eyes asking what came next.

Rosswell hovered over a small wood fire on a pile of rocks lying on the riverfront, although it wasn't for heat. It sufficed for that feeble bit of illumination in the waning dark and the smoky flames from the burning driftwood smelled better than the putrid stench rolling off the river. Wanting attention, he again whistled through his fingers, sounding like a trespassing alarm gone wild, panicking a flock of pigeons who happened to fly over at the instant of Rosswell's whistle.

Rosswell yelled, "Listen up!" The companions stopped chattering. "What is that?" His arm stretched out to the east, pointing to the low hills of Illinois. "Tell me what you see."

Sonya said, "I'm guessing it's the lights from cars. There's a lot of traffic over there this time of day. A whole bunch of people commute to work in Illinois."

Alexander strode up beside Rosswell. "May I say that it is the sunshine coming once again from the east? As it does every morning. At dawn. Every single day." He stopped for a moment, staring eastward, as if to affirm that the beginning of day had arrived on schedule. "So far. And if the sun doesn't come up one morning, then we all are dead. Or surely on the verge of dying."

"No," JoEllen said, glancing at her watch. "That's not the sunrise. It's too early for the dawn. Not by much but . . . still."

Maman Fribeau said, "Dawn. Been happening for billions of years."

Rosswell marked the progress of the light in the east as it began glowing more brightly, moving more swiftly, until it stopped over the companions. There it shined down on all them without casting shadows.

How does a bright light shining on me not cast a shadow? Is this the same thing Moses beheld when he stumbled on the burning bush that was not consumed by fire?

Rosswell concentrated on the phenomenon heading for him and the companions. He then understood that the thing, the phenomenon, was not a burning bush. A swift bird-like critter soared overhead, its head crowned with flowing golden feathers, its ivory talons dragged, barely skimming the water. A brilliant white shine in its eyes gave its face a luminescence greater than the sun. An odor of cinnamon followed the being, the scent reminding Rosswell of pies.

Father Mike hollered, "It's grown bigger. More beautiful than when I saw it in the church. I've never seen a bird that large nor that gorgeous." He took a moment to swallow and rub his eyes. "It's not a bird. It's an attendant of God."

Do they mean an angel? Should I believe that? Rosswell shook his head in disbelief.

A golden eagle would look dumpy next to the thing in the sky. As the being flew, it swooped and rose, then dived and turned, barely missing the companions. The cinnamon odor enveloped the whole part of the riverfront where they gawked in wonder. The creature's claws clicked as it flew, generating the noise of rhythmic marching, a pattern that all the companions enjoyed. The sound made them want to jump up and dance. From the structure of the tones, Rosswell now truly believed he was watching the angel that Father Mike and Reverend Ed had earlier reported to him, making him wonder if that was the same creature that saved him when he fell over the cliff.

Confirming what Rosswell had already surmised, Father Mike yelled to him, "That's what flew through the church." The priest stretched his neck to gaze upwards. "It's more beautiful now."

"An angel? Am I right?" Rosswell moved his hand between his eyes and the brightness of the critter now flying around the companions. "That's no demon."

Father Mike said, "You're absolutely right. It's not evil. It's an angel. Terrifying. But an angel. Angels are always scary because they are so holy. I know it's an angel."

The conversation could barely be heard over the noise of rushing wind and the musical clicking.

Rosswell said, "How can we tell for sure?"

The radiance of the angel—because everyone who could see it now knew it was an angel—shone greater, and its size increased beyond earthly proportions. The companions, all covered by the visitation, could see beyond its limits into the clear blue sky. Around the angel, the night sky had been ripped open wide where the sunshine showed plainly, although somehow still surrounded by the blackness of night. Rosswell noted that the fear and trembling reported earlier by Father Mike and Ed now seemed to be gone. Both stared at the being in awe and wonder, but not with trepidation.

"What happened in the church frightened me beyond belief. I know what I saw then. I know what I'm seeing now."

Again. *Click. Click. Click.* Pause for the angel to swing its head to stare at the priest and the minister. *Womp. Womp. Womp.* Another pause as the wings stopped. The air filled with the aroma of sweet incense. The dust that fell on the companions with each flap somehow reminded Rosswell of manna, although he'd never seen or smelled or tasted such a thing.

"In the church, I dubbed it The Demonic Nearness," Father Mike said. "I was so wrong. No more."

Rosswell said, "What do you see now?"

Father Mike said, "A creature blazing in pure light. It's neither male nor female. Dressed in linen, a belt of the costliest gold. A face like lightning, eyes like torches, arms and legs like molten bronze, and a thunderous voice sounding like a chorus of a million other angels. I'm not scared anymore!" He faced the being eye to eye. "What do you want?"

Bomb.

"Guessing games again," Father Mike hollered to Rosswell. Back to the angel, he said, "What about this bomb?"

Be not afraid.

"I'm not afraid. I know you're an angel and you know you're scary to human beings. And, I might add, the last time I saw you, you were mighty ugly for an Angel of the Lord."

I am not a demonic nearness.

"Yes. I know that now."

Murder.

Bomb.

"What?"

Apparently, the angel made certain that Father Mike heard all this, although it wasn't spoken in the way humans speak. Father Mike, however spoke to the angel in a normal voice. The angel must have heard and understood him or it would not have answered.

The priest persisted. "Aren't angels supposed to deliver messages to people? How am I expected to know what you are saying about murder and a bomb? Tell me. These little clues you're flinging down at my feet mean nothing to me." Rosswell heard the anger in the priest's voice, although he hoped Father Mike knew what he was doing. Irritating angels didn't sound to Rosswell like a thing that would ever be good.

The angel swooped down closer to the companions.

JoEllen.

The woman fell to the ground when the angel called her name. "What?" She jumped to her feet and yelled, "I had nothing to do with a bomb."

"Listen, JoEllen is standing right here." Father Mike jerked straight up so fast he nearly fell and then pointed to the angel. "Are you saying she knows about the bomb?"

JoEllen.

Maman.

The Hivite Horror stalks you both. The Hivite Horror makes this representation of the nearness seem like a sleeping baby. Beware the Hivite Horror.

"If we must, we will destroy the Hivite Horror!" yelled Maman Fribeau.

JoEllen pounded her ears with her fists. "I can feel him! He's on the train!"

CHAPTER 50

Day 10, continued
Almost dawn
Riverfront

R OSSWELL DECLARED HIMSELF HAPPY SINCE he hadn't been killed up to this moment. That and now he detected a touch of pink in the eastern sky, meaning the sun was indeed rising and not just an angel that happened to show up. Blues and yellows joined in, then whites when the wispy clouds showed up. Shortly, another big source of light—the sun—would be joining the angel. He said to JoEllen, "Who's on the train?" He didn't have to yell. The angel and everything around the area had fallen into complete silence. Light going up and sound going down. Rosswell also detected a pattern in the way angels and sunrises worked together. "Alex, what is happening? What am I seeing?"

"Begging your pardon, m'lord, but my name is Alexander Comana. I tend the charcoal at the cathedral. And during that tending, I have learned that men and women both look upon clothes and the face of the person before them, but God himself alone looks at the soul and the heart."

"Pretty lofty language, Alexander but look up there." He indicated and Alexander's gaze followed Rosswell's pointing finger. It could've been a mirage, Rosswell admitted to himself, but if his eyes weren't dancing in deception, the beginnings of an angel dome in the sky started covering the area where the fireworks may or maybe not go off in a spectacular end of watch.

JoEllen said, "Timothy Lockerbie is on that train."

"Is he the Hivite Horror?"

"Yes."

"It's a good thing I'm armed."

After rechecking his weapon, Rosswell said, "The Hivite is due for some extreme prejudice knocking him down."

Alexander spoke. "Again, there must be no killing. Timothy is the Hivite and everyone knows it. Yet that does not give us the right to take the life we did not give."

"Self-defense," JoEllen said to Rosswell and Alexander. "The Hivite Horror should die. He's the one who's been creating all the problems around here for a couple decades. Except for the time he was locked up in a Texas jail for a couple of years. He's a serial killer and he's coming this way. On the train. He wants to be a mass killer as well as a serial killer."

Rosswell said, "There's a difference?"

Of course, there's a difference, you dummy. You've forgotten all the continuing judicial education you sat through. You need to listen up. Your brain is getting rusty. Listen to JoEllen. You may learn something.

Rosswell listened, yet he couldn't recognize the something or someone who interrupted with a warning that the train was coming fast.

"Driving it is him," Maman Fribeau said. She stared up at the angel hovering over all the companions. "Wait! I see the bad boy, too! He's propped up on a big comfy chair, him. Driving the train from the front car. One-handed. With television sets in front of him in the cab, there. Buttons. Knobs. Computer controls. Levers. He wants to go faster. He's pushing something. Pulling something. I can't really see all."

Okay, now is Maman getting psychic pictures as well as JoEllen? How does Maman know all this? I thought she was science only. No iffy supernatural stuff like JoEllen. I'm confused.

Brian Reeves crowded in next to Rosswell. "Judge, what I'm hearing is that there's a bomb on that train. If we don't get it defused, all of Cape Girardeau and a lot of Illinois swampland will be gone."

"We?"

Brian picked Father Mike and Reverend Ed out of the group. "See them? That's why that angel is floating above us. They're the ones who were alerted to the murders in the first place. And now, the angel is telling us to stop the bomb."

Tina had slipped up next to Rosswell and Brian. "Can't we talk the angel into stopping it?"

"No," JoEllen said. "It doesn't work that way. I didn't make the rules, but it doesn't work that way. There are only two people needed to stop the bomb and one way to do it. If we co-operate with the angel, we can stop it, although I doubt that the angel would do diddly squat for us if we sat around twiddling our thumbs."

"She's right." Maman Fribeau had her hand on JoEllen's head. "Now she must lead and I must be her true companion. If we work that big thing in the sky, then we win. We don't co-operate, we die."

"There's only one way," JoEllen said, "that I know will stop the train. If the angel is telling me another way, I can't understand it."

"Tell us quick!" Rosswell said to JoEllen. "You best be hopping to it!"

CHAPTER 51

Day10, continued
Almost dawn
Riverfront

"WE NEED TO WEAVE." JOELLEN turned to Maman. "Weave." Maman nodded her head.

"Weave?" Tina said. "You mean as in lacing threads passing one way with others passing at a right angle to them? That kind of weaving?"

"Yes, exactly as you said—weave," JoEllen said one more time. "Here's how we'll do it. First, find the nearest optical scanner." Her fear obvious in the quiver of her voice, JoEllen spoke directly to Maman. "That's your area, isn't it? Nothing supernatural about optical scanners, is there? Seek and find." JoEllen pointed at the tracks. "We can stop it that way."

Maman shrugged, then she commenced to power-hiking down the tracks. After scouring over a half-mile of tracks, she stopped, raised both hands, and motioned JoEllen to join her. "There. That thing what it looks like a big smartphone. One on each side of the tracks. See those?" JoEllen nodded. Maman said, "I give you optical scanner. Sender and receiver. I gave to you. Now you give to us a way to stop the train."

"Hurry. Please," Tina said. "I'd suggest something low tech. We don't have time for searching out any electronic goodies."

"I'm way ahead of you." JoEllen scoured the tracks until she found a rock, big and heavy, mainly white quartz, which has always been known to hold strong psychic waves longer than any other natural substance. White contains all colors. Because of that, the unique power of the crystal to collect the energy of any situation is the most beneficial stone you can bring into your life for healing. "Here!" She lifted it above her head and with a yell, smashed the optical scanner into a billion (it seemed) pieces. "The train won't go past this point." She closed her eyes and covered her ears. "It's coming." She turned her back to the oncoming train. "I can feel its evil."

"Are you sure that rock will stop the train?" Tina, who'd been standing close to the tracks, moved closer to the floodwall. "A piece of quartz? It's strong enough? I think we're dead. JoEllen, tell me you're sure."

"No," said Maman, "she's not sure."

"Then let's beat it while our shoes are good," Tina said.

"We may not have many options," said Sonya. "I don't think running away is an option. We can't get to a safe space before the bomb explodes."

Tina said, "I can drive my car very fast."

"You are so right." JoEllen shook her head. "I mean Sonya is. If we don't stop this train, one of two things will happen. One is that we will die in an explosion. Two is that nothing will happen. In any event, I agree. You can't run fast enough now. And you can't drive or fly or swim fast enough. It's too late."

"Let me hear more about the bomb," Rosswell said, "Are you saying the bomb is super-powerful?"

"Yes," Maman Fribeau said. "In my network, The Warehouse, I see the notice for the box, as the bad guy calls the terminal, and I see its schematic, there." She closed her eyes and waved her arms and hands as if deluged by a cloud of hornets on a hot summer day, although what Maman swatted were the psychic messages smiting her from her own network. To an outsider, she appeared as if she were buffeted by a strong wind from the north. In fact, the wind pushing her had dropped the temperature by at least ten degrees. Possibly even fifteen. "There." She moaned, pointing her fingers and stabbing here and there in the empty space in front of her. "And there." Point. Stab. "Yes. And this. I see the connection, there, there, there." Point. Stab. Point. Stab. Point. Stab. "Weaving the cushion for the explosion. It must be made of quarks. The particles of the quantum elementary table—especially the charm and the strange—will fold themselves around each other and then around the package, which will then join in enclosing the whole matrix in an explosion-proof womb."

"Do I hear you saying using a bunch of jabberwocky that an electronic womb is going to save us from a bomb?" Rosswell's head hurt after listening to Maman's lecture. "Are you sure that will keep us all safe?"

"*Non!*" said Maman. "I'm not sure what kind of bomb it is."

JoEllen said, "Same here. I don't know anything about bombs."

"If I'm wrong," said Maman, "then that means boom. No more. Nothing is left. A pile of dust floating in the dark." She waved her flattened hand quickly at a forty-five degree angle, then a ninety-degree. "I say a fifty-chance that we boom like the big dirigible hitting the sparking antenna. *Poof!* All gone."

Rosswell closed his eyes and threw his head back. "Oh, the humanity."

"Thank you, Rosswell," said Tina. "All this gobbledygook we're getting from Maman and JoEllen means we're going to die."

CHAPTER 52

Day 10, continued
Sunrise is coming
Riverfront

"SOMETHING'S CHANGING," JOELLEN SAID. HER face was a study in pure serenity when she closed her eyes, gentle as a bunny. After a moment, her face twisted and she groaned. Tears ran down her cheeks. "There's violence and sorrow in the future but I can't tell who it affects."

Alexander said, "I can tell. It is all of us who it affects." He hung his head in prayer.

The sun's rising progressed slowly, as if the star had risen from a cold vat of sorghum molasses in January. Only a gentle wind blew with no prior hint of its speed increasing when the heat from the sun started sneaking up as quickly as it could. A cone of silence settled over the scene. No one—as far as Rosswell knew—heard anything but the soft murmuring of low voices running through the companions.

The angel, still surrounded by a scent of incense with a hint of cinnamon, undulated in a slow rhythm, the movement nearly hypnotizing Rosswell. The sights and sounds, together with words the angel ran through his head before he snapped to attention and tore himself away from meditating. The heat and humidity began rising, making everyone wipe their hands and face as often as they could. After touching the sweat rolling off them, however, many people expressed shock that the moisture was sweet smelling and felt like a fine oil. As a counterpoint to this scene,

Rosswell noted that the river kept rolling along, still muddy, still stinking, still floating unidentifiable objects down to the Gulf of Mexico.

JoEllen wiped her eyes with the back of her hands. "In my head, I see everything collapsing." She shook her head. "Nothing good can come of this. Nothing."

Possibly fearing a large crowd morphing into a large mob, Sonya ordered, "Okay, that's it. Everyone back off the tracks. Go stand on the sidewalk across the street." She pointed with her hand, although Rosswell could've sworn she'd signaled her directions with an old-fashioned nightstick. No. Merely a flashback of a police officer at a seminar, giving a history of batons and the fights over which one was best.

No one complied with Sonya's order. Rosswell knew why.

If people think they're trapped and about to die, they don't wander off, away from the excitement. They don't search out a safe space if they are convinced their fate is soon and certain. If your death is inevitable, you don't want to miss a single moment of the events preceding the outcome.

"Let them stay," Rosswell said to Sonya. "If we're all about to die, let us watch till the instant we're gone."

"Didn't I tell you that earlier?" Sonya tipped her head to Rosswell and winked before she joined the group. She turned her head and said over her shoulder, "I may as well get a good seat on the front row."

Things started to change.

Something was wrong. Bad wrong.

JoEllen froze in place. She stayed silent for a few seconds after she'd listened to the train's movements on the tracks. "The train is slowing. The train is slowing but the bomb is speeding up."

Maman agreed. "Yes, and it's because another optical scanner up the track detected the broken one you smashed down the track. The bomb ought to be booming right where we're standing."

"That's not good," said JoEllen. "Wait." She put her hands to her ears. "The bomb's doing something. I can't tell what."

"Hope for a safety measure of the railroad and not a... a... something that will set the big boom off instantly," Maman said. She pointed. "Take a look at that, there."

The angel hovered over the train car coupled behind the locomotive. The light train moved but barely. Maybe five miles an hour or even less. From the angel's hands, a veil like a golden silk blanket appeared in midair, floating over the car but not touching it. Not a ripple of wind stirred it. Then it started moving. After a few heartbeats of simply hanging in the sky, it drifted, covering the roof of the car with a sparkling wrap, then in one action, dropping and shrouding the entire train. Around the bottom of the car, the blanket sealed itself, leaving the car cocooned. Nothing in, nothing out.

"There's our womb," Maman said to JoEllen. "Me, I don't see how that thing take care of us. If it blows up, that flimsy rag will splatter both it and us all over the kingdom come and glory shines!"

When the train coasted to where the companions huddled by the floodgate, the locomotive shrieked to a stop, caterwauling up and down the same scale demons used when haunting a bloody European castle in Romania under a full moon.

Or, so Rosswell thought. He'd never been to Romania, much less heard demons there screaming.

I've never heard sounds like that anywhere before in my life. Even the war in the Middle East can't compare with the horror of these sounds.

"What now?" Rosswell yelled at Maman and JoEllen.

JoEllen leapt and pulled herself up on the freight car, then reached down and pulled Maman up with her. Rosswell stood gaping, wondering just where the smaller woman got the strength to hoist the woman onto a train car.

"It's back here!" JoEllen called out, pointing to the door of an enclosed car with a roof.

On each side of the car, a metal beam at the top supported retractable overhead side doors. The car ran equipped with a loading device for handling special commodities. Or, in this case, only one kind of commodity: A bomb prepared by the enemies of the Guardians of Dina nestled in a cube measuring one meter on each side. The explosive device could demolish a city block. Maybe, if the big shots who were controlling the thing had made a mistake in their quantum physics equations, the whole galaxy could collapse by destroying a few key supports. Mother Nature doesn't like it when mankind screws with the foundations of reality.

JoEllen and Maman pushed their way into the car to find the bomb anchored in the middle of the car. The cube spewed out an irritating frequency sounding like the ear-mangling squeal of a newly-sharpened blade on a glass window, allegedly the most excruciating noise to a human ear in all the world.

"Don't listen," Maman cautioned JoEllen.

"Not to worry," JoEllen said. Then after the awful noise quieted for a few seconds, she yelled, "What was that sound? Is it trying to kill us or warn us?"

"We walk around. Not dead yet. Take no chance. Don't mess with it."

JoEllen said, "Fear not. I'm ignoring it."

"You on one side of this cube baby in the womb, me on the other." Maman gestured to JoEllen, urging her to move into place.

When JoEllen had scooted to the opposite side of the cube from Maman, she said, "Grab my wrists." Leaning over the bomb, Maman grabbed JoEllen's wrist and JoEllen grabbed Maman's wrists. "Don't let go."

Rosswell had wormed his way into the car where he watched the two women drawing down the light from the angel overhead. The brilliance covered them and the inside of the car. Then the wind started. Although the air was calm outside the car, and the sun heating the day, the women were buffeted by a wind frozen by its journey from the north. The temperature plummeted. Frost began forming over the whole interior of the car.

Maman released JoEllen's wrists and JoEllen did the same for Maman. They both pointed their fingers at seemingly random places and then punching here, and there, in the empty space around them.

Maman said, "A womb weaving."

A spider dropped from somewhere, landing between Maman and JoEllen. Another spider. Then another. Soon there were hundreds—no, thousands—of spiders crawling over the two women.

"I can't take this!" JoEllen yelled. I hate spiders!"

"It's defenses of the evil," Maman yelled at JoEllen. "Don't pay attention to the spiders. They're pictures only, floating in the air."

Spiders now completely covered JoEllen and Maman. The evil critters—JoEllen shouted that she didn't believe for a second they were *pictures only*—began dancing on them, humming a strange sound. Both women swatted at the spiders, especially when they headed for their mouths and eyes and ears. Then the sound changed to a low pitch, shaking the insides of everyone around.

Maman coughed. "Can't ... breathe."

JoEllen slumped to the floor, not breathing.

After gathering her breath, Maman said, "The spiders have sucked in all the air. Break the spiders! Make them stop dancing. They will go away." JoEllen didn't move. "JoEllen, remember the angel who helped! Breathe now. Brush the spiders away."

JoEllen's eyelids fluttered. Yet she did not breathe.

"No!" Maman screamed. "Start breathing! Stand up!" Maman reached over for JoEllen and slapped her in the face.

JoEllen gasped and shot up and began stomping and hitting the spiders. There was no blood because the spiders were only electronic creatures, although creatures that caused great harm if no one fought against them.

Slowly, the spiders began disappearing. The two women breathed easier.

Rosswell then soon recognized the connections in different places in the air, the points glowing a bright yellow. Points speeded past other points, then turned around and caught the points that they had missed. Time after time, this happened. In a fraction of a second, he saw the pattern building. Around the cube, the points soon shrouded the entire construct.

They're weaving a buffer for the explosion. Maman said the particles will fold themselves around each other and then around the package, which will then join in enclosing the whole matrix in an explosion-proof womb.

He couldn't hold back the sob.

I hope this works. It looks flimsy. In fact, right down fragile. This isn't going to work. No bomb is going to be afraid of exploding because of bunches of light points flitting around. We're goners.

Sonya appeared then, at Rosswell's side, gun drawn.

He shouted at the women, "Step back. It's going to blow!"

CHAPTER 53

Day 10, continued
Very early morning
Riverfront

MAMAN, JOELLEN AND SONYA ALL ignored Rosswell's warning. Instead, they struggled through the strange landscape in the car until they stumbled onto steps where they jumped up to the cab of the train. If the women sacrificed themselves to save others, Rosswell would follow suit. If he could work up the courage.

His sight fell on the villain for the first time. Timothy Lockerbie lounged in the seat of the locomotive. His long black hair fell halfway down his back. His bluish-silver gray eyes not only matched his hair, but also Martha's eyes. *Could they be related?* Skin the color of a suntanned movie star. A smile curled his lips. Timothy started singing. "Let all you fools disappear in the mushroom cloud!" He sang the words repeatedly. All the while smiling, his bright teeth shining.

The acrid stink of expensive pot fingered its way into every pore of the car's insides. Rosswell coughed and hacked.

This guy sitting at the controls is trying to blow up the world and he's playing a game with songs and impersonations. And burning expensive alfalfa.

Pointing at Timothy, Tina, and Sonya shouted together, "Him! He's the one!"

Now those two are getting psychic vibes? And they're the same vibes? That should be pretty cool. Must be they're reading each other's minds. That could be dangerous. For me.

Father Mike, Reverend Ed and Brian Reeves had sprinted to the train. They climbed into the car.

Where had Brian Reeves come from? Roswell wondered. He had no time to think about this now.

Timothy, busy giving the evil eye to JoEllen and Maman, stopped when Father Mike and Ed interrupted his hate session. He set his eyes on the two approaching clergymen, singing, "You don't have the guts to kill the madman. You don't have the strength to murder the bad guy. You don't have the courage to chop my head off." Then he repeated. And the next time he repeated, he sang it faster. And louder. Faster and louder, he sang the haunting melody, again and again. Rosswell felt a migraine being aimed at his brain by the man who would blow the place up.

Together, Father Mike and Ed crowded the doorway of the locomotive. If Timothy had tried to escape, they could've pushed him down and held him for Sonya. Or other cops.

Ed pulled out his Glock.

"Sonya," yelled Rosswell. "Call back up. Now!"

Brian Reeves left his position next to Sonya. In a flash, he joined Father Mike and Ed. "Reverend Ed, shoot that guy. Aim for center mass. Kill him. He's going to destroy us if you don't!"

Ed examined the pistol in his hand. "I can't kill anyone." Turning to Father Mike, he held the Glock barrel-down, no finger on the trigger.

Rosswell cheered inside. Now was not the time for a good guy or girl to get shot by accident. Ed and Father Mike certainly had the bravery to rush the crazy man sitting in the engineer's perch. No question there. Could Ed shoot him? That was the question.

Someone must've been teaching Ed something about gun safety.

Father Mike grabbed the firearm from Reverend Ed.

Kill him! Did I say that out loud? "Kill him!" This time Rosswell knew he said it aloud.

The priest turned to Sonya. "I can't do it." She grabbed the pistol from him, stuck it down her belt at her back. She aimed her weapon at Timothy. Ed moved into Sonya's line of fire. Rosswell couldn't tell if he was clumsy, trying to commit suicide, or had accidentally tripped into a bad position.

Brian pulled Ed's pistol from Sonya's belt before she could react. He lunged toward Timothy, and stuck the Glock over the man's heart and pressed hard. "You're dead now, Hivite. A lot of people are waiting on your death." Timothy laughed.

"No!" Someone had yelled, apparently aiming to catch Brian's attention.

Rosswell watched Brian swivel his head for an instant, his attention being drawn away from Timothy Lockerbie for only a millisecond, yet that was all the crazy man needed.

Who's calling Brian? He's distracted. Timothy could kill him in an instant. Rosswell screamed at Brian, "Don't take your eyes off him! Kill him! Shoot now! Sonya, where are all the cops?"

Sirens in the distance began screaming.

Sonya said, "You're way behind, Rosswell. I had already called."

Someone yelled, "The gun!"

Brian, as it turned out, lost his concentration when the police cars began arriving on the scene. In that instant, before he could wheel around and kill the villain, a man (in the chaos, Rosswell couldn't discern his identity), grabbed the gun from the prosecutor, jumped down and scrambled to the riverside, tripping a couple of times on the cobblestones. Once at the water's edge, he wound up as if he were a big-league pitcher in the bottom of the last inning of a World Series game, and then power pitched the weapon into the river where it disappeared. Never again to be a temptation to anyone.

Timothy Lockerbie threw his head back and laughed.

"You can't kill me, no one can." he sang, and sang and sang.

Sonya took the shooter's stance, both hands on her weapon. "Don't be so sure, you bastard!"

That's when the train began to shudder violently. Everyone, including Sonya grabbed something to hang on to, as the shuddering increased. Then, came the noise, a sound so deep Rosswell felt it in the depths his soul. If he had one. The explosion was soundless, but lit the area with a white hot light. When the brightness subsided, Roswell stared incredulously at the headless body of Timothy Lockerbie. *How the heck did that happen?* He heard the *womp, womp* outside the window of the cab. They all rushed to look.

The figure rose with flapping wings, and from its talons, long black hair flowed blowing with the breeze.

Mesmerized at the sight, they stared as it rose higher.

A blazing white light enveloped the figure.

Then it was gone.

CHAPTER 54

A MIDST THE TUMULT, NO ONE noticed the dawn—this time the genuine dawn. It arrived and with it a soft whirlwind sprang up that wasn't damaging but was strong enough to cleanse the air. The whirlwind turned and swayed, transparent and soundless, banishing the odors that the hot night had generated on the riverfront. A few leaves jumped up into the cone, falling when the wind lost its power.

Rosswell, Brian, Father Mike, and Reverend Ed still gathered by the locomotive.

JoEllen and Maman, during the kerfuffle in the train's cab, had made their way to the street.

Sonya, calm as a fresh-picked cucumber, yelled orders to cops and civilians alike. At one point, she turned to Rosswell, gave him a thumbs up and saluted Tina, who stood with her arms wrapped around her man.

Hopefully to keep him from running off to a new adventure.

CHAPTER 55

R OSSWELL WATCHED AS FATHER MIKE sidled up to Brian speaking to him too softly for anyone to hear. But he did hear Brian's response.

"Father, forgive me. I almost sinned again."

Father Mike looked at Rosswell with a look that said, "*We'll never tell.*"

Rosswell nodded his acknowledgement as Father Mike stepped around him.

"Good pitching," Rosswell said. "Maybe you should try out for the Cardinals."

Brian and Ed turned and walked away.

———◆———

Rosswell stood with Tina upwind a ways, watching the police mop up the scene. Quiet fell on them like a wet blanket. Tina kissed him, reminding him of their early days when the only thing that seemed dangerous was tripping on the street as they walked to supper at The Purple Star.

Rosswell said, "I hope I don't see another angel until I die."

Father Mike, accompanied by Alexander, had quietly walked up to Rosswell and Tina.

Rosswell turned. "Where's Reverend Ed?"

Father Mike said, "He's got a lot of energy. He's walking home. The long way."

Rosswell said, "Did you and Ed really see that angel? In fact, did we all really see it?" Rosswell wasn't positive that he wasn't losing his mind.

"You and all of us saw it," Alexander said. "An angel. Yes. In a few days, you'll forget about this," Alexander continued. "Angels travel from a hazy land. Where is it they come from? One day you will all know. Their destination is a land where folks look so closely at the haze, that they miss the greatest wonders of the universe— human beings saving each other."

"You don't really believe that, do you?" Tina asked.

Alexander bowed and said, "Judge and Deputy—former judge and former deputy—Rosswell and Tina, enjoy your life. It's the only one you'll get. On this planet. In this reality. Goodbye. For now." Alexander added, "Just remember that a haughty look, and a proud heart yield the tillage of the wicked, which is sin."

"What?" Tina asked. "What does that mean?" Neither Father Mike nor Alexander answered. They kept walking.

She and Rosswell then heard someone behind them.

JoEllen walked up to Rosswell, and touched his arm. "Did we do it? Is the evil really gone?

Rosswell looked up at the sky. "Yes. It's gone."

For now. Roswell jumped.

Who said that?

THE END

ABOUT THE AUTHORS

BILL HOPKINS, author of the Judge Rosswell Carew mystery series, is retired after beginning his legal career in 1971 and serving as a private attorney, prosecuting attorney, an administrative law judge, and a trial court judge, all in Missouri. COURTING MURDER was his first novel and his second novel RIVER MOURN won first place in the Missouri Writers' Guild Show-Me Best Book Awards in 2014.

Bill's poems, short stories, and non-fiction have appeared in many different publications. He's had several short plays produced. Bill is a member of Horror Writers Association, Missouri Writers Guild, SEMO Writers Guild, Heartland Writers Guild, and Sisters In Crime. Bill is also a photographer who has sold work in the United States, Canada, and Europe.

SHARON WOODS HOPKINS is the author of the Rhetta McCarter Mystery series. featuring mortgage banker Rhetta McCarter and her '79 Camaro. Her first book, KILLERWATT was nominated for a 2011 Lovey award for Best First Novel and placed as a finalist in the 2012 Indie Excellence Awards. Her second book, KILLERFIND, was a finalist in the

2013 Indie Excellence Awards, and won first place in the Missouri Writers' Guild Show-me Best Book Awards in 2013.

Sharon is a former branch manager for a mortgage office of a Missouri bank. She also owns the original Cami, a restored '79 Camaro like Rhetta's. Sharon's hobbies include painting, fishing, photography, flower gardening, and restoring muscle cars with her son, Jeff. She is a member of the Mystery Writers of America, Sisters in Crime, Guppies, Thriller Writers of America, the Southeast Missouri Writers' Guild, Heartland Writers, and the Missouri Writers' Guild. Sharon also spent 30 years as an Appaloosa Horse Club judge, where she was privileged to judge all over the US, Canada, Mexico and Europe.

Besides writing, Bill and Sharon are involved in collecting and restoring Camaros. They live on the family compound near Marble Hill, Missouri.

Contact Bill and Sharon on Facebook.